"I see you brought a [...]

There was not the slightest [...] her gawking at him, nor that he even cared. "If it is all the same to you, I'll be reading through these papers for the bulk of our travel. I trust you can entertain yourself?"

So formal. So distant. Elizabeth nodded slowly, at a loss. Who was this man in front of her? Certainly not the carefree gentleman who'd visited Grandmother and chided Elizabeth's bibliophilism. Nor was he the mischievous boy who'd yanked her pigtails and dared her to climb Grandmother's tallest oak.

No, this man across from her, with his long legs encased in shiny Hessian boots and his serious brow fastened to the work before him, was not the Miles she had always known.

A chill started at the base of her toes and rippled upward. Suddenly the prospect of meeting new people appeared far less da[...] [...]n a future spent with a man who h[...] [...]plete and utter stranger.

Jessica Nelson believes romance happens every day and thinks the greatest, most intense romance comes from a God who woos people to Himself with passionate tenderness. When Jessica is not chasing her three beautiful, wild little boys around the living room, she can be found staring into space as she plots her next story, daydreams about raspberry mochas or plans chocolate for dinner.

JESSICA NELSON

A Hasty Betrothal

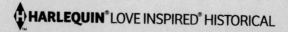

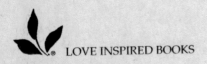

LOVE INSPIRED BOOKS

Recycling programs for this product may not exist in your area.

ISBN-13: 978-0-373-28373-6

A Hasty Betrothal

www.Harlequin.com

Printed in U.S.A.

But let it be the hidden man of the heart,
in that which is not corruptible, even the
ornament of a meek and quiet spirit,
which is in the sight of God of great price.
—*1 Peter* 3:4

I first want to dedicate this to my little brother, Hunter Schwirtz. When I started this story, I never would have guessed that you would be gone by its completion. Your struggle and your pain have given me an empathy I lacked. Your bright beauty is missed by so many. We grieve the loss of you.

Thank you to Anita Howard, for being the best, most fantastic POM in the world, and for catching all my echoes. Also, a huge thanks to Ane Ryan-Walker for taking the time to read the story and refine my Regency knowledge.

I also want to give a shout-out to my fantabulous aunts: Laurie Fontaine, Ellen Begin and Rosemary Begin. When I was a visiting child during multiple summers, these ladies indulged my voracious appetite for reading by making sure my world was fully stocked with books. Thank you.

Thank you to Emily Rodmell, my wonderful editor. She truly makes my stories shine.

And finally, to God, who sees us in our deepest sorrows, who comforts us in times of need. We are never alone, because of Him.

Chapter One

Balls were the worst sort of social event.

One month after Lady Elizabeth Wayland's arrival in London, the Season began full force. She received her voucher to Almack's, that most-coveted place of stale biscuits and overeager girls in search of a groom.

As in Seasons past, Elizabeth loathed Almack's on sight.

Tonight's rout at Lady Charleston's was bound to be just as detestable, but refusing the invitation would have been a slight too large to justify. Elizabeth's father, a wealthy earl, and her mother, the daughter of a duke, were well liked by the haut monde. Their pristine reputations kept their calendar full. Her brother, John, was also making a name for himself in political circles.

Quite unlike Elizabeth, who preferred a secluded life at her grandmother's estate. She'd been caring for the dowager duchess nigh unto fifteen years, ever since she was sent to live at Windermar as a young girl. Her mother and father resided in London for much of the year, but spent the heat of summer rusticating at their own estate in Kent.

Elizabeth adored her grandmother's spacious home. Located in Cheshire County of Northern England, it was a three day ride to London. Escaping her parents' abundance of charitable events caused Elizabeth a great feeling of accomplishment. They insisted her looks did not matter, but she could not help but feel that the large birthmark on her face made others uncomfortable.

No, it was far better to remain with her books and her adorable if decidedly eccentric grandmother.

Except each year when the Season rolled around.

Unfortunately, her parents refused to budge on the notion she should marry, despite her pleas. They cited reasons such as decorum, responsibility and her future. But Elizabeth knew that no man would ever want her, except be it for true love. Still, to satisfy her parents' demands, every year she gathered her pluck and attended soirees, balls and dinner parties. She only went to enough to appease her parents. Once she'd participated in a few select events, they often let her return to the country before the end of the Season.

Frowning now, she picked her way across Lady Charleston's overly crowded, giggle-saturated ballroom. Nothing was worse than being forced to dance with multiple partners who either stared at the large pinkish blotch covering her right cheekbone in pity or avoided looking at her altogether. Indignation burned through her, little salving the hurt that scraped the surface of her emotions.

She dropped her dance card to the floor, deliberately sliding it away with her slipper. Let someone else dance the night away. She longed to be finished, to return to Windermar and meld back into her normal life routine.

She left the ballroom, certain she remembered a library nearby from Seasons past when she'd made a similar escape. Spotting a familiar door, she sighed with relief and pushed it open.

The welcome scent of leather and paper greeted her. *The library.* She finally felt as though she could breathe. She inhaled deeply. Her corset stretched with the movement, and her lungs filled with less-congested air. Sweet Jenna had kept the strings loose. Elizabeth made note to give her lady's maid a gift.

It had been trying indeed, attending dress fittings, fixing her hair, ordering new bonnets. Two fat curls dropped over each of her shoulders, and her pale blue gown had been designed with one goal in mind: to fetch a husband.

As if she planned to do such a thing. She would finagle some reading instead. She doubted her mother would notice her missing. After several minutes of perusal, she selected a book. Bound in cracked leather, the novel looked decrepit and, oh, so very intriguing. She could not recall ever reading this one before. She would merely take a moment, really only a few minutes, to traverse this story before returning to the ballroom. Very gently, with the tip of a finger, she eased to the first page and lost herself in a world far more exciting than the one she presently inhabited.

"Head in a book again, eh?"

At the sound of Miles Hawthorne's husky voice, she looked up from what was actually a fascinating treatise on African populations. A wayward strand of hair fell across her vision, and she blew it away. Her brother's friend, and her childhood nemesis, stood in the doorway. His clothing was neatly pressed, his fine black Hessians polished to a spit shine.

She glanced at her own skirts, creased from sitting.

Most likely, she looked a fright. "Hawthorne, what a surprise. Have you taken up dancing?" she asked.

Not bothering to wait for his response, she eyed the book in her lap, trying to find the paragraph she'd been reading before his appearance. She traced the letters lovingly, each curve and bend a precious entrance to another world. Ah, there she'd been. The Maasai threw a rungu. She frowned at the page. How utterly painful. But a natural weapon, to be sure. She certainly would not want to have to dodge the aim of one of those warriors.

A crude line drawing on the next page sent her imagination wandering into the wilds of the Sahara. Stumbling over broken pieces of...well, whatever was in the Sahara? Perhaps it was better to imagine dredging through dark dunes of rust-colored sand. The grains scraped the palms of her hand as she stumbled up a hill. Skeletal shrubs snagged her dress. And then a lion appeared, its mighty mane—were there lions in the Sahara? And would she be wearing a dress? It seemed she might wear something more luxurious and strange... More research was required.

This might even be a topic the Society of Scientific Minds would be interested in reading. Her last article on astronomy had been well received by the group.

"Bitt, did you hear me?"

The nickname filtered through her daydreams. Snapping the book closed, she dragged her gaze to meet Miles's remonstrative glare. "I have repeatedly told you not to call me that horrid name. What are you doing at a ball, anyhow? Do not tell me you are in search of a wife?"

"I will never get married again." He chuckled lightly, though she had the feeling that his words carried a deep weight. He meant them, certainly.

She did not blame him one whit. She had heard rumors about his tempestuous marriage. She studied him now, wondering why he looked different.

Same lanky frame. Gray eyes, though she'd seen them turn green when he was in a temper, and unfortunately, his tempers happened often. Nothing violent, just long silences and tempestuous looks. She preferred his authenticity to the sticky disingenuousness of the haut monde.

What she actually preferred was isolation.

His eyes held seriousness tonight. Despite his moody temperament, he managed to sport sun-streaked hair as though he spent time outside rather than brooding indoors. The blond strands must be from horse riding. Crooked smile...wait...she paused, eyes narrowed, and then gasped.

"Why, Miles, whatever did you do to your mustache?"

His lips dented at the corners. "It's been gone for more than two months." He paused. "I'm wounded, well and truly hurt to the core of my being, that you have just now remarked upon my new style."

Elizabeth reluctantly put the book she'd been reading back in its place on the shelf.

He did look handsome without the facial hair. More dashing and younger somehow... She put the thought to the side. It was artificial and irrelevant to the moment.

"Tell me, sweet Bitt, why are you hiding in the library? Your grandmother sent me to find you. It's not seemly for a dowager duchess's granddaughter to be poring through literature like a bluestocking." His smile grew more crooked.

"You are a thorn in my side," she said testily, rankling again over his use of that detested moniker. "It is not your business what I am doing here. I don't need watching over, and I don't like your hovering, smelly presence."

"Why, Bitt..." He pressed a hand to his elegantly tied cravat. "Another insult?"

Truth be told, he smelled quite nice, but she'd rather be gored with an elephant tusk than admit such a thing to him. The boy who used to pull her hair, steal her books and then lose her spot in them.

"Mr. Hawthorne, stop the pretense. Tell Grandmother I shall return shortly."

"And if she asks why you did not come with me?"

She sighed heavily. "Very well, if you insist on being difficult." She stood, brushing out her skirts as best she could, knowing the rest of the evening would prove to be a great bore. Nevertheless, duty must be fulfilled. Perhaps she might claim a megrim... It would certainly not be unexpected.

Miles held out his arm as she neared. "I know that look. Plotting escape, are you?"

"Not I." She felt his gaze upon her. "Do stop staring," she murmured, taking his arm and allowing him to escort her back to the ballroom.

"You really should not be wandering alone, especially at a crush this size."

"Please, Miles, not now." He was right, of course. She risked her family's reputation, but staying in that horridly stuffy ballroom had proved unbearable. Besides, she was older than many here. Nothing untoward would happen.

"Shouldn't you be entertaining a bridegroom by now?" Miles asked.

She rolled her eyes. He acted as though he were her guardian rather than an old family friend. Oh, how she despised his pristine, well-kept appearance! The cravat that was always tied just so and the unblemished features he'd been born with. It was not his fault that he knew nothing of her struggles, of her insecurities.

But to mention her lack of prospects…how utterly uncouth of him. The audacity of his comment rendered her speechless for a moment. This was why she preferred never to see Miles. His blunt ways and teasing smile bothered her to no end. Then there was the unfortunate incident he'd witnessed her fifteenth year… Yes, she avoided him whenever possible.

But most importantly, he possessed the greatest fault of all: the man never opened a book.

That thought uppermost, she leveled a lofty look at him, the one she reserved for ill-trained butlers and staring housemaids. "I will marry for love or not at all."

"Why, Elizabeth? Love can come with time." They paused in the doorway of the ballroom, his eyes searching her face. "Don't you wish to have a family, your own home?"

"Not with someone who does not love me." She broke their shared gaze, searching the room for her mother. Why wouldn't Miles just leave? His questions poked tender scars from years ago.

"Haven't you had several Seasons now?" He continued speaking as though he had no notion of how his words affected her. And maybe he didn't, for she was well versed in decorum.

A lady did not show her emotions in public places.

"Perhaps I shall start a rumor that you are a heart crusher," he said.

"Tittle-tattle, all of it," she responded quietly. She'd experienced many Seasons—though it was no wonder he strove to remember. She was worse than a wallflower.

This time of the year was always terrible, but she managed to muddle through. Oh, why didn't he leave? She had little patience for Miles and his irreverent ruminations. "Go away."

"You are filled with sharp words today, sweeting." Before she realized what he intended, he drew her to an alcove to their right, which held a small bench situated behind a potted plant. He released her arm and, gratefully, she sat.

From this vantage point, she could watch the dancing without being noticed. "It is this time of year. I suppose I am irritated with my parents. They are always trying to marry me off."

Elizabeth dropped her chin into her hands and surveyed the attendees. They chatted and swirled, preened and giggled. The gentlemen wore starched cravats, crisp breeches and such serious expressions one might think the world would end if they didn't snag a bride. Or rather, a fortune.

"What are you brooding about?" Miles settled beside her, his cologne intoxicating.

"Avariciousness."

He made a sound akin to a laugh. She scowled at him. "It's not funny—it's ludicrous. What do these people hope to become? To dream about? The latest French fashions?"

"Very judgmental, my lady."

"I'm in a foul mood." She focused on the people milling about. "My parents refuse to see reason."

"This is regarding your marital prospects?"

"The lack thereof."

From the corner of her eye, she saw his hands lift, palms up. "You're an heiress. Surely you've had offers."

She sniffed. "When I marry, it shall be for love. *If* I marry. No one shall force me into the cage and if my brother's career suffers, if my parents' reputations hold the tiniest smear of disgrace simply due to my hermitude, I care not a whit."

"Harsh words, my lady." He leaned forward, mimicking her bent posture. "Marriage can be rewarding. It is not all doom and gloom. If you choose wisely, you will spend the rest of your days residing on a country estate. Why, you might even be allowed to move your bed into the library. Then you may cozy up to your books without interruption and never be parted from them again."

"You are silly, Mr. Hawthorne." She scrunched her face at him, realizing that an unacceptable giggle gurgled within. She tamped it down. Firmly. "This is no time for laughter. Do you see those dowagers and my mother watching me? They are assessing my value. Planning, no doubt, for my sale to the highest bidder."

"Come now, Bitt, that is hardly fair."

She straightened, suddenly annoyed. "You are not a woman. You do not know what it is like to be picked apart and looked over, only to be found wanting." Her eyes stung, and she blinked. Oh, rats. Why did this happen when she talked to him? Perhaps because he knew about Luke. He knew what had happened so long ago. "What are you doing here, anyway? This is hardly the place for a widower who has vowed to never marry again."

As she faced him, she caught the grimace crossing his face. Was that regret in his eyes? Guilt barreled through her. "My brother told me of your commitment to work."

"I acquired a new factory near your grandmother's estate, actually. I don't have time to cater to a wife." His eyes were dark, stormy, as though a mood had come upon him.

If she was honest with herself, she'd always enjoyed looking at Miles. Almost in the way one admired a violent sunset splashing across the horizon. When she was around him, she felt freer somehow.

As if she too were a myriad of colors spilling into the sea.

"If you are not here for a wife, then you must be here for some other nefarious purpose." She squinted at him, allowing a bit of mockery in her smile. "Tell me truthfully: Did John send you here to spy on me?"

"Your brother is too busy for meddling."

"Do not be vague with me, Mr. Hawthorne."

"Despite my lack of title, I also received an invitation. Does that surprise you?"

"As you are a gentleman, it is not surprising at all." She stood, suddenly tired of their banter, of the constant irritation that had plagued her from the moment she'd arrived in London. Nay, before that. "I'm in need of fresh air. Do not follow me. If you see Grandmother, please tell her I took a turn in the gardens."

"Without a companion?"

"Perhaps I shall conveniently snag one on the way out," she said crossly. She really should keep a companion near her at all times, but what she wanted most was to be alone. Who would bother a wallflower, anyhow?

Miles chuckled, the sound warm and inviting. She steeled herself against any feelings of friendliness toward him.

"You laugh, yet you have never known the restrictions of womanhood."

"If you mean spending your days reading, shopping

and talking, you're correct. I have never known such freedoms."

"You mock me!"

"Nay, but I beg you to consider the benefits of your station in life. Most have not the comforts you enjoy on a daily basis."

"I know that," she said hotly. Who did Miles think he was? Always needling her, acting as though she was some spoiled, ungrateful wretch. "Would you have me sacrifice myself to the cold system of our society? A system that prefers breeding over character, purse over heart? I think not, Miles. Now, if you would be so kind as to bid me adieu…" She trailed off, for Lord Wrottesley headed toward her, a disconcertingly aggressive look to his gaze. "I really must leave now. Lord Wrottesley has called on me twice since we arrived in London. I do not wish to speak with him."

"Who is he?"

"A fortune hunter." Without wasting another moment in useless conversation, she twisted to the right, desiring to dodge several patrons, but she caught her reflection in the large mirrors that gilded the ballroom: a pale wisp of an heiress, the strawberry birthmark covering her right cheekbone, glaring out from the whiteness of her skin.

Averting her eyes from the sight, she charged toward a set of French doors she'd seen earlier.

The exit promised solitude. A rest from the noise of congestion, the odor of too much perfume that clogged her windpipe. She dared not glance back to see if Wrottesley followed her.

She prayed he did not. When he had called last Wednesday, it had been the most stifling thirty minutes of her existence.

Grandmother insisted God heard prayers from every soul, and Elizabeth dearly hoped the duchess was right.

The doors shuddered beneath the force of Elizabeth's exit, but the damp earth welcomed her slippers a bit too readily. She sank deeply into the ground and, in her haste, almost fell. Catching her balance, she hurried forward to the garden walk, ignoring the sucking sound her slippers made in the mud. They would be ruined, but she owned at least twenty more.

The scent of rain clung to the air. Lighted lanterns cast eerie shadows upon the path ahead, but the stones promised dryness for her feet and where they led, she would follow. Lord and Lady Charleston's back lawn was a lovely respite, the gardens a comfortable touch for guests. Though situated in London, they'd made good use of their small plot of land.

Oh, for quiet from this dreadful press of a ball. Vaguely it entered her mind that she risked her reputation by entering the gardens alone. Surely a brief rest could not hurt, though. She would return shortly. She reached the stone walkway and heaved a sigh of relief, for her toes squished and the sad, sodden state of her slippers reminded her of her future. Equally dark and muddy.

She should pray. Grandmother exhorted her to do so. Glancing up at the night sky, she saw that the moon hid behind clouds, painting them shades of dark blue and gray. *Lord, please guide me tonight. Give me wisdom for I am beset by worries.*

She picked her way down the path, passing a couple sharing sweet whispers on a bench. The lanterns guided her feet to a ribbon-festooned gazebo sitting on the edge of what looked to be a pond. Out here, beyond the maddening noise of festivities, she finally felt she could draw a breath. The air was sweet, humid. Crickets welcomed her, their song harmonious and gracious.

She stepped into the gazebo, and it was as though a weight lifted from her shoulders. The half-circle bench beckoned her to sit and wait out the night. Perhaps a half hour, and then she could beg off the event by claiming malaise. A megrim, perhaps, or blisters from too much dancing. Sinking onto the bench, she watched the shimmering reflection of the now-unveiled moon on the water.

Blessed peace descended. It was only her and the night and God's watchful eye. He had answered her prayer and for that, she thanked Him. She sat for some time, her heartbeat lulled into synchrony with her breaths. She propped her arms on the edge of the gazebo, laying her head down, knowing she smashed the curls Jenna had worked so hard on and hoping her maid would forgive her the transgression.

She did not wish to think of marriage nor her parents. She wanted only to rest here and pretend that their desire to marry her off could be circumvented.

In the midst of her thoughts and the swirling anxiety that never seemed to quit, a twig snapped, cracking the silence.

Her head lifted, her pulse ratcheted. "Who's there?"

More scuffling, another twig snapping and suddenly she realized just how secluded she was. Perhaps no one went missing at balls, but plenty had been ruined. She stiffened as a shadow fell across the entrance of the gazebo.

"Alone, my lady?"

Chapter Two

Perhaps Miles ought to follow Bitt. He sipped his punch while eyeing the dandies who stood a few feet away, laughing within a circle of young misses.

Who was this Wrottesley Bitt spoke of? If he was related to the earl who lived near Windermar...no wonder Elizabeth did not like him. They were a slatternly bunch who were facing a mountain of debt, if he recalled correctly.

Elizabeth's happiness was important to Miles. He hoped her parents allowed her to choose her marital partner. She was kind and naive. He did not want to see her married for her inheritance. Her husband had to pass muster. A Season carried all sorts of disasters of which she knew nothing. Within that time frame, Elizabeth's future could be decided forever.

She wanted a marriage of love, she had said.

Well, she deserved one, if there was such a thing. She deserved something like he'd had, once upon a time.

A frown tugged at his lips.

He took another swig of punch to hide his mood from the group with which he stood. The ladies chatted with the gentlemen. One particularly forward lady kept sidling curious glances his way. Prospecting for a future husband.

She did not realize that he was infinitely far from husband material.

Miles's displeasure deepened. Bowing, he pushed away from the wall and decided to find Elizabeth. She shouldn't be without a companion.

"Miles Hawthorne." Elizabeth's grandmother, the Dowager Duchess of Windermar, rapped his shoulder, effectively halting his pursuit.

He bowed. "Your Grace."

She nodded to him, then turned to the couple on her left. "Venetia and Adolphus, you remember young Miles? And, Miles, certainly you have been introduced to Bitt's father, Lord Dunlop?"

"A pleasure," he said, bowing yet again in their direction. He had met them briefly during various stages of his childhood. Like most parents of the ton, they did not overly concern themselves with their offspring until the children came of an age to be married off or taught the family duties. As a result, they'd paid little attention to whom their son played with. Now that he was grown up, however, perhaps they were surprised that the friendship between an earl's son and a factory owner's son had survived the years.

Surprised and disapproving.

Lady Dunlop sniffed, and he detected condescension from Bitt's mother. No doubt due to his being a man of business. For some, the ultimate black mark in the ton. Hiding a wry grin, he turned to the other man beside Bitt's parents. His shock of white hair framed a narrow face and deeply set brown eyes. He looked familiar.

The duchess gestured to him. "This is Mr. Hawthorne. He owns a factory in Littleshire. His father and I were great friends."

"Lord Wrottesley." The earl held out his hand.

"A pleasure," said Miles, hiding his surprise. So this was Wrottesley's father. Standing with her family… Did they not know of his debts? The man did possess a reputable lineage and a well-respected title. Though the family had come into hard times, possibly due to a streak of gambling that ran through their bloodlines, a well-matched marriage could fill their coffers once again.

Elizabeth's future was becoming alarmingly clear. Did John know of his parents' machinations? Surely he wouldn't approve such a match for his little sister.

"I would not expect to see someone such as yourself at a ball. Are you looking for a wife?" Lady Dunlop fluttered her fan while waiting for Miles to answer.

"Not at all. Lord Charleston and I are business acquaintances," said Miles.

Her nose wrinkled at the word *business* as though it might contaminate her reputation.

Hiding his smile, he gave her a curt nod. "A pleasure."

Turning to the dowager duchess, he offered her a warmer smile. She responded by putting her quizzing glass to her eye. "Now that you've bought the Littleshire Mill, I expect to see you more often. It is between our estates, is it not?"

"I'd hardly call my plot of land an estate," he said.

"It's your home." She waved her glass through the air. "What it is called is neither here nor there. Now, did you find that bookish granddaughter of mine?"

"She went out to the gardens," he murmured. "I was just on my way to fetch her."

"Very good. A ball is no place for a lady to wander off alone. And well she knows it." The duchess sniffed, her powdered cheeks wiggling.

"She will return shortly." Miles excused himself and continued his search for Wrottesley, but the man had disappeared. He threaded his way twice around the room before concluding that his quarry had meandered into the gardens.

Where Elizabeth had claimed she'd go.

He stepped outside, the humid air clinging to him like a tightly tied silk cravat. The recent spring shower served to muck his boots and hinder his walk through the grass to a stony path at the edge of the lawn. He believed there to be a pond nearby. If Bitt had gone there alone, she'd been unwise, for a young lady should always be chaperoned. She was testing her limits, he supposed, and he could not blame her for it.

He had never known her to shirk duty or behave unwisely in the past.

Wrottesley's disappearance worried him, though. He strode along the path, his boots clipping the stones impatiently. The chirping of crickets and the full moon created urgency rather than calm. Bitt shouldn't be out here alone. She ought to know better.

He came to the end of the stone pathway, but there was nowhere to sit here and no sign of Bitt, only a quiet pond adorned with lily pads and the reflection of the moon. He turned, scanning the landscape until he caught sight of a gazebo on the other side of the pond. Movement rippled the shadows around it, and then a high-pitched gasp interrupted the steady song of the crickets.

He bolted forward, pushing through the plants lining the walkway and finding another stone path that lead to the gazebo. His pulse thrummed in hot beats through him, his body strained to reach the sound of that anguished cry. It couldn't be Bitt, he told himself as he ran down the path, but instinct told him it was her, and that she needed him.

He finally cleared the path and emerged in front of the gazebo. One quick glance told him everything he needed to know. A man's hands dug into Bitt's arms. She was kicking his shins.

He pounded up the stairs and yanked him away from Bitt. The man fell away easily, stumbling backward and plopping onto the bench. Miles advanced, his vision hazy and his knuckles aching to connect with the coward's face.

"Miles, no."

Elizabeth's tugging on his shirtsleeve broke his concentration. Her face looked unbearably white in the shadows of the gazebo, her eyes huge and shiny.

"All is well. Leave Lord Wrottesley be."

Miles dragged in a ragged breath, willing his body to calm so that he might deal with this situation. Not daring to move too far from Wrottesley in case the man attempted to leave, he cast a careful eye over Bitt's visage. She appeared unharmed, but everything was askew from her hair to her dress. One sleeve appeared to be torn, though he couldn't be sure.

Scowling, he crossed his arms in front of him. "All does not appear well. Are you hurt?"

She shook her head, and her hand dropped from his sleeve. "Lord Wrottesley was under a mistaken assumption."

The strength of her words roused Wrottesley from his lethargy on the bench. He lunged upward, face contorting. "Now see here, I only came to check on her, but she attacked my person."

Miles squinted. Upon closer look, he did spot an outrageously long scratch along the man's cheek. A sound from Bitt prompted him to look at her. She did not bother hiding her disdain.

"You well deserved what I gave you." After delivering that arch reply, she glanced at Miles. "Mr. Hawthorne, I would much appreciate your escort to the house, as Lord Wrottesley seems incapable of gentlemanly behavior."

Wrottesley shot them a withering look. "You will regret your actions tonight, Elizabeth."

"I did not give you leave to call me by my Christian name." Her chin notched up in a way that filled Miles with pride, despite the urge still barreling through him to smash Wrottesley's face to pieces.

He sneered at Miles. "And you...we will see what is to become of you." The man pushed past Miles and disappeared down the pathway.

Exhaling a breath he hadn't realized he'd been holding, Miles took Bitt's hand and pressed it between his. Her cold skin filled him with concern. "Are you sure you do not need to sit, my lady? Perhaps find your composure?"

"I'm quite composed. Just take me to my mother, please. I feel the press of a megrim and wish to leave at once."

"As you will, madam." He tucked her arm beneath his, only too aware of her small stature. If he had not come outside, there was no telling what Wrottesley might have done to her.

The dread pooling in his gut did not dissipate, even when they neared the house. Before entering, he pulled Bitt to the side and faced her. The familiar lines of her features struck him tonight in a different way. He had the strangest desire to run his thumb along the line of her lips, to press his cheek to hers and feel the sweet warmth of her skin. She stared up at him, eyes wide and trusting. For all her bluster, for the many times he knew he'd upset her, they shared a childhood closeness. He needed to be sure of her safety.

Needed to make certain she was not terrified.

"Whatever is the matter with you, Miles?" She pulled her arm away. "I'm perfectly well."

"Lord Wrottesley's actions… I must know—did the man compromise you?"

Even in the darkness, he could see the flush upon her cheeks. "He forced a kiss, but that was all."

Miles restrained a growl. "It will not happen again. I shall make sure of that."

"And so shall I. A foolish thing for me to wander alone. I realize that now, but you must not worry for me." Her gaze softened. "Truly, I appreciate your presence and hope your rescue shall sufficiently satisfy your need to protect me."

"Your hair is mussed."

She patted the unruly strands. "It cannot be helped. Thank you again, Miles, and while I feel I should be miffed at you for following me… I cannot help but be grateful you appeared. It was something out of a story, perhaps, and surprisingly expedient."

The soft light from candles shining from the windows flickered across her features. If she had a husband, this would not have happened. "Very well, if you are not harmed…"

"I truly am not." Her pretty mouth curved upward. Her hair spilled in wisps from its confines, brushing her high cheekbones. The strands were darker than he remembered. The last time he'd seen Elizabeth was several weeks ago and her hair had been put up. Between childhood and adulthood, the color had deepened to a pretty auburn. Perhaps it became so dark from never venturing outside. She had skin the color of cream and often complained about the sunlight, but he knew her appearance bothered her.

More so than she'd ever admit.

He shifted on his feet, remembering an episode when she was fifteen and he'd been visiting John at Windermar. He'd heard crying in the stables one evening, the quiet kind of weeping designed to mask deep distress. Not one to ignore someone in need, he listened carefully and finally pinpointed the source of the sound coming from behind a bale of hay. He walked over, unexpectedly finding Elizabeth, who covered her mouth in a desperate bid to hold in her sobs. Even now he remembered the pain that had lanced through his chest at the sight of her tears, and the frustration he'd felt when she refused to divulge the reason for her weeping.

Discomfited, he retreated, but he determined to find the cause of her pain. The information came quickly enough from a foolishly loquacious groom who lost both his job and several teeth on the same day. The lad had broken Elizabeth's heart. Told her he could never love a woman who looked as she did.

Miles had never divulged that he knew what had happened. He would do anything to never see her cry again.

"Enjoy the rest of the ball, for I shall be doing my utmost to leave immediately." She offered him a saucy wink. Taken aback, he followed her into the ballroom but stayed near the wall, watching as she tracked through the crowd to find her mother. People turned to look at her. Then they looked at him.

Rather odd.

He pushed away from the wall, passing a familiar face as he headed for the doors. "Good eve, Lady Swanson."

The countess did not glance at him, but gave him her back. A cut direct. The first he'd ever received. How very strange. Surely there could be no rumors already. He tried to remember exactly how disheveled Bitt looked, and how quickly he'd entered the ballroom after her. Casting the countess a befuddled look, he continued to the door, where he gave instructions for the bringing of his rig.

Lord, watch over Elizabeth. God could certainly do a better job than Miles. As for Wrottesley, Miles planned to take care of him.

Elizabeth rose late the next morning, almost missing the array of food on the sideboard. She meandered by the eggs and finally decided on a generous helping of porridge coated with sugar and fresh cream. Her stomach rumbled. Last night's dramatics seemed a distant dream, slightly disturbing yet infinitely less important than the demands of her belly. She inhaled the rich scent of sausage as if she had not eaten the very same thing yesterday.

There were a great many toils associated with being an heiress, but having an abundance of food was not one of them. Pushing the events of the previous evening to the back of her mind, she forked two sausages onto her plate and decided to scoop up eggs, as well. Thus fortified, she found a seat at the little table where she'd placed a gem of a book she'd checked out from Hookham's Circulating Library. The novel promised the wonder of an adventure.

The Arabian Nights.

It was a classic she had not yet explored, but passing the Season by delving into it seemed a pleasurable way to avoid the haute ton. She opened the book, relishing the thick texture of the page and the sweet smell of leather binding that rose to greet her. The endearing scent almost surpassed her desire to eat, but her stomach quickly rebelled against such an inane thought. She managed to hold the book open with one hand and fork food into her mouth with the other.

She was deep in a riveting scene between the merchant and his wife, who were arguing over his laughter, for he'd heard animals talking, when the morning's gossip rags were slapped over the words of her book.

Startled, she dropped her fork on the plate. She looked up. Mother stood above her, cheeks scarlet and lips pressed tightly together. A most unnerving sight. Elizabeth pressed her napkin against her mouth. Unlike Grandmother, her mother did not give in to fits of emotion. The obvious anger in her eyes torqued a nervous clench in Elizabeth's belly.

She preferred avoiding conversation with her parents. Four years ago, during her first come out, she overheard them expressing their embarrassment at her visage to callers. It was a conversation that, at the oddest times, repeated in her mind like an unceasing headache. Old, familiar pain palpated within. She tightened her posture and looked her mother in the face.

As usual, Mother's eyes skittered to an invisible speck upon Elizabeth's shoulder. Far be it that she must see the shameful birthmark upon her daughter's face.

She wet her lips. "Good morn, Mother."

"Read the gossip."

Elizabeth's gaze fell to the paper lying atop her book.

The front page headline filled her with dread: Heiress Returns Disheveled.

The writer did not name her, but it became obvious as the story progressed that it was about her, Lady Elizabeth Wayland. An heiress returned from Lady Charleston's gardens disheveled, hair almost undone, followed by a notable factory owner. The writer then speculated that a rendezvous had occurred... Elizabeth tore her eyes away, appetite dead.

Worry raced through her in uneven clops, like a startled horse galloping without restraint.

"You understand how close you are to being ruined, do you not?" Mother slid into the chair opposite Elizabeth. "If this becomes fodder for the gossips, it will damage John's position in the House, his career aspirations and our family's reputation. This is disgraceful." Mother took a shaky breath and Elizabeth wondered how she could breathe at all when a steel vise had tightened around her own ribs, making inhaling almost impossible.

She did not want to marry, but that did not mean she wished to be ruined. Not to mention the damage she might cause to her family's reputation, sullying all that they'd worked for... She squeezed her eyes tight and tried hard to think.

"Are you sure it is me they refer to? There is no mention of—" the words hurt to emit, but she forced them out "—my birthmark."

"There will be. Soon enough."

Elizabeth winced at the defeat lacing Mother's answer.

Venetia rubbed her brow. "I must ask—are the rumors true? Was there a dalliance with a man last night? Who could it be? Is that why you claimed a headache and practically forced me to bring you home early?"

Elizabeth pushed her plate away. "Dalliances are the furthest thing from my mind. Trust me, I want nothing more than to return to Windermar and take care of Grandmother. This Season is a farce. I'm an heiress, not a fatted calf."

"Elizabeth." A sharp edge tipped her mother's tone. "Every young woman deserves a home of her own, children and a stable future. Accept your responsibility as the daughter of an earl, the granddaughter of a duke. We will have to decide what to do with *this*." She tentatively tapped the edge of the paper as though it were a hot plate. "Your father must be told at once."

Her lids fluttered as if the colossal import of the situation weighed upon her. "Have you perhaps considered Lord Wrottesley? He has expressed interest in you."

Elizabeth flinched. "He is the last person I'd ever marry. Besides, he is a fortune hunter."

"You do not know that."

"I suspect it."

Mother sighed in a way that suggested Elizabeth was a great drain on her energy. "You cannot afford to be picky now. I shall speak to your father. Perhaps we can arrange terms."

Elizabeth swallowed back a retort, for she knew no way of escaping the rumors that had forced her into this situation.

Despite her brave words to Miles, she found that deep within, she truly could not subject her family to such a scandal. A betrothal might put the gossip to rest, but could she put aside her own happiness for the sake of her family? Every fiber of her being shouted *no*. Martyrdom lacked appeal. Especially with Lord Wrottesley.

Who else would want to marry her, anyway? A reclusive heiress with an unsightly birthmark?

She was going to have to give up her dreams of love because of one foolish action. After returning from the gardens, she'd entered the ballroom, gone straight to her mother and they'd left immediately.

Who would have spread such tittle-tattle about her? Perhaps a man out for revenge? A man who had discovered a way to put his greedy hands on her money?

Wrottesley.

She shuddered. Had he succeeded in ruining her?

Chapter Three

Wrottesley was not home.

Annoyed beyond reason, Miles rode back to his house with the urge to box the cad itching his knuckles. When he arrived home, he saw John's carriage.

He had barely gotten in the door when John appeared in his hall. "I suppose you've heard the news?"

Miles handed his coat to his valet. "News?"

"Regarding Elizabeth." Her brother pivoted, disappearing into Miles's study.

Biting back exasperation, he followed John. This was not how he'd intended his morning to go. He hadn't intended to tell John of Wrottesley's perfidy against Bitt either, but since he was here, perhaps he already knew.

Did he want Miles's assistance? He rubbed his palms together, anticipating the moment Wrottesley learned the consequences of assaulting Elizabeth. He entered the study. As he made his way inside, his mahogany desk greeted him like an old friend, staid and reliable in the familiar room. He'd inherited this office from his late father. Sighing, he sank into the plush chair accompanying the desk.

John watched him steadily from his own perch on a less comfortable chaise at the side of the room.

"What's this about Bitt?"

His old friend leaned forward, resting his elbows on his knees, hands clasped. Expression serious. "She has been compromised. But I suppose you know that already."

Miles felt his brows lift. "She has been in London only a month. What happened?" His mind raced. Last night, the cut direct he'd received, Elizabeth's disheveled state…still, that should not be enough to get tongues wagging so quickly.

Unless someone started the gossip. Someone intent on making her look bad.

"It's in all the papers. Not her name, specifically, but it might only take a few days for the ton to realize who this heiress is, and once that happens, she will be ruined. She was seen in the company of a factory owner." John's mouth tightened. "You were at that ball last night."

"What are you saying?" Miles asked flatly. But he knew. How foolish he had been.

"No one knows that I am whatever man was described in the papers. And you say her name is not mentioned? There is no reason for you to be here, John. You're distraught. Give it a day or so. The gossip will die down." Though they had been good friends since childhood, they rarely saw each other now that John stayed busy with his estates and his work with the House of Lords.

"I am here to demand honor for my sister."

"You believe I dishonored her?" Miles straightened in his seat. Shock curled through him. "I would never treat her in such a way."

"No, you wouldn't." John's laugh was dry. "But according to that article, the ton believes you have."

"My name is not mentioned. I fail to understand how Elizabeth's predicament is my concern." And yet, even as Miles spoke, he realized that he did indeed see the part he had played. For if she really was on the verge of ruination, then his actions last night had partially caused the problem. He should have insisted she straighten herself. Or perhaps he should have returned to the ballroom by a different way.

It had been so long since he'd attended a ball or paid any attention to society's strictures. Not since Anastasia... and he would not have gone last night if it were not for the personal invitation.

John dragged in a deep sigh. "I have come to insist you marry Elizabeth, should the need arise."

Panic, sharp and visceral, sliced through Miles.

"Politics have turned you daft," he said in a casual tone, hiding the terror rushing through him. He knew he owed John a great deal. He had been a bastion of support for Miles years ago when Anastasia died. As the powerful son of an earl, John had made sure the circumstances of Anastasia's death were kept quiet and out of the gossip rags.

But he could never marry again. He simply could not.

"I know that your marriage was less than ideal," John continued. "I would not demand this of you if I did not think it necessary." He shoved a hand through hair a shade lighter than Bitt's. "There is a chance the gossip shall pass. I have not spoken to my sister as of yet, but from what I've garnered, there is little to support the accusations."

"Speak to Elizabeth. It could be that she will happily retire to Windermar with the dowager duchess."

"Grandmother left for her estate this morning. She doesn't stay in London long. I can't imagine the uproar that would occur if she heard of this. Things are not so simple as you imply. There are other factors to consider."

"Your reputation?" he asked drily.

"Yes, my reputation." John narrowed his eyes. "I've worked hard for the latest bills that have passed the House. There is so much to accomplish and something like this...well, it tarnishes credibility. My parents come from a pristine lineage. Impeccable bloodlines. This is something that would drag our name through the muck for years to come."

Miles studied his friend. He cared little for reputations or the idle gossip of the ton, but would Elizabeth be able to live with disparaging her family? Would they ever let her forget what her lapse in judgment had caused?

Not that he truly blamed her for her nighttime excursion. Wrottesley was the culprit, and the urge to soundly thrash him still ran through Miles. Revealing how Elizabeth left the ballroom and went outside alone would be indiscreet, though. And what would it accomplish to tell the full story? Then John would demand honor from Wrottesley, and Miles absolutely would never allow her to be joined to such a man.

He owed John, though. His friend had shielded Miles and Anastasia's family from gossip. He had used his influence to hide the truth of Anastasia's death. Miles swallowed hard, hating what was to come, and yet knowing it to be necessary.

Mouth dry, he said, "I shall speak to Elizabeth. I make no promises."

John left quickly after that. Miles called for his rig. The sooner he spoke to her, the sooner he could rid himself of this terrible sense of duty.

Marriage.

The very word turned him squeamish.

He was shown into the Dunlops' residence with little fanfare. He found Elizabeth in the library, surveying a shelf of books. He acknowledged that her lustrous hair and unique eye color were not so difficult to gaze upon. Her lips were delicately shaped and rosebud pink. John's demand echoed in his mind.

Miles enjoyed Bitt's company. Felt a measure of affection for her.

Perhaps a marriage of convenience was not so preposterous, after all.

But he greatly hoped she rejected the notion. For all he knew, she had an admirer in the wings, waiting to rescue her.

"Good morning, Bitt."

She heaved a sigh much too big for her tiny frame. "Miles Hawthorne. You are up early today."

"I went to take care of Wrottesley."

"And?" She turned to him, eyes questioning, wary.

"He was not home." He cleared his throat. "Another matter has been brought to my attention."

"I daresay it has to do with this morning's gossip?"

"John came to see me."

"He is overly worried about many things. It shall blow over. This talk of ruination—" she fluttered her fingers as though waving off a bothersome bug "—is nothing. I have no desire to be married. Surely, being a widower, you understand."

Miles blinked, gathering his wits, trying to rein in

his reeling thoughts. It was a smidge hard with Bitt staring up at him so wide-eyed and upset. She'd always had enormous and expressive eyes. Such a pale blue they were almost crystalline.

Unfortunately, he doubted any suitors ever saw Elizabeth's eyes as, more often than not, she kept her face trapped in novels.

"What I don't understand," he said slowly, "is your flippancy. You are not worried?"

"Certainly I'm a tad concerned. This gossip will bring out desperate fortune hunters." She planted her hand on a shapely hip. "It is paramount I find a way to fix this. I will find a way. I must." A trace of panic edged her words. "No man shall want me for myself, Miles, and you know that *is* the truth."

"I did not think you so vain." Miles spoke slowly, knowing his words would incite her. Better to face her irritation than to hear that panicked note in her voice. "Assuming no man will want you based on your appearance is presumptuous."

She whipped a hand acrobatically through the air. "Presumptuous? Vain? How dare you criticize me when the woman you married was always called a diamond of the first water. I may have been in the schoolroom, but Anastasia's attributes were often remarked upon in my family. One could hardly travel through London without hearing of her beauty."

Miles's jaw clenched. "Anastasia's looks had nothing to do with our marriage."

"Nothing?" Her hand fell and she gave him a glare that turned his stomach queasy. It was as though she saw through to his inner depths and found him wanting. Her accusation was a slap to his conscience.

"I fell in love with Anastasia because of her laugh," he said tightly. It was true. She'd giggled infectiously during their courtship and loved to tease. If only he'd known that her heights of happiness were often followed by depths of sadness he had no power to rouse her from.

Bitt's head bent, as though she regretted her harsh words. "I recall her laugh and it was quite lovely. I apologize for my impetuous words. Of course you loved her for more than her beauty. It was unkind of me to suggest otherwise. Perhaps my own insecurities have blinded me to what a man desires in a wife."

"Any man would be fortunate to have you as his bride." Miles tapped his fingers against his thigh. "This situation you find yourself in... John and I are concerned."

"He is overprotective. He need not worry though, because I have no intention of marrying anyone, and if my parents try to force me into it, I shall simply run away."

Miles did his best not to scoff. "That would hardly solve anything. Besides, how would you support yourself?"

"I have been saving money for several years. If the need arises, I shall use that to find a post somewhere. A companion position, I suppose." Perhaps she saw the doubt on his face, for her brows furrowed.

"No legitimate family will hire a ruined woman."

"I am not ruined yet. Gossip has a way of trickling off. I simply must wait for a juicier tittle-tattle to occur."

Miles could not stop incredulity from barreling through him. Perhaps the reaction showed, for Bitt scowled deeply.

He returned her look with a glower of his own. "You hate attending society events, you shun the outdoors and you deny an audience to anyone who is not family because of a mere birthmark. I do not believe for one second that you will become a companion or a governess. Marriage is a position every lady of gentle breeding has been groomed for since birth. Will you really subject your family to great reputational harm rather than marry?"

A dark flush suffused her cheeks, creeping around the large birthmark that covered the right side of her face and coloring the rest of her fair skin an angry scarlet.

She gave him an arch look, completely belying every notion he'd ever entertained about her timidity. "Unless it be for love, I shall never marry. No matter the consequences."

"Even at the expense of your family?" Miles asked.

Elizabeth winced. Tearing her gaze from the books, she looked at him. She'd spent all morning in this library, hoping and praying the gossip would die down. And then he appeared, reminding her of the entire predicament.

It was unfair how handsome he looked when she found him so bothersome. His crisp waist jacket lay becomingly over dark breeches that were paired with shiny Hessians. She didn't know why, but suddenly the lack of his dreadful mustache struck her anew. A little shiver coursed through her at his appearance.

From his full lips to the dimple in his cheek, formerly hidden by the mustache… She shook away the awareness that rippled through her at his changed looks. This was *Miles*. Childhood nemesis and annoying man who most unfortunately turned out to be her hero last night.

"I don't know," she whispered.

He returned her look, unblinking. She patted her hair, certain it must be in place. Jenna had been dressing it for years. Why else did he stare at her so? Was he terribly disappointed in her?

"Since you are here, I feel I must thank you for rescuing me," she said to fill the silence.

"By all means, do not force your thanks."

Did she hear mockery in those words? "It is not forced at all. I am sincerely thankful you arrived when you did. Wrottesley was out of line, and I believe he also partook of too much punch. You will see—the gossip will die down, and my family will be fine."

She prayed it to be so, for she did not truly wish for their reputations to be harmed because of her. If the rumors affected only herself, she would have been happy to live at Windermar for the rest of her days.

But this could affect her family for years to come.

Marriage.

Bah! She likened the institution to a velvet cage. An image from the tribal book she'd read filled her mind. The young women carried baskets on their heads. Of all things! Every culture had its societal expectations and dictates, she supposed.

A footman appeared in the doorway. "My lady, Lord Wrottesley is here to call on you."

She suddenly felt faint. She had no desire to see the man. Words refused to form. Miles's gaze was on her. She blinked.

"I had hoped to take the lady for a ride in Hyde Park," he said, never removing his eyes from her.

She nodded faintly, catching her breath. "Yes, that would be lovely. Please tell him I am indisposed, or out." She waved a hand dismissively. Thank goodness Mother had gone out shopping or else she would not have allowed Elizabeth to go with Miles.

The footman disappeared.

Miles held out his arm. "A ride, then?"

Suddenly the thought of fresh air and sunshine seemed smart, indeed. She took his arm, noticing how much taller he stood than she. His arm felt exceedingly strong.

Which was neither here nor there, she told herself firmly.

It did not take long to leave.

Miles helped her into his rig. His fingers lingered on her knuckles, and she sent him a sharp look. Did he realize the small impropriety? Still feeling warm, she withdrew her hand and found her seat. Once they were settled, and Jenna had handed in her bonnet and taken her own seat, they were off.

"Hyde Park is beautiful this time of year," Elizabeth said inanely.

"We've never taken a turn by ourselves, have we?" Sunlight lit the chiseled planes of his profile.

She glanced at her lap, fiddling with the ribbons of her bonnet.

"You do not need a cap to hide your face, Bitt."

"It is for shade, sir."

"I see." His tone suggested he thought otherwise.

She cared not a whit what his tone said, though her hands were clammy.

They left the tree-lined road as Miles turned the rig into Hyde Park. Sunlight bloomed immediately upon their faces, warm and inviting in the still-cool spring air.

She situated the bonnet upon her head, but as she pulled the ribbons forward, Miles touched her hand.

"Allow me, my lady." His eyes darkened. Some tempestuous emotion spiraled through them, though Elizabeth had no idea why. She dropped her hands to her lap.

Miles parked the rig to the side of the pathway. Setting the reins on his lap, he pulled the ribbons of her bonnet gently, tying them neatly beneath her chin, the skin of his knuckles the briefest whisper of a caress against her skin.

"I had wondered…" He paused, his face only inches from hers, his gaze earnest. "If you might consider a betrothal."

Chapter Four

Elizabeth stiffened. The bonnet hid most of her face but the sudden frown turning her pretty lips downward remained visible. "I shall not be marrying Lord Wrottesley, no matter what occurred last night. I do hope my parents have not sent you to persuade me otherwise."

Miles wanted to take her hand, but the knowledge that they were riding in a public place and bound to encounter peers stayed him. He tapped his fingers against his knee instead, debating the best way to phrase his question.

Perhaps a simple business proposition?

That might be best, as it most described the purpose of the proposal. He picked up the reins, guiding the horses back onto the path.

"Nay, Bitt, your parents know nothing of my actions. The thing is…" He gathered his courage, which seemed to have deserted him. "I have come to see if you would consider a betrothal to me."

Her mouth rounded. Miles took a curve in Rotten Row, passing an early rider he did not recognize. He felt compelled to fill the silence of Bitt's shock, to assure her of his honorable intentions. And perhaps to convince himself that such an offer was in both of their best interests. Hard to imagine; nevertheless, he felt honor bound to offer.

"John came to my house this morning. He is concerned."

"Yes, yes, you told me he saw the papers."

Miles's mouth tightened. "He worries for your family's reputation."

"He should have expressed his worries to me." She pulled out a fan and began waving it vigorously against her face. "I truly feel that the gossip shall pass. After all, the column was quite vague, merely mentioning an heiress. That could be a number of people, including debutantes. It is known that I shall inherit, of course, but the amount has been kept quiet to discourage fortune hunters."

"Do you speak of an inheritance or a dowry?"

"Both, really. My grandmother has settled a dowry upon me, but I am also to receive an inheritance from my grandfather. It was in his will. We were very close. He made me feel loved for myself, and in fact, it was he who introduced me to the wonder of novels." Her eyes briefly closed as though she remembered a sweetness Miles himself had never known.

His own experiences with reading encompassed contracts, bills and legal papers. He took a quiet moment to study her. She sat to his right and the birthmark did not extend to the left side of her face. Her high cheekbones hinted at aristocracy, at a regal breeding that did not enrich his own blood.

"Your grandfather sounds like a wonderful man."

"His life was too short." Elizabeth opened her eyes, training their brightness upon him. "Tell me, Miles—why propose to me? I had believed you to be firmly settled in your widowerhood."

He dragged in a breath. "It is true. Marriage is the last thing I want. But you are an old friend, Bitt, and I do not wish to see you ruined. A betrothal seems a smart proposition. The article did mention a factory owner. Not only will the rumors subside and your reputation remain pristine, but you will be able to continue with the life you have known. With me, you might reside in the manner to which you're accustomed. We are comfortable together, having known each other since childhood. I wished to discuss the idea with you before going to your parents."

"While I appreciate the sentiment, you make marriage sound cold and heartless, a calculated business decision rather than a joining of hearts." She edged away from him.

The morning sun felt unbearably hot. He tugged at his cravat. "Because that is what it would be, Elizabeth. A proposition." He cleared his throat. "Do not mistake me. I do not want to ever marry again, but should the rumors increase, I want you to know that I am here to assist you by whatever means necessary. I do have a few requests, of course. Requests that would assure me you could be a suitable partner."

"Such as?"

"If forced to marry, I would want a wife who is not a ninny, one who might keep my home warm but not interfere with my social and political activities, promising a beneficial arrangement. You would have the protection of my name and the comfort of my acceptance."

"Forced to marry? And this is what you think I want?" The high pitch of her voice indicated that he'd upset her, but he could not fathom how or why. "I have not been ruined yet, sir, and if I were, it is doubtful I would accept such a proposal. Even from an old friend. How very distasteful."

"It's practical, Bitt. We get along well enough."

"That is an exaggeration if I've ever heard one."

His cravat grew tighter by the second. His head pounded. "You are a woman of excellent taste, refined but timid, one whose biddable nature would do well in housewifery. If it is acceptable to you, I would ask your parents for your hand in marriage—"

She reared back. "Have you lost your senses, Miles? We have nothing in common. Nothing at all. And I shall never marry unless for love. The matter is as simple as that. There is nothing that could induce me to marry you. Nothing at all."

"Not even scandal?"

Her face flushed but she did not respond.

He shifted on the seat, wondering if Bitt's lady's maid had heard her exclamation. "Your vehemence is unnecessary, my lady. A simple *no* will do. This is not my idea of fun. I simply thought to help."

Beneath the brim of her hat, her eyes flashed. "If I have wounded your ego or offended your pride, I do apologize, but for you to take me on this ride and hold out marriage as some kind of business offering…it is uncomfortable, Miles. What would Anastasia think of such a proposal?"

"Anastasia is gone," he bit out, "and has no place in this conversation."

Elizabeth's arms crossed her middle. He would like to imagine she was sorry for her harsh words, but he began to think he'd assigned to Elizabeth a heart that perhaps she did not truly possess. All for the better that she found marriage as abhorrent as he did. Her family could deal with her. He was done.

She sounded strained as she said, "I am merely pointing out that I want to marry only for love. Rumors abound in the ton. Let the gossip run its course. My parents and John shall be fine. They shall not suffer for my actions."

"And if the rumors don't subside?"

"I cannot marry someone who feels forced into the deed."

"You are being naive, Elizabeth." He felt unruly inside, unsettled by her unexpected irritation, her complete lack of faith in his husbandly virtues. Not that he had faith in them himself. This was all for the best, he told himself. He turned the horses for Bitt's home.

"Better to hope for the best than settle for the worst," she said.

"Indeed," he muttered. The worst meaning him, of course. "It was merely an idea to keep you from ruin, but since you feel it unnecessary, then we shall not discuss this again."

"I do so appreciate your putting aside your distaste for marriage in order to help me, but fear not. All shall be fine." The hopeful lilt of her tone did not comfort him.

John could still pressure them into marrying, citing honor, but at least Miles had offered before the request became a demand. He had fulfilled his obligation, but where he should have felt relief, he merely felt a deep emptiness, a wrenching certainty that things had not turned out how they were supposed to.

Elizabeth wished to face life on her own terms. He could understand such a goal, and yet, watching her proud posture as they rode back, he could not shake the nag-

ging feeling that this Season was bound to interfere with
his life in a most uncomfortable way.

Life did not unfold as Elizabeth hoped. Neither did
the rumors abate.

She was sitting in the library the following day, con-
gratulating herself on her newest find from Hookham's
Library, when her mother blasted into the room.

Or so it felt.

Mother snatched the book from Elizabeth's hands,
prompting a startled gasp and immediate irritation. She
straightened, eyeing her mother carefully. The older
woman paced the library. The calm she usually carefully
exuded was gone, replaced by a tenseness that perme-
ated the room and ruined any vestige of comfort Elizabeth had felt.

"Is something the matter, Mother?" She played with
the lace on her dress, dreading the answer.

Mother swung around, slapping the book down on
the nearby desk. "As a matter of fact, Elizabeth, there is.
I was denied a voucher to Almack's today. Denied. Do
you have any idea how humiliating that was? To be told
my family does not have the prestige to enter? We have
never been denied entrance. Never."

Elizabeth's hopes imploded. "Was a reason provided?"

"I know what the reason is. You are still in the gossips' line of fire. There is only one way to remedy this."
Elizabeth did not miss the imperceptible tightening of
her mother's lips.

The coiffing of Venetia's hair must have taken her
lady's maid at least an hour to fix. She wore her favorite
emeralds, as well, handed down to all the wives in Fa-

ther's family. His affluent earldom more than made up for Mother's step down from being the daughter of a duke.

She quietly waited for the woman who birthed her to speak. There had been a time Elizabeth longed to know the mother whom she resembled so closely, but that desire no longer existed. Not for many years, not since the evening she'd overheard a conversation that revealed her parents' true feelings toward her.

"Your father and I are in agreement that Lord Wrottesley might be willing to marry you."

Venetia's eyes, the same shade of ice blue as Elizabeth's, implored her to listen.

"He is a viscount who has already shown an interest in you. There is no reason to believe that has changed." Her mother paused, but not in a dramatic way. No, Mother did not put on airs. Her calmness quite made Elizabeth want to stomp a foot. "If Lord Wrottesley offers for your hand, your father and I are prepared to accept the proposal."

Elizabeth gasped. She'd suspected her parents' plans, but for mother to speak them in such a way, with such finality… She clenched her skirts, readying to retort, but Mother held up a hand.

"This Season, to my utter dismay, is proving more disastrous than your first one. An intervention is in order. Due to your unique situation, finding a husband is nigh impossible. Thankfully, Lord Wrottesley is in need of funds to bolster his estate, and you are in need of a husband to provide for your future and save you from ruin. This is a solution that will prevent further harm to the family's reputation." Mother bent her head, looking at Elizabeth in a not unkind way. "We worry about what will become of you, our only daughter."

How was it possible to wear such an air of concern

while shattering Elizabeth's world into a million unalterable pieces? A looking glass dropped to the floor could not be more broken than she felt at this moment. Her skin tingled, from temper or hurt, she was not sure. Her mother's insinuations bristled every ounce of pride Elizabeth contained.

"The reason I have no suitors," she said in a tight, emotionless voice, "is due to a lack of desire for them. Should I want a man to secure my future, there are plenty of impoverished earls to choose from. There is no reason for you and Father to concern yourself with me."

Had she said such a thing to her mother? Yes, those words issued from her mouth, daring and bold and perhaps a very big mistake, for Mother drew herself to her full height, a scant inch above Elizabeth's, and eyed her forcefully.

"It is time for you to marry. Not only is it what is expected, but your actions have left us no choice in the matter. What of our reputations, Elizabeth? Your brother can not afford to be ill spoken of at this time in his career. A good name is pivotal to his success."

"What about Grandmother? Who will take care of her?" The fight was leaving her body, seeping away like morning mist. "And have I no say in who is to court me?"

"If Lord Wrottesley offers, and we have reason to believe he will, then we shall accept on your behalf. A thanks would not be too much to ask."

"I should be thankful that you are forcing me into marriage with a cad?" Her cheeks flamed as she struggled to keep indignation from her voice. "He is the reason I find myself in this dilemma."

"Whatever are you talking about?"

A hot flush of shame spiraled through Elizabeth. "He

forced a kiss on me. At Lady Charleston's ball. Mr. Hawthorne interrupted Lord Wrottesley's ungentlemanly behavior, but it is because of him that I returned to the ball disheveled." The admission cost Elizabeth her composure. Her fingers trembled. "Please do not encourage the viscount. He is dishonorable. I wish to marry for love, and love only."

Mother's brows lifted. "I am dismayed. Why would you be alone? That is what a companion is for. To protect you from the likes of overly zealous gentlemen."

"He is no gentleman," Elizabeth said darkly.

"Regardless, you shall not marry a man of business. Mr. Hawthorne is an unsuitable candidate. Wrottesley is a viscount, heir to an earldom. There is no adequate reason to reject his courtship." Mother waved a hand, dismissing further argument on the matter. "And what is this talk of love? That has nothing to do with a marital contract. Have you been reading that ridiculous poet again? Byron, is it?"

"No, I simply long for a love like Jacob and Rachel's in the Bible. Or perhaps Hermia and Lysander…"

"Shakespeare? Really, Elizabeth, there is much more to the world than books."

And yet books had been her dearest friends. She felt drawn to Hermia from *A Midsummer Night's Dream*. A girl kept beneath the thumb of her father. They held even more in common now that Elizabeth's parents wanted her to marry Lord Wrottesley.

Only she had no Lysander waiting to rescue her.

She looked away from her mother, counting the seconds until she could leave this house. Even walking in a park full of people would be more bearable than this wretchedness.

The thought bolstered her resolve to extricate herself from the perfidy her parents planned. Her chin notched upward. "Will you take away my books just as you are stealing my freedom?"

"Do not be melodramatic, Elizabeth. It doesn't suit you." But a fine blush swept her mother's cheeks.

"My lady." The footman, whose name Elizabeth did not know, entered the room. His gaze skittered away from Elizabeth to land on Venetia. "Lord Wrottesley has arrived to call on Lady Elizabeth. Do you wish to receive him?"

"Very good, Stockton. Show him to the parlor."

Stockton bowed and then left. Once again Elizabeth was reminded of her failure as an earl's daughter. She should know the servants' names, but most often she found herself avoiding them. There was that dreadful time during her fifteenth year...

She sighed. "May I go back to reading?"

"No." Her mother studied her. "This is as we hoped, and sooner than we expected. Go upstairs, put on your best dress and then return to meet Lord Wrottesley. I shall welcome him and see that he's made at home. Do not tarry." Mother swiped a scornful glance at Elizabeth's morning gown, a simple cotton dress she'd been wearing for years.

"I cannot believe that you are actually going to make me see him. After what he did?"

Mother had the grace to look away from Elizabeth. "It is not uncommon for a man to lack self-control. In the future, keep your lady's maid or companion nearby. It is your job, as the more refined gender, to keep a man's base instincts in check."

Clenching her jaw, Elizabeth rose, grabbed her book and went to her room. Jenna dressed her speedily.

Elizabeth's nerves coiled. A great wall of anxiousness descended upon the anger she felt with her mother. The utter betrayal. As she slunk to the parlor, she realized her palms were damp and her jaw sore. She rolled her shoulders back but the movement did not ease the kink winding up her neck.

Odious Wrottesley. She prayed he came to apologize for kissing her. For putting his hands upon her person in an unacceptable manner. Couldn't he find some other heiress to annoy? A quick rap of her knuckles and the parlor door swung open. It had not stuck closed as she'd hoped it would.

Lord Wrottesley looked up as she entered. Mother was not in the room. The scratch upon his cheek had rather disappointingly faded. Elizabeth suppressed her chagrin at not leaving her mark in a more permanent way. An elaborate cravat decorated his shirt. True dandy fashion. His smooth cheeks and empty eyes reminded her of a book without words. Or perhaps a gossip rag. Yes, full of lies and cruelty. Though his lips tilted in a facsimile of a smile, she detected triumph. Her nerves flamed and for the briefest moment, she was tempted to begin carrying smelling salts.

Oh, to be able to faint at the slightest upset. It was truly disheartening that Grandmother had not passed down the condition.

Pushing the thought aside, she curtsied. Lord Wrottesley performed his requisite bow.

"You are looking much better than you did the night of the ball." He eyed her carefully, as though examining her for evidence that his actions then had greatly affected her.

She kept her features placid. "My headache has subsided."

Was that dissatisfaction crossing his features? She dearly hoped so. He clasped his hands and walked toward the fireplace, face tilted to study the portraits on the wall. "I will come straight to the point of why I am here."

"Please do," she said.

His form stiffened, but he did not look at her. "Yesterday morning's gossip rags were distressing, to say the least. To think I have called on someone capable of such misbehavior."

"You caused it by manhandling me."

"Ah, so you also recognized yourself in the column." He turned to her and now she was certain of his disdain and his gloating. "There is a way to solve this, to keep your family's name intact and preserve your future. I have spoken with your father in the past and have been patiently waiting, but I will not wait forever. Now seems the time to right the unlikely situation which has presented itself."

Knots twisted in her stomach. She could only stand immobile, heart pattering in uneven beats against her ribs, fingers clenching her skirts… She could not marry this man. Could not. He repulsed her in every way.

Memories from the ball crowded her mind. His sour breath upon her face, his fingers digging into her skin and his laugh… He had found it funny to frighten her, to catch her unawares.

She wanted to speak but found that her lips had numbed, her tongue had swollen. He advanced. He put his hands on her shoulders and, because of their difference in size, she felt even more threatened. Her pulse galloped within her skin.

"Ah, Lord Wrottesley." Mother's voice sounded behind her and Elizabeth thought she really, truly might faint from relief.

He removed his hands and moved forward to greet her mother, kissing the top of her presented hand.

"Good to see you, Wrottesley." Father emerged in her periphery, shaking hands with the dreadful viscount. "I see Elizabeth has made it down. Have you two discussed… anything?"

"I was just getting to that." Lord Wrottesley flashed his supercilious smile and Elizabeth battled the urge to run as far as she could. "I would be honored if Lady Elizabeth would accept my proposal of marriage. In light of what's being said, now is the best time to put rumors to rest and I am prepared to offer her the security of my title and hand."

"Daughter?" Father peered at her.

She swallowed. Though her parents were in many ways strangers to her, there resided a deep need to make them proud. To show them that she was not just a deformed castoff who brought shame, but a productive member of the family. Could she marry for that alone?

Her dire predicament struck her fully as the three stared at her expectantly. Waiting.

"I…" She faltered beneath their gazes. Her mind raced. "I thank you, Lord Wrottesley, for your generous offer. It is with regret that I must decline it."

"But we will be ruined!" Mother's sharp exclamation was cut off by her hand to her mouth.

Father's brows furrowed. "There is no room for scandal in this family, Elizabeth."

"I know that and I would never cause you such pain.

The truth is…" She gulped deeply, knowing her next words would change the course of her life forever. "The truth is that I am betrothed to another."

Chapter Five

"Lady Elizabeth to see you, sir." Powell announced the news quietly, but the words punched Miles out of his deep study of contracts and into the present. He blinked at his valet.

"Lady Elizabeth Wayland?"

"The very one. She has requested your presence immediately." Powell paused, his serious features perplexed. "She claims the matter to be most urgent, and if I may say so, she appears rather…winded."

"Thank you. Tell her I will be there shortly." Miles pushed his chair out, gut twisting. He could not forget yesterday morning's ride. What had he been thinking? Offering marriage? He must have temporarily gone insane. Thankfully, she'd refused. He'd done his part, as he'd scribbled in a quick note to John when he returned home.

Should Elizabeth need to marry, there would be plenty of willing suitors. His gut twisted at the thought of Elizabeth in a loveless relationship, but he pushed the feeling aside.

He well knew how love brought pain. He frowned. He

did not wish to see Elizabeth today, but he could think of no reason for her to be at his house, alone, except for some unexpected predicament.

Had she changed her mind? Panic shot through him. He prayed not.

He found her pacing his library, hands wringing and dress fluttering with the force of her walk. Her hair escaped in disorganized ringlets around her cheeks, and when he entered her gaze flew to his.

"Miles," she breathed.

He hardened himself against the relief so clearly etched on her face. Perhaps his pride still rankled from her cold dismissal. "Lady Elizabeth, won't you have a seat?"

Surprise fluttered across her face. Perhaps she'd expected a less formal greeting.

"I cannot sit. Something dreadful has happened. My hand is being forced, you see, and I said what I had to but now... I'm truly at my wit's end. I know not what to do. I pray you forgive me."

He did not move from his position in the doorway. What was happening here? Fingering his cravat, he gave her a questioning look. "Surely things are not so terrible."

"Oh, but they are." She stooped and plucked a paper from the chair. Marching to him, she held it in front of his face. The words blurred without his spectacles, which he'd left at his desk.

"What is it?" he said irritably.

"That article. They are referencing me." She lowered the morning rag. "It's still the gossip this morning, though there is no more mention of a factory owner. There is simply the implication that I..." Her face blanched. "Behaved inappropriately. They do not go so far as to write something to my complete ruination, but a betrothal is the only option to fix this, for if it continues as a topic of conversation, or widespread rumor, then I could very well be ruined and throw my family into the worst sort of scandal."

"Did you not say you cared 'not a whit' about your family's standing?"

Elizabeth wrinkled her face. "Empty words. I wish I had not uttered them." She drew a deep breath, looking down at his feet. "Lord Wrottesley has offered marriage, and my parents would have me accept."

Miles's spine went rigid. He held up a hand, stopping her midspeech. "The same man who so cruelly mauled you and caused this fiasco?"

Bitt flushed. "Do not repeat this, please, but I believe he may be the one behind the rumors. They are too expedient. I cannot marry him, Miles. I dare not."

"After what he did to you? Do your parents know?"

Her blush deepened. "I told Mother, but she feels I brought his behavior upon myself. I will say that he was a gentleman in the library, in the presence of my parents. I told him I could not marry him. That I was not at liberty to do so."

"At the risk of ruining your family?"

"Not quite." Her eyes, a startling crystal blue, shone in the morning light streaming through his library windows. "I know you believe me spoiled and selfish and that I care nothing for my family's standing, but you are mistaken."

"Bitt." A lump rose to his throat. "I do not think those things of you."

She smiled, but it was halfhearted and sent a pang

through him. "Nonsense. You said as much the other day. My concern for my family is precisely the reason I am here this morn."

He waited, knowing her well enough to trust that she'd circle to her purpose at her own leisure.

"I was hoping your proposal still stands," she said.

Miles couldn't control the shock that pierced him.

Bitt walked to him and placed a hand on his sleeve. "When Lord Wrottesley arrived today, I knew I would do anything to avoid being joined to that odious toad. So I told him we were betrothed."

Shocked by her words, he wrenched away from her and glanced out the study door. There were no servants to be seen. "You were adamant you'd never marry me. Yet now, in a moment of desperation, you have changed your mind?" A curious hurt resided in his chest. From whence it came, he knew not, but nevertheless it was there, a heavy pressure beneath his sternum that turned his stomach sour.

Why did he care? He did not want marriage.

Bitt winced. "My hasty words hurt you. I see that now. It is simply that I never thought to find myself in this predicament. I felt that I would never marry in order to appease my family's need for good standing, but now that the moment has come and I have seen the pain I would cause, I cannot bear to be the author of such scandal."

Miles walked to the window and peered outside. His view faced the street. A carriage pulled to the curb. He recognized the crest as Dunlop's. "Your parents have arrived."

Bitt's silence weighed on him. He knew she wanted him to renew his offer, to ignore her earlier rejection of him and pretend that they could move forward. They very well could marry. He knew that. He also knew he would fail her, just as he had Anastasia. Then again, a marriage of convenience was different than what he and his deceased wife had shared. Their relationship had begun with him already mired in the pit of love.

Or infatuation.

Whatever it had been, once married, reality had set in for both of them. Perhaps he needn't worry about that with Bitt. Swiveling, he took in her unkempt hair, her begging eyes and nervous fingers. He remembered her laughter in childhood, followed by somber silences. And that day he'd heard her sobbing…

If he married her, she'd have his protection. No one would dare mock her or make her feel ugly. But she'd told him that she only wanted to marry for love. And that was the one thing he could not give her.

"Miles." Her voice caught, the tang of guilt residing in her broken syllables. "There is something else you should know."

He regarded her carefully. Quiet, unobtrusive Bitt. When had she grown into such a stubborn creature? "Yes?"

Her fingers knotted in the folds of her dress. "I did not only tell Wrottesley I'm betrothed to you. My parents believe it, as well."

"You lied." His jaw hardened. Every tendon in his neck tightened. This explained her sudden appearance at his door. She'd dug a hole and expected him to rescue her from its trap.

"No, I have simply changed my mind. I hoped your offer might still stand. I—I promise to be a good wife,

Miles. If you will only understand that I did not know the repercussions when I rejected your kind offer. Although I hoped to marry for love, that is no longer an option."

Mouth dry, he said, "Anastasia was unhappy married to me."

So much so that she took her own life. But he could not utter that terrible truth. Could hardly bear to remember the depths of misery she'd endured in their relationship. Marrying for love, as he'd learned, was a foolhardy reason for what essentially amounted to a contract.

"I do not know the truth of your words," Bitt said quietly, "but I would rather be unhappy with you, a man who sees past my visage and cares for my soul, than unhappy with one who would empty my pocketbook and treat me with cruelty." The sounds of her parents' arrival in the hall filtered to them. She lowered her eyes, knotting her fingers. "They shall be in here in a moment and if you can find it within yourself to marry me, then I will proudly take your name."

Miles studied her. Surely she lied to herself, whether or not she knew it, but he owed John a great deal, and if he married Bitt, his debt would be paid. No doubt her parents would demand he marry her, as well. Especially since she'd rejected Wrottesley. He blamed her not at all for such a decision.

He could not forget his own part in her situation either. Had he pressured her to take a companion with her, Wrottesley would have not found her vulnerable. What a mess he'd gotten himself into. John was right. There was only one acceptable solution to this situation.

He expelled an uneven breath. "It will be a marriage of convenience. A business contract. No more or less."

"I understand. I take that to mean that…well…that there will be no wedding kiss?"

He understood her question. He remained silent at the hesitant inquiry. By offering her a marriage of convenience, he would save her reputation and yet steal her chance for the intimate love of a husband and wife. Let alone the experience of a first kiss.

"Forgive me," she rushed on, before he could respond. "I will not ask such assurances from you. It is enough that my family shall remain in good standing."

He nodded slowly. "If you recall, I mentioned certain stipulations. I need to be certain that you can be moderately happy married to me."

Miles did not care for the strain on Bitt's face, but it had occurred to him that if their marriage was to have any success, he should test their compatibility. Make certain she could fulfill the duties of a gentleman's wife. Nothing strenuous, just enough to set his mind at ease. After all, he was about to be shackled for life. Not his idea of a happy ending, but he could not leave his childhood friend in distress.

He waited for her to respond, every muscle tight and clenched.

Footsteps pounded down the hall. Bitt's parents appeared in the doorway. Her father's face wore somber lines as he advanced into the office. "Is it true, Hawthorne? Are you set to marry my daughter?"

Bitt looked at him, a mix of fear and desperation plastered on her features. She gave him a slow nod, and he knew that she had accepted his terms without even knowing them.

A stiff foreboding crawled down Miles's spine. He

bowed crisply. "Forgive me, Lord Dunlop. I meant to speak with you sooner. If you will allow so, I shall marry your daughter."

"Why, Miles, this is positively insulting." Elizabeth scanned the paper he handed to her. Ensconced in his barouche, they were to discuss the "business" of marriage while taking a trip to Gunter's for ices.

It was all very tedious and though she did enjoy sweets, she'd much rather be curled up on her bed with a good book than sitting in this rig, looking at a list of tasks she must accomplish in order to be considered suitable for marriage. How like Miles to create a list. So very methodical. She found the entire business humbling, for he was changing his life to accommodate her. She worked hard to squelch the irritation throbbing within.

"You agreed to this arrangement," he said, his voice unusually hard.

Wincing, Elizabeth dipped her head in concession. "Quite right. I did. Though may I remind you that I was under a great deal of pressure at the time? Is this truly necessary? A house party? To celebrate our betrothal? That is farcical."

"You and I will have a marriage of convenience. Nothing more."

A pang hit Elizabeth square in the ribs. Indigestion, no doubt, brought on by the stress of her future being destroyed. She peered at the paper more closely, attempting to decipher his scrawl whilst acknowledging the terrible fact that due to her own irresponsible actions, she had given up her dreams of true love forever. A surreal realization, to be sure.

"Instead of writing what you want from me in overwrought detail, you could have simply told me." She handed the paper to him, thankful her fingers did not tremble. She had not slept well last night, strange dreams troubling her sleep. "Am I to understand that you ask only three things of me?"

"That is correct." He steepled his fingers, his face dark and brooding. "Are you certain you can do what I've asked?"

"I said that I would." She drew an unsteady breath. Miles had been backed into a corner. He had done an honorable deed, one she should be thankful for. It was her duty to make this as painless for him as possible. "Visiting your new factory shan't be an issue, I'm sure. But planning a betrothal ball is a bit excessive. And I confess I fail to see why I should visit Vauxhall Gardens with you, as well. These are odd and unlikely requests. They will not make me a better wife." The very thought filled her with dread. Her shoulders slumped. She could never measure up to Anastasia.

How could a homely caterpillar ever compare to a fragile, colorful butterfly?

He held up a hand. "Familiarity with my business and associating with others in social settings is something you may be called upon to do. If you can't handle these situations gracefully, it is better to know now, before we are bound for life."

Elizabeth didn't dare look at Miles. When he'd picked her up this morning, she'd felt the darkness of his demeanor. He was in a mood, to be sure, and it did not reassure her of their upcoming nuptials. It was no surprise that marrying her brought him great irritation. If she had any other option, she would not have accepted his reluctant proposal.

The thought sparked her temper. "If marrying me is such a daunting task, why did you ever ask in the first place? I did not compel you to act the honor-bound gentleman." She dared not go so far as to offer to back out of the nuptials.

"I am still asking myself the same question."

His words sliced her. She was truly in a mess of her own making. Oh, why had a walk outside seemed like a good idea? That dreadful viscount had ruined everything.

She swallowed hard, summoning the reserve she'd been taught to carry, the fortitude to face unpleasant situations with grace and regal bearing. "You're avoiding answering me, but the truth is that your response no longer has any bearing on the situation we find ourselves in. There are three things you ask of me. I shall do them regardless of how I feel. And if I do these tasks, you will marry me and not break our betrothal?"

"Yes," he said.

She found the courage to look at him. His eyes were unreadable, his jaw set in a stubborn line. It reminded her of the time he took the punishment for breaking cook's favorite bowl when he and John were fighting over the last bit of dough. John had let him take the punishment, too, which she'd deemed quite dishonorable at the time.

Miles would go through with marrying her, no matter how unpalatable he found the union. It was in his nature to fix situations and help others. She lifted her chin and met his troubled gaze.

"This is not ideal for me either. I am giving up the possibility for true love. At least pretend that we are on somewhat good terms. I shall not bother you overly much, Miles. After these first few months, we may go our separate ways."

His brows lowered and if possible, his glower deepened. "Trust me, madam, I shall not forget that you are only marrying me out of desperation."

The barouche jolted to a stop just in time, for Elizabeth did not know how to respond. She had assumed he found marriage to her a cumbersome burden, but it almost seemed as though her first rejection had tainted his view of her. But how could that be? He was as resistant to marriage as she, though for quite different reasons.

Befuddled by his response, she waited for the barouche door to be opened. She took the footman's hand and descended. No matter. They had chosen their course, and there could be no turning back.

She glanced around her. People crowded Gunter's. It was April, after all. The start of a fabulous Season, and everyone who was anyone knew that ices on a warm day were a perfect opportunity to see and be seen.

She braced herself for the stares and conversation, taking the parasol Miles so kindly handed to her. He had managed to wipe the moodiness from his face and looked the perfect gentleman with his chiseled features and neatly tied cravat. She half expected her skirts to be mussed, but no, as she glanced down, she saw that the silks were in perfect arrangement about her slippered feet.

The purpose of their visit to Gunter's was twofold. To discuss what Miles expected of her and then let all those who had read that unfortunate gossip see that Mr. Hawthorne was far more to her than an illicit liaison during an overcrowded ball.

Her parents wasted no time in informing her that it was her duty to spread the word that she was betrothed, even if only by action. They were quite unhappy with her betrothal to a man of business but since she'd rejected Wrottesley, they had little choice in the matter. Unless they wanted to bring scandal on the family, her marriage to Miles was the only possible solution.

Mother had refused to speak to her this morning.

Wincing, she forced herself to take in her surroundings. Her windpipe shrank.

Well-dressed ladies milled about the emerald grasses of the park, some carrying their own parasols, others wearing broad-brimmed bonnets. Gentlemen strolled beside them, using stylish canes and carrying ices. Servants darted back and forth, and even the waiters looked pristine in their uniforms as they brought treats to those who'd rather sit in curricles.

Clouds provided the perfect shade for those who chose to walk the paths designed for couples and families. Not everyone wanted to be cloistered on such a lovely spring day. Elizabeth clutched her parasol closer, battling the urge to turn her head at an angle. Why had she agreed to this?

The overwhelming sense of inferiority and failure that accompanied public appearances pounded through her. A duke's granddaughter should be poised and, if not beautiful, then regal. She supposed she should be thankful she had not been sent to a country house to live out her days, free of the stares of those who had never experienced mottled, discolored skin. She supposed she should be thankful...and yet she was not. How often she wished to live in solitude, with only the company of unseeing books.

This morning's escape from her parents' disapproval had seemed a smart choice, but now she wasn't so sure.

Panic edged her throat, circling her thoughts like a vulture feeding upon her sanity.

Pressure on her arm caused her to glance over to see Miles offering her a tender look. "All will be well, dear Bitt. Hold your head up and show these people how the granddaughter of a duke behaves."

She nodded stiffly. He was right, of course. His confidence bolstered her as she gripped his arm and let him lead her to a pretty little bench situated on the side of the hill. He left her there to get ices, and when he returned, he settled beside her and handed her one.

The treat was as delicious as she remembered. Almost enough to take her mind off the curious glances they received. At last one woman meandered over. Elizabeth knew she should recognize the striking blonde, who was dressed in an outfit that must be eminently fashionable, covered in ruffles and lace and shrieking wealth.

Her lady's maid followed behind, eyes averted. Oh, yes, certainly a woman Elizabeth should know. A sense of failure threatened to take hold.

"Lady Elizabeth, how good to see you out. And with a suitor, no less." The woman's eyebrows twitched, and Elizabeth thought she saw a frown in her smile. She waited, presumably for Elizabeth to introduce them.

Miles had stood in the lady's presence. Elizabeth forced herself upward, racking her mind for the lady's name. For something. Anything. But a name failed to form.

"Lady Englewood, is it not?" Miles offered her a crisp bow, to which the lady held out her hand for his perfunctory kiss upon her silken glove. He straightened, offering Elizabeth a twinkling smirk. "We met the other evening, I recall."

"Ah, yes. Mr. Hawthorne. Lord Wrottesley mentioned you in passing, and I do believe you were a part of our little group at Lady Charleston's. Such a fashionable woman." The lady turned her sharp words to Elizabeth, who wavered beneath her peer's scrutiny. "It is good to see you in the fair weather, my dear. Your parents have expressed concern for your health, citing it as the reason you've been in the country for so long. Though I do remember you coming out last year, did you not?"

"I have been out for several years now," Elizabeth said carefully. And now to play her parents' plan to perfection. "Mr. Hawthorne has graciously extended me an offer of marriage, and so we are celebrating with ices. There will be invitations going out for a celebratory ball. An event you will not want to miss. It's sure to be a crush of the most gigantic proportions."

Miles made a noise that sounded like a cough. She quickly patted him on his nicely muscled arm. "My affianced is quite excited to meet my parents' circle of friends."

"Is that so?" Lady Englewood's nose thrust upward and Elizabeth could almost imagine a quizzing glass stuck to her eyeball. "We shall most eagerly await the invitation." She gave them one last look, her gaze lingering upon the right side of Elizabeth's face, as though perhaps wondering how any man could possibly want such a marred human being.

Miles was not any man though, as annoying as he could be. Suddenly Elizabeth felt happy to be out with him. They shared a conspiratorial smile as they returned to their seats and watched the loose-lipped lady spread the word that the heiress had found a gentleman.

And for a moment, as Elizabeth tasted the tartness

in her ice and inhaled the aroma of Miles's cologne, she quite felt that all was right with the world, and that perhaps life would not be as horrible as she anticipated.

Chapter Six

Miles had certainly wasted no time in making Elizabeth's life miserable.

She scowled at herself in the mirror.

"Be calm, my lady." Jenna came up behind her. She touched Elizabeth's hair, which she'd put up earlier that morning. "You look lovely and shall enjoy yourself."

"Now that I'm betrothed, you won't need to go with us everywhere."

"Quite fortuitous for me." A shy smirk edged Jenna's lips in the mirror's reflection. "I have several duties to complete before I meet you at Windermar." Jenna would be leaving the next morning for the estate. "Your pink chiffon is in need of an update. I was thinking roses and silk stitching."

Elizabeth waved a hand, her gaze straying to her birthmark. In the glare of morning, the rippled redness appeared remarkably noticeable. "I despise that dress. Destroy it."

Jenna laughed. "Nonsense. I know of several lower maids who are in want of a fancy dress. Why, Betsy is marrying in two months. She could use the material for something quite lovely."

A twinge pinged Elizabeth, but not enough to take her attention from the face staring back at her. "Just get rid of the dress. Is there no other way to disguise this…?"

"I purchased a new powder but hesitate to try it on a day you're going out with Mr. Hawthorne, on the chance you have a negative reaction. You have such sensitive skin, my lady."

Elizabeth frowned, tracing the outline of her birthmark. The edges scraped her fingertips, the texture quite different than the rest of her skin. Indeed, if it were not for this infernal marking, she might have quite beautiful skin. Naturally creamy and pale, with cheeks that blushed easily and required no rouge. Her lips also were often full colored, requiring none of the dreadful lip antics she'd seen other ladies resort to.

Jenna put a hand on Elizabeth's shoulder as if to comfort her. "We will try the powder tomorrow. Will that do?"

"After so many years, one would think we could find a way to hide my blemish." Elizabeth pushed up from her seat and faced Jenna. "You have been a most excellent lady's maid. Give that dress to Betsy, finish whatever duties await you and then take the afternoon off."

"Really, my lady?"

"Of course. You are leaving for Windermar in the morning?"

"I had planned to."

"Grandmother can spare a maid to help me when I arrive." Elizabeth forced a smile to hide the dread curling inside as the time to visit Miles's factory drew near. His arrival was imminent. Their trip would be an all-week affair, as the factory was located in Cheshire County, near her grandmother's estate.

After Miles informed her of their upcoming factory visit, she'd written to Grandmother, procuring permission to stay for several days. Elizabeth was looking forward to returning home. She had procured a telescope several months ago but had not been able to use it nearly as much as she'd hoped.

"Thank you, my lady." Jenna curtsied and left the room. Reluctantly, Elizabeth followed. As she trudged downstairs, she heard Miles's voice coming from her father's study. The sound of his husky, deep tones sent an odd shiver through her.

Nerves, of course. For being forced into a factory tour, surrounded by strange staring people... She shuddered but then squared her shoulders. A small price to pay for what Miles had given up to keep her from ruin.

That niggle of guilt did not leave her as she reached the hall. She determined to make the best of today. At least she no longer had to put up with Wrottesley. He'd turned his attentions to a country baron's daughter rumored to be in possession of an impressive dowry. She hoped the poor girl's parents possessed some sense.

Her stomach pinched and she was aware of a tight, painful feeling beneath her breast bone. Nausea rose as she stood near the front door. She battled the feeling down, not wanting Miles to see how horribly uncomfortable she was. He might back out of the betrothal if he thought she could not handle being his wife.

Though she hadn't read the gossip rags this morning, she was sure they must be worse. Unless some other unsuspecting debutante had made the grievous error of venturing out alone, making herself ripe for ruin. Less than two weeks ago there had been speculations about a betrothal announcement and a veiled threat that should it not be done soon, a certain heiress risked ruination.

Their visit to Gunter's several days ago had helped in settling the rumors. For the past week, Mother had been making calls and the banns would be announced soon enough.

Elizabeth had attended another ball last night, and it had been a tricky business. She'd tried her best to smile, to engage, but she had not danced a single dance and she'd felt the speculative gazes of matrons and debutantes alike. No one had cut her though, and for that she was thankful.

Miles had not attended the event, for he'd been busy working.

"There you are." Father emerged from his study, followed by her betrothed. "Your mother has left to pay calls and find out where we stand with your...situation." He cleared his throat, his immaculate visage contorting with the supposed pain of having to think of his daughter's less than stellar choices.

"Are you ready?" Miles walked toward her, his expression inscrutable.

Wordlessly, she nodded. His gaze lingered on her for a moment longer than she thought necessary. She wrinkled her face at him. His lips twitched. He turned to her father and held out his hand.

"I trust I've answered your questions thoroughly, and that we may proceed with our contract?"

"My man of business will be in touch."

The two men nodded in a masculine code that, frankly, Elizabeth had no desire to understand. It did not escape her that Miles probably had a man of business, too. He probably spent hours each day immersed in contracts, which she'd never really considered before.

What a lot of boring reading.

Give her a good piece of fiction or an informative article on the newest technological advances…but contracts? She repressed a shudder.

Her father returned to his study, hardly glancing at her. It was time to leave. She felt quite sick, and moistness slicked her palms. Surreptitiously she swiped them against her dress. Miles took her arm gently. Warmth radiated from him. His cologne surrounded her. And it seemed as he looked down at her that his eyes held unexpected compassion. Their gray calm reminded her of a quiet sky, overcast with no wind and plenty of shadow.

Did he guess how difficult this journey was for her? How inept and terrified she felt? She swallowed and forced herself to stand straighter, to look brave when she felt perilously close to bursting into childish tears. The last thing her family needed was for Miles to withdraw his offer because he thought Elizabeth incapable of being the kind of wife he wanted.

Soon they were situated in the carriage. Elizabeth clutched her novel, hardly speaking as the rig rolled down the road, heading out of London and toward Cheshire. Bright skies promised safe travel and little to fear on the journey.

They had mapped out which inns to stay at, should the journey require more than one night of rest.

Elizabeth swallowed, very aware of Miles's proximity and the lengthy travel ahead. His satchel bulged with papers. Her book felt light in comparison.

Who was this man she'd pledged her life to? Busy searching his satchel, Miles did not appear to notice her perusal, for which she was thankful. He was not in a brooding mood. Of that she was sure. But not once had he cracked a smile or teased her. His solemnity concerned her and added to the coiled rigidity of her emotions.

He set a pair of spectacles on his fine nose and drew a thick stack of papers from the satchel. He looked up, catching her open gaze.

"I see you brought a book." There was not the slightest hint that he'd noticed her gawking at him, nor that he even cared if he had. "If it is all the same to you, I'll be reading through these papers for the bulk of our travel. I trust you can entertain yourself?"

So formal. So distant. Elizabeth nodded slowly, at a loss. Who was this man in front of her? Certainly not the carefree gentleman who had always chided Elizabeth's bibliophilia. Nor was he the mischievous boy who'd yanked her pigtails and dared her to climb Grandmother's tallest oak.

No, this man across from her, with his long legs encased in breeches and shiny Hessians and his serious brow fastened to the work before him, was not the Miles she had always known.

A chill started at the base of her toes and rippled upward. Trembling, she pressed her lips together and stared out the carriage's window, scarcely seeing the change of countryside as they traveled north.

For suddenly the prospect of meeting new people appeared far less dangerous than a future spent with a man who had become a complete and utter stranger.

Miles exhaled with relief when the carriage pulled up to his newly acquired factory. The journey had been smooth but long. He was a little ahead of schedule, arriving before his man of business expected him. He'd decided not to send a post, the better to keep Mr. Shapely on his toes. Though such underhanded tactics were not a common method for him, his father had taught him that it sometimes paid to be unpredictable. It kept employees accountable.

Not that Shapely had given him any cause for worry. His longtime man of business sent detailed reports and kept meticulous records. Miles had no reason to doubt his abilities.

When he'd first toured the factory months ago, he'd decided to buy it. He'd known he'd need to make changes, because the sight that assailed him had been heart wrenching. Vacant-eyed mothers and emaciated children worked the bulk of the machinery.

Not only were the employees ill-treated, but the factory was dirty and mismanaged. After the contracts had been settled, he had given the factory manager a month to improve conditions. That time was almost up. He'd planned to return to oversee the changes, and in the meantime, he'd left Mr. Shapely to facilitate the process.

Inheriting the family business was a responsibility Miles didn't assume lightly. His father taught him and his brother to treat their employees with respect and fairness. Unfortunately, not all factory owners valued their workers. Then again, not all owners had risen from the depths of poverty to become wealthy men as had his father. He had left his children not only with a financial inheritance, but with a reputation of being worthy of the title gentleman. It was a responsibility Miles did not assume lightly.

He put aside the studies he'd been perusing and watched Bitt. Head bent, she read with a quiet ferocity that befuddled him. Her hair was twisted in a neat auburn chignon that allowed two pretty curls to drape over her petite shoulders. She had not noticed that their carriage had stopped.

The footman opened their door. Sunlight drenched the innards of the rig. Bitt looked up, blinking like an owl caught unawares. A strange and unwieldy emotion knotted in Miles's chest. There was something so intensely feminine and gentle about Elizabeth.

After their visit to Gunter's, he wasn't sure he'd done the right thing in agreeing to this betrothal. She was a rare flower, a fragile bloom of womanhood in need of protection. He may not be able to give her his heart nor his time, but could he provide a safe haven for her soul?

"Thank you, Thomas." Miles held out his satchel to the footman, who took it before stepping to the side while Miles exited the carriage. The sound of the mill greeted him. Water charging over the mill wheel created a constant rushing noise.

Once on the ground, he beckoned Bitt to step out of the rig.

Clutching her book, she held out a hand.

"Leave the novel," he said.

"Must I?" The timidity he'd so often seen on her in the past had returned. Her obvious fear clawed at his resolve to remain distant when every instinct propelled him to comfort her.

Feeling grim and tamping his emotions down to a more manageable place, he took her hand. "The book may be ruined or destroyed if you bring it in. A cotton mill is no place for dreams."

Her chin quivered for the briefest moment before notching up as though she'd found some starch in her spine. She set the book on the seat and then allowed him to help her out.

He caught a whiff of her perfume, wildflowers and honey. He set her quickly on the ground, releasing her, forcing himself to forget how soft her skin had felt against his, how tiny her waist beneath his palm.

"This belongs to you?" She offered him a tremulous smile as she pointed toward the factory before them. An imposing brick building, it offered little in the way of gentility. The first time Anastasia had seen his other factory, she'd had a fit of the vapors.

Bitt was made of sterner stuff, he guessed, for her color remained healthy and her eyes direct.

"Yes," he answered. "I've some changes to make. It was in disrepair and not producing a profit." He shifted on his feet, shoving his hands into the pockets of his jacket. Perhaps he should have waited to bring her here. Waited until flowers and shrubs had been planted in the barren landscape. Anything to escape the illusion that they were about to enter a prison. An illusion he hoped to change very soon.

"Owning a factory seems as though it requires a great deal of time."

He grimaced, fighting the urge to look down at her lest she see his discomfiture. One of Anastasia's greatest complaints had been his lack of time spent with her. "Most of my reading involves articles regarding profit and loss, how to run a mill in the most efficient ways. Sometimes I enjoy a good, scientific discourse on new inventions."

She shot him a look of surprise, which he couldn't decipher. A part of his preoccupation during their travel was because he had wanted to avoid conversation that might turn toward uncomfortable topics. It was bad enough that her perfume had filled the interior of his carriage, making focusing impossible because all he could think of was the woman sitting across from him.

"This is it." He held open the factory door, his breath captive while he waited for her denouncement. This was his reason for bringing her, wasn't it? To prove that while she wished to avoid ruin, marriage to him could be a far more riskier matter. "What a man of business does while the beau monde sleeps."

Bitt tossed him a frosty look, no doubt catching the gist of his words and taking offense. Let her. He didn't have the time nor the inclination to tiptoe around titled snobbery. Unlike some people, he worked for his money.

Thus armed with that bit of logic and bitterness, he surveyed his acquisition, trying to see it through her eyes. Or rather, smell it.

As they entered the breaking room, noxious heat slammed into Miles. He was ready for the change, used to the odor of machinery, human sweat and dirty cotton, but Elizabeth was not prepared for such a blast. She halted immediately. The sounds of the machinery were muted in the front entrance, but as soon as they entered the spinning room, the clamor would be ceaseless.

She fumbled in her skirts, pulling out a lacy handkerchief and pressing it to her nose. Her eyes were saucers. "How can anyone work here? Surely this is unhealthy."

Lips pressed together, Miles surveyed the breaking room. It was wide and open. On one side, hundreds of bales of cotton were stacked up against the wall, waiting to be broken open in the blowing room and carded. The door on the other wall swung open.

"Mr. Hawthorne, good to see you." His manager, John

Grealey, hurried over. His slight frame and pallid skin testified to his history working in the mills. The man's knowledge was a boon, which was why Miles kept him on when he bought the factory. Unfortunately, Grealey was used to horrid working conditions, and since he'd been a child laborer himself, he displayed neither sympathy nor compassion toward his workers. He had become hardened toward humanity.

An attitude Miles sought to remedy.

"Good day, Grealey. This is my betrothed, Lady Elizabeth Wayland."

His manager's smile froze when his gaze alighted on Bitt's face. He stared too long, attention fastened to the birthmark on her cheek. Anger surged through Miles in hot, undulating waves. The man's nose twitched and he quickly bowed, perhaps to hide the play of emotions on his face.

"My lady," he said.

"Mr. Grealey." Elizabeth's eyes flickered. Miles noted the flash of hurt, followed by resolve. She nodded to Grealey, the tilt of her head regal and cold.

"I wish to look in on things," Miles said as his manager straightened, eyes averted from Bitt. "We will be touring every room. I trust my changes were implemented speedily?"

"Oh, yes, sir. I've been working on it, sir." Grealey swept his palm through the air. "We installed windows and thoroughly washed the walls. That did cut into processing time, though. We are behind and hired out extra positions to fill the gap. Mr. Shapely was by just yesterday to approve the changes."

Miles nodded. He'd check the books himself. Mere maintenance should not be such a detriment to production. He touched Bitt's elbow and, nodding a goodbye to Grealey, they left the room. They turned into a hallway. The sounds of the machines grew louder. Before taking her into the gut of the factory, he stopped at a small square of a room on his left where his employees ate during breaks.

Four women sat at the table. Their tired gazes met his. One woman raised her hand in greeting. Beside him, Bitt was silent. The swish of her dress was a faint sound. She looked like a bright flower, clean and fragrant, in this dank room.

There were only four windows and the grime kept out the sun. They had obviously not been cleaned in years, despite Grealey's assurances.

Something akin to regret filled Miles. He gestured to his employees. "Good morning, ladies. I am Mr. Hawthorne. This is my betrothed, Lady Elizabeth Wayland."

Several *my lady*s were uttered, but he did not miss the suspicious eyes nor the resentful gazes of the women, whom looked to be Bitt's age, though one could not tell it for the lank hair and gray skin.

There were several more changes to be made here, he determined. The people in his father's mills had been happy and healthy. Indeed, his other factory was productive despite the humane changes he'd implemented, changes which other mill owners had warned him against.

Elizabeth performed a curtsy, expression shuttered. They left and traversed the long hall to the door at the end, which would lead downstairs to the main part of the mill. To fill the silence which Bitt so readily allowed to bloom, Miles talked of mechanics. How the bales of cotton arrived and must be sifted through in the blowing room. The way the children pulled twigs from it to make it ready for carding and spinning.

"Children?" Her head snapped up.

"Well, yes, most families work all day here."

"But children? Miles…" The disapproval in her voice set his teeth on edge. He guided her to the door, pausing before opening it. He did not need his employees to hear her remarks and start a riot like the ones happening in other parts of the country. One of the reasons he wanted her here was to gain a feminine perspective, but he had not expected accusation.

The air here was no better than in previous rooms. He struggled to take a deeper breath, knowing part of the problem was his irritation at Elizabeth's criticism.

"I told you there are changes to be made. Laws are being created to help the underprivileged and protect them from being taken advantage of, but in the meantime, it's my duty to provide these people with a wage so that they can eat. Do you understand? I purchased this factory knowing I had much to change in it."

"Thou doth protest too much, sir." Bitt's eyes flashed at him in the dim hallway.

He crossed his arms over his chest. "I did not bring you here to criticize my work. This is how I make money, Elizabeth. I'm not some titled earl who lives off his wife's dowry. Nor am I a wastrel making my fortunes at the gaming table."

"And how did you come to be in possession of your factories? Did not your father start this family business? In essence, you are living off his hard work."

Miles felt not the slightest hint of amusement at her jab. "It is my own work ethic that has continued the prosperity of my mills. And what do you know of our business?"

"I know many things." Her chin lifted. "I know you've a brother who also owns factories, and that you have a reputation for being a gentleman who treats all who meet you with fairness and courtesy. I know your father died while you were at university." Her voice faltered and despite the glare still residing in the icy depths of her eyes, the cut of her lips softened. "I was sorry to hear of your loss."

"You came to the funeral." He remembered her hair, still the bright red of youth, and the sorrowful look she'd shared with him at the grave site. As though she understood his pain. Though they had not spoken, it had been an odd moment of comfort he'd never forgotten.

"Yes." She looked down. The concrete floor was dirty and littered with all the dregs of a cotton mill.

What was she thinking? Did she hate this place? Even he disliked this aspect of business, but he saw too many possibilities for betterment to let the factory go. "These people deserve a better life, Bitt," he said quietly. "With God's help, I can give them that."

"By hiring children? By exposing them to noxious fumes and long hours of labor?" She glanced behind him, to where they'd left the exhausted women. "Their youth is gone. What joy can they find in life? How do they even have time to read?"

"Read? My dear Bitt, the majority of these employees are illiterate."

Her lips flattened into a frown. "I don't understand why you insisted I visit this place."

"I want you cognizant of what my life is. What my daily duties consist of. I hoped for a feminine viewpoint, not a lecture on impractical ideals. Marriage will make turning a blind eye to my business impossible."

"I turn a blind eye to nothing," she said crossly.

"You are irritated."

Mouth set, she looked away but high color tinted her cheeks. "Show me the rest of your factory, then."

"Bitt…" He hesitated. Despite his earlier thoughts of protecting her, perhaps it was better if she did not marry him. A place like this lent no protection for an innocent heart. He had entertained the small hope that she would add womanly softness to the factory. Perhaps a kinder ambience. "If you want to reconsider our betrothal—"

She gave him a sharp look. "And be ruined? I think not. I can certainly manage a factory tour without succumbing to hysterics. I understand your logic in having me visit. These requirements you've set forth are all a part of your stubborn plan to force me from the safety of my library."

"Not safety," he said gently. "Confines."

"Our perspectives are markedly different. Open that door on which your hand has been resting. Show me all that I have missed whilst *hiding* in my library." Her words reeked of bitterness.

Miles grimaced. "Are you really so naive that you did not know who made those fancy fabrics you wear?"

"My dresses are specially ordered from Paris. Grandmother's doing, not mine," she added, as though it made a difference.

"And who do you think makes them in France? Silkworms?"

She did not laugh at his words. Indeed, her mouth was altogether too grim. Dread pooled in his gut. If she hadn't liked what she saw with the women, then she would not like this next room at all. He hadn't expected her reaction. He'd anticipated sorrow for the people, not enragement at the unfairness of life. Not anger toward him. He only wanted her to see the world as it was and not colored by fancies caused by too much reading.

Now he wondered at his own wisdom. Perhaps Elizabeth was better off staying in her comfortable world. Maybe God had put her there for a reason.

He turned the knob to the next room, the handle as cold and hard as the life his employees led. As the door opened, the sounds of machines assaulted them. The aggressive clacking, the constant hawing of the looms set up throughout the room. From one end to the other, they were lined like sentries. At first no one saw him. His employees were busy emptying spools, refilling them. Checking threads and tying knots.

He'd been debating how to change the flow of duties. Unfortunately, little boys were best at doffing, but climbing on the machines to remove lint was dangerous. As was the spinning the girls did. His brow pinched. He was in a conundrum of sorts, as the families needed the income from their children, yet he could not countenance the employment of these little ones when the risk of harm remained high.

His other factory had been opened by his father. No child was allowed to work unless over the age of twelve, and then for a maximum of six hours per day.

But this place proved to have different needs. The families counted on the children's income to make ends meet.

Elizabeth gasped, drawing his attention from his thoughts. He glanced at her and winced at the accusation in her eyes.

Miles clenched his jaw. For all Bitt's angry words and

verbal jabs, he'd always known she held a measure of affection for him. He had never felt that she truly despised him.

Until now.

Chapter Seven

A child without a smile cracked Elizabeth's resolve to stay detached. She stared at the room filled with noise, cotton and children. There were both women and men in the room, but it was the children who snagged her attention, their tiny faces painfully hooking her like the trout John used to catch from the stream at Windermar.

Wan, listless, they were sprinkled around the machines like faded versions of everything a child should be. She did not know much of children. When she went into the village, she avoided them. But always she heard them. Running and screaming and laughing. Hardly ever holding still, that she could tell.

These children stared at her with large, soulful eyes, as though begging her to take them from this dungeon, this horrid, terrible place. How could Miles allow this? Her heart felt like it might split right down the seams.

She wanted to close her eyes or cover them, anything to block out the sight of suffering. Miles claimed to pay them, but then why were they so emaciated? So bent and pallid? A little girl wobbled forward on bent knees, looking like an arthritic old woman.

She asked a question, her voice reedy. Her accent was too strong, her grammar too improper, Elizabeth supposed, for she could not understand her with all the noise in the room. Reluctantly, she looked at Miles.

It was quite unfair that he could stand there and be so vibrant and strong, all piercing eyes and vigor when everyone else acted like automatons. She recalled reading a book once about a cadaver animated by electricity. The being came to life but he was not human.

It had been a frightening novel and yet the theme of the story, of unconditional love and the power of kindness, quite affected her for some time to come. She must make a note to look for that novel when she returned to Grandmother's.

If she returned.

Such a depressing realization that her former home was no longer home.

A tug on her dress brought her back to the present. She looked down. The little girl peered up at her and asked the question again.

"She wants to know if you'll meet Sally, her doll," Miles said in a monotone.

Too surprised by the request to worry about Miles's strangeness, emotion tugged within her chest. She nodded, allowing the little girl to take her hand and lead her to a door on the far side of the room. They descended a flight of stairs, entering a dim room with dusty air and lint everywhere. Far from the chattering looms, this room teemed with people sifting through cotton, plucking out impurities. There were machines here, as well, and the dirtiness of it all bothered her.

The little girl chattered, dropping down next to a pile of cotton and digging through it until she found what she was looking for. Smiling broadly and showcasing several missing teeth, she brandished a surprisingly neatly stuffed bit of rag. The sound of scuffling feet alerted Elizabeth to the presence of other children.

Their small statures gave little insight into their ages, but she supposed by their eyes that they were older than they appeared.

"Katie loves her dolls," one boy said. "Mr. Hawthorne gave them to her."

Elizabeth repressed her surprise at that information. It explained the even stitches on the otherwise ragged doll. How very kind of him.

"Sally is beautiful." Elizabeth felt no remorse at the exaggeration. The rag was lovely to Katie, and that was all that mattered.

The little girl pressed the doll into her hand. Tufts of cotton peeking out from the doll's worn clothing warmed her palm. Katie obviously played with this doll often. Memories transported Elizabeth to her own childhood, to the frolicking openness of it. What must it be like to work from sunup to sundown? She guessed these children must, for their skin bore no trace of sun exposure.

Elizabeth looked more closely at the doll, marveling at the fine stitching of the cloth that made up its head. Someone with a fine hand had made this.

"Beet."

"Beet?"

"She means Bitt." The little boy moved closer, followed by the other children.

Elizabeth's eyes prickled. She'd always hated that name, but for some reason, hearing that a little girl's treasure carried the same moniker filled her with unaccountable emotion. She glanced at Miles but he was speaking with that ferret-faced man they'd met earlier.

Mr. Grealey.

She turned her attention to the small group surrounding her. Apprehension rippled through her. Taking a deep breath to steady herself, she handed the doll back.

"That's my name, too," she said.

"Your name be Bitt?" Another child spoke. An older girl with long, dirty braids and bright eyes.

"You may call me that, if you wish," she found herself saying.

The children were silent, studying her, measuring her, she thought.

But no, as one pointed at her face, she realized they were looking at her birthmark. Realization barreled through her. In the midst of her shock at what it meant to work in a factory, she'd forgotten all about the disfigurement. How silly to think the children wouldn't notice it, though.

"My name is Louise," the older girl said. "Did your man do that to you?"

Katie reached out and touched Bitt's cheek. Alarmed, she pulled back, out of the range of the little girl's touch. She covered her cheek with her fingers.

"My man?"

"Mr. Hawthorne." Louise's gaze was far too grave for a girl her age. "Did he scar you?"

A flush washed through Bitt. She shook her head forcefully, making herself meet the girl's eyes when she truly wanted to run and leave this place. "Oh, no, not at all. This is not a scar. It is a birthmark. I was born with it. A great-aunt of mine had one, as well, so it is hereditary."

A terrible thought occurred to her as she spoke. If she

had chosen a love match rather than a marriage of convenience, she could have passed this monstrosity on to her own children.

Another reason that marriage to Miles was the wisest course of action.

Swallowing hard, she shrank from the eager faces of the children. They seemed closer than before, surrounding her, trapping her.

Her pulse pounded, and her mouth dried. *Stand up*, she told herself, but her legs refused to obey. Heat accosted her. She became aware that her clothes were damp. The children were all talking now, pointing at her, but she couldn't understand most of them. Why didn't they speak proper English? Why were they pointing?

"Elizabeth?" Miles parted the children, holding out his hand.

With a relief so profound it shook her, she grasped his fingers and stood. The stifling air remained, but she was once again taller than the little people around her. They dispersed, perhaps going back to their jobs.

"Thank you," she murmured, slipping her hand from his comforting grasp.

As they left the room, he asked, "Are you ready to see my office?"

"Please." Faintness pressed in on her. The unwavering sounds of machinery beat against her skull. She could not allow this weakness to best her though, or Miles might think her too incompetent to marry. All she wanted was the quiet of her home. A good book. A spot of tea.

By the time Miles took her to his office, located on the first floor at the rear of the building, she was more than ready to leave. She was tempted to sink into the chair he offered her, laying her head on his desk and closing her eyes.

She didn't, though. Nay, the wife of a mill owner must possess more stamina. Battling the exhaustion, she meandered through the small and sparse office. There were no personal effects to be seen.

"Is this where you work?" She traced the edges of the sturdy desk.

"No, Mr. Shapely and Grealey handle the operations of the mill from here. This is essentially their office, but I thought you'd like to look at the ledgers and get an idea of how we make our money. The costs involved. I know you handle your grandmother's affairs and thought you might be interested in seeing the numbers." There was a slight burnish to his cheekbones, as though the profession of his knowledge of her habits embarrassed him.

The quietness of the room steadied Elizabeth. She finally felt that she could draw air without breathing in millions of cotton fibers. Unaccountably, she relaxed.

Miles moved to a cabinet on the far wall and pulled out a huge tome. An accounting book.

A wriggle of excitement threaded through her. She did enjoy numbers. They were steady and unchanging. After the exciting challenge of figuring sums, there would be a precise and unalterable answer. Completely objective.

"This is very thoughtful of you." She sat in the chair at the desk, fingers itching to flip through the pages. He plopped the ledger in front of her and when she glanced up at him, she caught the tail end of a satisfied sparkle in his eyes.

Perhaps the old Miles did reside in this strange man before her. As she ran her fingers along the ledgers, asking questions, checking sums, another part of her was very aware that Miles smelled of sandalwood and clean soap. The heat from where his arm rested near hers was quite distracting.

"There are a few discrepancies here." She peered closer at the paper, relieved to have something to occupy her mind other than this man beside her. "Do you have a pen?"

He opened a drawer, removing quill, ink and paper. As she jotted figures, Mr. Grealey poked his head into the office. "Sir, the new machine you ordered has arrived."

"I am fine here," Elizabeth assured him, seeing the concern in his expression. "Do you order machinery often?"

"It is the newest version of a loom. I'm eager to implement it."

She heard the excitement in his voice and almost smiled, but caught herself. Could she so easily forget the people he employed? That he'd chosen to keep children on staff? Narrowing her eyes, she shot him a hard look and returned to the books.

He left without saying another word.

Miles stomped back to the office. The new loom worked perfectly, and he'd received a discount because he'd been one of the first twenty-five buyers. He should be happy. Giddy.

Instead he dreaded facing Bitt and her accusatory frowns. What did she know of owning mills? Of being responsible for the livelihoods of hundreds? Nothing, that's what.

He pushed open the office door. Bitt was deep in concentration, the lights casting shadows over her pretty hair as she scratched out numbers with the quill. "It's getting late," he said.

His curt tone startled her. She glanced up, lids flickering. "Very well. I am just about finished here."

"So soon?"

"I'm quite good with numbers." The tiniest hint of a smile played about her mouth until she firmed her lips. Always the duchess's granddaughter, he thought unkindly.

"Indeed. So is my steward. Let us go now, before dark descends. It is at least an hour's ride to your grandmother's estate."

"I didn't realize she lived so near." She placed the quill and ink back into the drawer, closed the ledger and, standing, held it out to him.

He was forced to come deeper into the room to take it from her. After putting it away, they left the office. Bitt was withdrawn and, despite his usual instinct, he felt no compulsion to tease her out of her pique.

He'd hoped this trip would not only prove that she'd make an able wife, but also that she could offer more ideas for improvements. Instead all the journey showed was that Bitt was incapable of accepting who he was and his place in the world. Bringing her here had been a colossal mistake, one he was sure to pay for with the waspish end of her tongue.

He clomped upstairs, Bitt behind him, annoyance making his footsteps heavy on the stairs. When they came into the hall, near the break room, the sound of a man's voice reached them.

From the sounds of his tone, he appeared to be chiding a child. They were almost past the room when Miles realized Bitt had not followed him. She stood near the break room door, face arrested.

"I cannot allow this," she said. Giving him one of those looks he recognized from childhood, the one that never failed to send his pulse rocketing, she pivoted and went into the room.

He hurried after her.

In the break room, Grealey loomed over a small girl. Miles could hardly see her for the way the man overpowered her. He entered just in time to watch Bitt as she reached over to poke Grealey on the shoulder.

The man twirled around, his face red. When he saw who'd poked him, he bowed. "My lady, how may I help you?"

"For one, you will stop yelling at that child. Your voice carries into the hallway."

Miles had never heard Elizabeth sound so cold.

Grealey didn't like what she said. His face hardened. "The child was playing when she should have been working. That is dangerous for everyone." He looked past her to Miles. "Sir, I am only doing my job. There is no excuse for this youngster to have put others in harm's way."

"A simple warning will do in the future."

"Yes, sir." Grealey glared at the little girl, who Miles could now see was a very grubby Becky, a child he'd met before. Her deep brown eyes gazed woefully up at him. The painful-looking scar from what looked like the incomplete repair of a cleft lip twisted her lips into a quivering frown.

As she scurried away, Grealey grunted. "She doesn't talk so good because of that ugly face but her ears work just fine. I should have fired her on the spot. Homely critter."

A small sound issued from Elizabeth. A flush deepened her color, and Miles noticed that her tiny hands were fisted at her sides. Reacting quickly, he took her by the arm and moved her toward the door. "Refrain from personal remarks, Grealey, and focus on safety and production. I will return tomorrow morning to go over a list of repairs that are still needed."

He ushered Elizabeth away, out of the building and into the cool, moist air of an English afternoon. Gray wisps of clouds drifted across the hilly horizon. Tension radiated through his betrothed's body. He felt her arm quivering beneath his fingertips.

Once they were safely out of earshot, she yanked her arm from his grasp and pointed to the factory. "You allow that…that oaf…that cad to work with your employees? He is a terrible person. Unkind, unfeeling. How could he say that about her, and so callously? What do you think he has said to her face? You must fire him at once. I insist." She drew a breath, her chest heaving, eyes flashing.

Feeling rather grim himself, he crossed his arms. "They are in need of an overseer. Grealey knows the running of a mill in minute detail."

"He is a detriment to your company," she said hotly.

She looked every inch the hoyden he remembered from childhood. Where had this Elizabeth disappeared to in the last few years, he wondered. Had too much reading destroyed her capacity to feel until this moment? He couldn't help the grin that cracked the surface of his resolve.

"Of course, you would laugh." Her haughty tones reminded him of the duchess. Casting him a disgusted look, she allowed his driver to help her into the carriage.

As soon as he climbed in, she wasted no time in continuing her diatribe.

"That horrid creature must go at once. I am insisting upon it. I will personally find another supervisor more skilled and more compassionate than that ridiculous ninny. I shall read about other— Why, are you laughing at me?"

Miles tried very hard to hide his smile. "Not at all. I admire your determination to remedy the situation. I had hoped you might have ideas on how to make the mill a better place for the workers."

She gaped at him. The carriage hit a rut and she gripped the seat. He had the feeling she'd like to grip his throat by the look in her eyes.

"Try not to look so murderous," he said mildly. "I'm sure if you pick up that book beside you, soon all the injustices of life will be forgotten and you can lose yourself in a story where all is right with the world."

Her mouth moved but no sound issued forth. She was well and truly vexed. He knew he should feel remorse for egging her on, but he had clearly told her that he was making changes at the factory. She should, at least, give him the benefit of the doubt.

If her eyes shot bullets, he'd be dead.

He chuckled at the thought.

Wrong reaction. She swung her reticule at him and it very nearly took out his eye. Only his quick reflexes saved him from a wallop.

A flicker of irritation lit.

She pursed her lips, placing the reticule-turned-weapon next to her in a prim movement. "Next time you shall not be so fortunate. As I recall, my aim has been true in the past, and if you continue your dastardly teasing, it shall be again."

Shooting her a rueful look, Miles leaned back against the squab. "It is one thing for an immature young woman of four and ten to hit her brother's annoying university friend with her purse. It is quite another for a betrothed woman to do so. Do you find yourself subject to these fits of rage often?"

"You beastly man!"

"Better to be a beast than an ill-tempered woman."

She made a sound that came close to a snarl.

The corners of his lips crooked. He stretched his legs and gave her a considering look. "I do not recall your temper being quite so vile, Bitt. I believe this to be a direct result of quiet, restrained living. Much like a pot sitting on the stove, slowly simmering. You've been simmering too long, and now that the heat has turned up, you've boiled over."

"That is an odd and incomplete metaphor. It makes no sense."

He shrugged. "I am simply trying to understand you."

Suddenly, her face wrinkled. Not in the "I'm going to laugh" way but in the way a face does just before water starts streaming down one's cheeks. She pressed both hands against her brow, hiding herself from his view.

"Are you going to cry?" Miles heard the strangled note in his voice, but little could repair it.

"No" came the muffled answer. And that was all.

Eyeing her, he shifted on the seat, straightening in case his assistance was needed. Though for what, he had no idea. Her weeping was his fault, of that he was certain. He should not have teased her so, but it seemed better to tease than to engage in an argument. He did not disagree with her sentiments.

He studied her carefully. After a long moment, she removed her hands and met his look. Yes, her eyes sparkled unnaturally bright but he caught no sight of tears.

"I had thought better of you, Miles," she said quietly, "than that you'd allow such treatment in your factories."

Gut twisting, he barely restrained himself from punching the seat. "I am sorry to be such a disappointment."

"We will muddle through somehow." She picked up her book and poked her nose into it.

Holding back an oath, Miles forced himself to silence. There was much he could say, but all his words would prove hurtful. She insisted on seeing only what she wanted.

Truthfully, Grealey's treatment of the child was beyond the pale. It was a small droplet in a full bucket of injustices. The power to fix such problems remained beyond his grasp, at least for now.

If only Elizabeth understood. They were not even married yet, and he keenly felt his lack. It did not bode well for their future.

Chapter Eight

Ruination was so very inconvenient.

Elizabeth was still fuming behind the pages of her book when a shudder shook the entire carriage and it came to a grinding halt. The betraying sting of tears had eased, allowing her to set the novel to the side with some semblance of dignity.

"What happened?" she asked. Miles was already rising and opening the door.

He exchanged words with the driver. Then he hopped out, leaving her alone.

Heart pounding, she willed herself to stay seated in the side-listing vehicle. It would not do to have an attack of hysterics. Today had been quite nerve-racking enough without the added bother of an overwrought constitution.

If only she had inherited Grandmother's gift for fainting. To bypass the pounding heart, perspiring palms and dizzy spells and slide into blackness seemed more desirable right now than panic.

Instead she practiced deep and steady breaths, as Grandmother had taught her many years ago. The pressure above her sternum eased. Surely they were not too far from Windermar or its village. They'd been traveling over thirty minutes.

Miles thrust his head inside. "Broken wheel. It will take time to repair. Tom is riding into the village of Windermar as we speak."

She gathered her book and reticule. "Shall we wait here, then?"

His eyes crinkled at the corners. "That we shall, unless you'd rather fly to the estate."

Her stomach rumbled, reminding her that her small repast had been many hours ago. "I'd rather dinner and a warm bed."

"That is several hours from now, dearest."

She tamped down the tiniest delight at the way he said *dearest*. He meant it in a purely general sense, she was sure. Standing, she went to the door. "Help me down, please."

He did so, his grip firm. Once safely on the ground, she adjusted her hems, shook out her skirts and smiled up at Miles. "I wish to walk to Grandmother's."

His brows shot up. "Now? At dusk?"

"It will be faster than waiting for aid, and I'm hungry. We can pass through the village and perhaps pick up mutton pies or fresh stew."

"I suppose the idea has merit."

"But of course, it does." She fastened her reticule more securely to her wrist. Unfortunately, the novel did not fit within the small purse, so she would have to carry it. "Come along, Miles."

Giving the lopsided carriage one last glance, she began marching toward Windermar. The rough road proved treacherous to her slippers, though, and she moved onto the grassy bank. Trees sporadically lined the road and deep fields of emerald grass surrounded them. She drew in a satisfying breath.

How beautiful and fresh this was compared to the cotton factory. Those poor children. They should be frolicking and climbing trees. Picking flowers and laughing. Not cooped up in stuffy rooms that echoed with unnatural sounds and held dangerous machines.

She became aware of Miles walking beside her, his cologne a sweet addition to the land's natural scents.

"Are you still angry with me, Bitt?" he asked some time later.

The village could be seen. Only a few more minutes and they'd be within reach of food. She took time answering him, for after her outburst earlier, she realized her unfairness toward him but could not fathom how to fix it.

"I was surprised," she said carefully, using every ounce of self-control to contain her anger at what she'd seen.

"You think me capable of great greediness, I suppose."

His words sullied their companionable walk. Elizabeth frowned. "I do not think such a thing of you, but surely there is a way to run the mill without exploiting the populace and destroying its youth."

He laughed, but the sound was dry and without humor. "If such a way existed, I would be the first to find it. I bought this factory several months ago and am still making renovations. Tell me, Bitt, what would happen if I fired all the children today?"

"You'd make less cotton, which means less money," she answered promptly. An uncomfortable heaviness invaded her. His questions felt like a test of sorts, one which she would certainly fail.

"And?"

"And what?" she answered a tad too crossly. She had never known herself to be quite so shrewish as she had been today. But he deserved it, she reminded herself. What kind of man employed children? Stole their childhood?

Not the kind of man she wanted to marry, she thought grimly.

"Think deeply about it."

Gritting her teeth, she stomped forward. She was thinking about it, wretched man. He acted as though she was half-witted.

She dodged a root poking out of the ground. She glared at him. "If you fired them, they'd have nowhere to go. I suppose they do not employ nannies."

Miles made a rather annoying sound, almost like a barely restrained cough. She crossed her arms and willed herself to reach the village. Her stomach rumbled, cramping. If only she could eat. Her toes stung and every step brought a new pebble to dig into the tender flesh of her feet. Her patience for Miles and his desire to defend himself threatened to flee.

Setting her shoulders, she silently willed him to drop the subject.

He did not.

"You're jesting, I hope?" He came up beside her, reaching for her reticule. He jogged the reticule in front of him and the coins clinked. "I daresay, Bitt, my workers could live on what you have in here for a month."

"Nonsense."

"Is it?" He cast her a look, the deepening shadows lining his face with disapproval. "With all your book reading and skill with numbers, it is a certainty that you must be aware of finances and the necessities of living."

Uncomfortable, she trudged on, saying nothing. Once again, Miles treated her as a spoiled, ignorant lady. "I am not interested in hearing your disparagement of my character."

"But you are interested in the plight of my employees." He released the reticule. He cut a dashing figure at dusk. Tall and lean, striding forward on sturdy boots that were no doubt more comfortable than her flimsy slippers.

"I am angry about their lifestyle," she corrected him. "Especially since you have the power to change it."

"As do you." He gestured to the reticule.

They were entering the outskirts of Windermar. "Throwing money at people has never solved poverty. Education, literacy. Those are practical solutions."

"And I ask you again, what would happen if the children in the families did not bring home income?"

Elizabeth blinked, his meaning sinking in. "Their families would starve."

"Exactly."

The firm, more finely combed roads of Windermar's village offered her feet a respite. "Mrs. Rose at the inn makes a fabulous meal. Perhaps you'd like to stop there before going on to Grandmother's?"

"Before we eat, I'll make arrangements for transportation at the livery."

She ducked her head out of habit as they passed cottages. The townspeople knew her and had always treated her with fairness, if not a bit of reserve.

When they stepped into the sweet warmth of Mrs. Rose's dining area, the last bits of tension seeped away.

"Lady Elizabeth, to what do we owe this visit?" Mrs. Rose met them halfway in, curiosity creasing her flushed features as she surveyed Miles. "Mr. Hawthorne? Is that you, sir?"

"Mrs. Rose, it's been a long time." He took her hand and kissed the top.

Silly gallantry, but Mrs. Rose giggled. "A bite of food for you two? Ye all appear right famished."

"Indeed, you know my appetite." Miles flashed his signature grin. It always looked just the slightest bit crooked, as though he planned a spot of mischief.

Elizabeth felt herself relaxing. This was the Miles she knew. Flirtatious and charming, a hint of mockery in his smile and no trace of that serious, irritable businessman. She set her reticule on a roughly hewn yet clean table near a wall. She settled into a chair.

"I'll arrange for travel and then I'll be back," said Miles. He went to speak with the man at the door as she sat, enjoying the quiet. It was a lovely feeling to soak in silence. Or rather, to live in her own bubble without outside interference.

Although the dining area was not empty, no one spoke to her as it would be unseemly to approach one above their station. She was able to lose herself in her own comfort. A steady bustle enlivened the atmosphere and a fire had been started in the pit at the other end of the room. Mostly commoners ate here at this hour. She doubted she'd see any peers passing through. Grandmother did not often entertain visitors, but when she did, it was at her London house.

Elizabeth wondered how her parents fared. Had they succeeded in tamping down the gossip? Perhaps Lady Englewood had spread word that she'd seen them at Gunter's. The betrothal was scheduled to be announced in next week's papers.

Then Elizabeth would begin planning the betrothal ball. She did not relish the task, but since Miles wanted her to do it, she would. She owed him a great deal. But hosting a betrothal ball... She shuddered. The very thought made her squirm. At least today had not been so terrible, she supposed. She propped her chin on her hand, watching Miles across the room. She could not reconcile her childhood friend with the man across the room. He had grown up. He had changed.

Sometimes she felt as though she were still the same girl, marred and simple.

Today had opened her eyes, and perhaps that had been his intention all along. How many times had he reprimanded her for her reclusiveness? Caused her to feel overindulged and spoiled?

Miles turned and caught her staring. She gave him a little flutter with her fingers. No anger stirred. She'd always found it hard to stay perturbed with him.

If he wanted what was best for his workers, then his words regarding child employment made sense. He was truly in a quandary.

Miles waved back and a tiny flicker of warmth in her belly caught her by surprise. Of course, she held a measure of affection for him. He had, after all, been a part of her life for a long time. But what was this feeling inside, this unsettled tumultuous churning of her stomach, the uptick of her pulse when he smiled at her?

Horrified, she jerked upright.

Was she attracted to Miles? It could not be so. Was it because he'd shaved off that infernal mustache? Creating a younger-looking, less refined, more dashing hero?

Blinking hard, she opened her book, but the inn's

lighting was too dim. The words fuzzed and, annoyed, she slapped the book closed.

"Nothing worth reading?" Miles pulled out a seat, obviously done with finagling a ride home.

"It's too dark. Were you able to request a hackney?"

"Even better. The owner's son is riding to your grandmother's estate with a note from me and will hopefully return with her carriage."

"Perfect. I have not yet ordered food."

"I took the liberty." His lips lifted, revealing his white smile. "You did well today. I regret that the state of my factories shocked you, though."

She lifted a shoulder, tracing the crevices on the table with her fingertip. "It was not so horrible. I have simply never seen such miserable surroundings."

"I know," he said quietly.

A restlessness filled her. "Is it so everywhere? Surely there are societies designed to assist the poor?"

"Dearest, you truly have locked yourself away."

She stopped tracing as indignation flared through her. "Not at all. I am aware of the state of the world. I simply did not realize…" She trailed off because a dreadful squeeze had taken hold of her heart. Those children. Their haunted eyes. That ragdoll worn into a mangled, stitched-together cloth by innocent hugs. "Children find joy even in their dark circumstances."

"They do."

"And that dreadful man…you cannot keep him, Miles. He called her *ugly*." Her voice caught. She had heard that word about herself too many times. By her own parents, though they had not known she stood on the other side of the door.

"Do you think she is ugly?" Miles trained his gaze on her.

Mrs. Rose brought their food, setting the steaming bowls of stew before them with a hunk of bread.

"Thank you," said Miles, but he did not take his eyes from Elizabeth.

Her stomach twisted. "Of course not. But I question God. Why does he allow such circumstances? Not only hers, but all those who suffer?"

"Would you have every flower be a rose?"

"You avoid the question, but I understand the point you wish to make. Comparing people to flowers does not explain why some have so much, and some have so little."

His eyes flickered. His fingers clenched, and she thought perhaps he might not respond.

But then he said, "I have no answer as to why one child grows up in a well-fed, comfortable estate and another sleeps on cobblestones. But I do believe that beauty cannot be measured by one opinion. Becky, that is the child's name, by the way, is a perspicacious child who is thankful to be alive. When she was born, she found it difficult to nurse and for many years no one knew if she would live. Eating is problematic. Her family treats her with a great fondness. She is beautiful to God and to all those whose lives she touches." He spooned his stew. "Do you honestly think because one man calls her a name, his words will influence her entire life?"

"Sometimes that is exactly what happens. You are being condescending."

"You're upset with Mr. Grealey, and rightfully so, but Becky has borne more than one man's half-witted insults."

"What goes on in her heart may not show on her face."

Elizabeth looked down at the stew, filled with carrots and potatoes and a delicious-smelling broth. "Once again, I feel as though you are chastising me when it is your manager who spoke unpardonably."

"We are both tired and perhaps overly sensitive. We can speak of this later."

"We will, indeed." She draped her spoon with stew, mindful that while her opinion of Miles had risen, her opinion of herself had dropped.

How was such a thing possible? Was it because he knew the little girl's name and history? He cared about the details of the people he hired.

Yet she knew nothing of the servants in her grandmother's household, the place where she had grown up. She had felt ugly for so long, and now she was beginning to realize why.

It was not the birthmark on her face.

No wonder Miles had set forth strictures. No wonder he hesitated to marry her.

She ate the stew, but it went down tasteless.

Perhaps ruination was not such a terrible thing, after all. It certainly beat realizing what a horrid human being she'd allowed herself to become.

Chapter Nine

"What did you do to my granddaughter?" The dowager duchess eyed Miles.

He stopped himself just in time from wiggling beneath her eagle-eyed gaze. He was not a young lad anymore, tearing through her gardens and climbing her trees. Still, when she gave him that look, dipping her face and peering at him through that infernal quizzing glass, he felt like a scrawny, high-pitched child again.

Miles set his quill down while weighing his answer. Rather than having him travel to his own property, the dowager duchess had kindly allowed him to sleep at Windermar. His childhood home was farther away from the mill than her house. They had decided to stay an extra day as he wanted to oversee more changes at the mill. "Is there something wrong with Elizabeth?"

Lady Windermar swept into the chair across from the desk that she'd so kindly allowed Miles to use. Her perfume billowed outward with the expansion of her voluminous day dress. She pursed her lips. She tapped her quizzing glass gently against her knees.

"She's moping," she finally said, as though the responsibility for it lay directly on Miles shoulders.

Rubbing his eyes, he leaned back. What did one say to such a pointed remark? When he said nothing, the dowager leaned forward.

"You are her betrothed, though I must confess to a certain confusion as to how such an event happened right beneath my nose, without my consent. That is neither here nor there. The matter remains that as her betrothed, it is your responsibility to cheer her up. I've sent her out to the gardens. You must go to her now."

Miles frowned. Cheering up women had not proven to be a capability of his. He straightened and glared at the paperwork on the desk. "I don't have time."

The duchess made a sound that resembled a refined growl. He dragged his gaze off the desk to see her standing up, her shoulders squared.

"Young man, I did not ask if you had time. If you care for my granddaughter, which I suspect you do, then you will make time for her feelings. You will consider her thoughts and emotions and you shall treat her as your most valuable friend while in my home. Is that clear?"

Miles rose. "Eminently clear, Your Grace. I shall go to her at once."

He bowed and rounded the desk. Dread weighed his walk but he found his way to the gardens. The sun hid behind clouds though it was not quite afternoon. Rain might find them soon. The damp weather cooled his heated skin and the regret that had poured over him at the duchess's words.

It was not that he wanted to ignore Bitt or her feelings. He simply hadn't realized she was upset. She'd seemed tired and quiet last night when they arrived. When they

broke their fast this morn, she brought a book to the table
and hardly spoke to him. He assumed she'd spend the
day in the library.

Strolling down the manicured walkway, he scanned
the area for her. Flowers grew in profusion, the April
weather encouraging blooms to spring up everywhere.
The bright, cheery colors and floral perfumes encased
him in beauty. It had been too long since he'd walked
outside.

"Lovely, is it not?" Bitt's voice came from behind him.

Surprised, he swiveled and found her holding a lush
bouquet of flowers, her lips curved in a soft smile. "Besides the library, this is my favorite place.

"I know a bank where the wild thyme blows,
Where oxlips and the nodding violet grows,
Quite over-canopied with luscious woodbine,
With sweet musk-roses and with eglantine."

Miles squinted. "Was that a recitation?"

"Shakespeare." She shrugged and still that sweet smile
painted her face. "What are you doing out here? I had
thought you working."

"Even a working man is in need of sunlight and roses."

"Why, Miles, that is a lovely line of prose." And now
her teeth showed and her eyes flashed up at him, the
muted sunlight dimming their beauty not one bit.

A sense of shame rolled over him. He did not wish to
tell her the duchess had sent him out to check on her. He
looked more closely at his betrothed. Her bun was unkempt, and it appeared as though she'd rolled through
a carpet of wildflowers, for bits of grass and colorful
petals interlaced with the burnished strands of her hair.

His arms ached, as though filling them with an arm-
ful of Elizabeth might ease the pain.

Elizabeth had never enjoyed being stared at, but when
Miles did so, she felt different. Not ugly nor ungainly.
She simply felt *seen*. She was suddenly aware of the heat
in her cheeks and the succulent scent of the blooms in
her hands.

There were emerald shards in his irises, and they
glinted in the sunshine. His mouth looked soft and yield-
ing, relaxed, even. Perhaps he did not find her so dreadful, after all. He had shed his overcoat, probably in the
office Grandmother let him use, and his breeches were of
fine quality. They fit him well, molding to his fit frame.
She supposed his mills gave him first choice of fine fabrics. He lacked the pasty quality many gentlemen sported.
Evidence of their indoor lifestyles, which was why she'd
always assumed Miles spent a good deal of time outdoors. She had not realized just how involved he chose
to be with his business, assuming him to be a sports-
man because of his complexion. Now she realized he
simply enjoyed riding outdoors, whether in the country
or in London.

Since his businesses did mean so much to him, he
might be interested in hearing what she had discovered.

Once she had witnessed firsthand the environment of
his mill, she felt honor bound to change things, or to at
least support Miles in his goals.

"Would you care to take a turn about the gardens with
me? I had hoped to speak to you today and am relieved
to see you out of the office," she said.

"You are? It was my understanding that you were
miffed with me."

"An understatement, Miles. I was positively perturbed." She meandered down the path, smiling a secret smile, for time had given her space to consider his actions. "I overreacted. You were right to remark upon my purse, and I was wrong to demean your ambitions."

Silence behind her. Was he listening to what she said? Feeling the first prick of doubt, she kept walking. A rose trellis waited ahead, interlaced with thorns and blooms. Quite like how she felt when she was around Miles, never knowing if she'd inhale sweetness or be stung by an unseen thorn.

It was all rather disconcerting. She inhaled deeply, but the indignation that had filled her yesterday had seeped away, replaced with a resolve to change things for the better.

"It pains me to think of Becky and Louise and the other children working in cotton mills. Spending their entire lives bent over machines, little knowing the joys of the rest of the world. Like what it means to have an ice at Gunter's, or to stand at the harbor and breathe in the pungent salty air."

"You have done such a thing?" A trace of laughter filled his words.

She threw back a look, catching the quirk of his lips and the amused flash of his eyes. "Indeed not. But I have read of pirates and smugglers. I have a fair idea of how a harbor must stink."

She reached the trellis. It arched over her, a tangled weaving of scarlet petals that looked soft as velvet. A perfumed spot on her trek.

"Reading something is not the same as experiencing it." Miles touched a petal, his large hand incongruous and yet surprisingly gentle as he stroked the rose.

"It can be close," she said, caught unawares by the motion of his finger.

"But when you read of something, you do not get the full effect." He turned to her then, and she saw that he was not all humor as she had supposed, that something more drew his brow together. His voice was rough and the hand that had been touching the rose moved to her hair.

She could not move. Everything within her stilled at his proximity. Something like lightning raced through her, sizzling down her legs, electrifying her to this very spot on the ground. It was the oddest feeling, a drawn-out moment when speckled sunlight and rosy hues colored her entire being.

And Miles.

His fingers in her hair. His gaze on her. Grave and remote and something else, something she could not put a finger on, but the unnamed emotion lingered in his movements.

He held out a leaf to her. "Were you rolling in the grass, Bitt?"

And now there was the humor she frequently saw in his eyes. This was the thorn, then, to tug her back into reality and far from the romantic place she'd been swept to, a place where she thought he actually might want to kiss her.

Her lips tingled. Her stomach quavered.

"I would never roll in the grass," she said primly, summoning every ounce of pride she possessed. She pivoted, marching out from beneath the trellis as quickly as possible. "There are two things I wished to discuss with you. First, your employees' education. They are in need and I'm quite certain there must exist a precedent for establishing a curriculum for the illiterate. Second, the figures in your ledgers are incorrect."

Disgruntlement sharpened her words, but she cared not one whit. What a foolish girl she was, thinking Miles might actually kiss her when really he was laughing at the state of her hair. She kept marching upward, toward the house, hearing the crunch of Miles's boots behind her but not pausing. There was only room for one on the path, forcing him to stay behind her.

Which she preferred, as she didn't wish him to read the longing on her face, a longing she'd only just recognized.

A *very* irritating longing.

"One thing at a time, Elizabeth. Could you stop walking so we can discuss this?"

"I must get these blooms in water before they die. I'm decorating the dining room table. Usually I have someone else handle the task but I felt up to fresh air." The house loomed before her. Perhaps by the time they reached it, she could look Miles in the face without her every nerve vibrating.

How had this attraction happened? It was his lack of mustache, she surmised.

He must grow one back, and soon.

She entered the house through a back door, one the servants often used but she made use of it, as well. The walk to the kitchens was shorter this way. She'd hardly entered when a young woman rushed over to her.

"Oh, miss." The girl bobbed a curtsy. "There's been a dreadful accident with the housekeeper's son. She's having a fit of the vapors and we can hardly calm her. She's in the village, and there's still next week's menu to be planned and all sorts of other—"

"What is your name?" Elizabeth interrupted.

"Macie, my lady."

Elizabeth handed the flowers to Miles, who stood directly behind her. "Take those to the kitchen, please, and put them in water." She cast Miles one last look, soaking in the familiar and yet decidedly different angles of his face. He was too handsome for comfort, she decided. "We shall discuss the ledger at supper."

Gathering her skirts, she addressed the young maid. "Take me to her at once."

Chapter Ten

Miles returned to the study, but his thoughts kept straying to Bitt. The muddle of feelings she evoked drove him to distraction, and he was thankful when he received a post requesting his presence at the mill. He borrowed a horse, a young mare whose canter was smooth and quick, and left.

Elizabeth was nowhere to be seen when he passed through the village.

While at the mill, after reiterating his expectations to Grealey, adjusting his workers' schedules to allow for more breaks and fresh air and speaking to Shapely about expenses, he grabbed the ledger. Bitt's words echoed in his mind. She would not have mentioned an incongruity if there was none.

He would look further into the matter because when it came to numbers and reading, there was no one he trusted more than Elizabeth. He meandered back to the estate in the evening. Dinner at eight, he'd been told. He should have time to freshen up and pore over the ledger to find exactly what Elizabeth had seen. He'd return it to Shapely tomorrow.

A sweet English wind scurried across the acres of the duchess's estate. Hopefully the housekeeper's son was not badly hurt. He had not heard news of the injury while passing through the village. Then he'd veered into a forested area, finding a trail he used to ride as a child from his family's estate to see John on rainy afternoons.

And there'd always been Bitt, stowing along for the ride. Trailing her big brother, watching him with wide, curious eyes. He remembered clambering up trees just for the excitement of hearing her squeal in fear and chide him to get down. She had been younger, but that hadn't stopped her from ordering him and John about. Not that she would climb a tree.

She much preferred to read about one rather than do it herself. A thinker, a dreamer but not a doer.

And he was going to marry her.

The knowledge pressed against his skull, deep and irksome. Between John's demand and Bitt's unfortunate situation, he'd been roped into a cage he'd wished to avoid altogether. He pulled on the reins, guiding his mare to the right, onto a grassy hill that led straight up to Elizabeth's house. He comforted himself with the thought that once married, he wouldn't need to see her much.

This afternoon had been risky. Knowing her so well brought an unanticipated affection that could only complicate his life. An image of Bitt beneath the trellis tormented him.

For the briefest moment, an overwhelming urge to place his lips upon hers had raced through him, a mad temptation to taste for just one moment that sweet mouth, to feel his cheek against hers, to hold her close.

Madness! He pressed his heels into the mare's sides and they raced up the hill.

Madness to even contemplate engaging in a relationship with Elizabeth. He couldn't make her happy. He was not husbandly. Furthermore, she already thought ill of him. Nothing good could come of this attraction, of that he was certain.

The wind tugged at his skin, brisk and refreshing and altogether real. Certainly more real than this ephemeral state he found himself in regarding his betrothed. He would just have to do his best to stay away from her.

Ascertain that she was able to fulfill the tasks he set before her, that she could be the kind of wife he needed when life called for it, and then keep far away. The worst thing he could do would be to lead her on. To make her think that they could build any kind of romance together.

Regardless of their friendship, which truthfully was little more than a shared childhood affection, their marriage must remain platonic.

It was his duty to keep their friendship at a comfortable level. Thus, when he entered the dining room that night after freshening up, he was prepared in every way to be distant and calm.

That resolve didn't last. The dowager duchess sat at the long table, her hair piled high and candlelight flickering across her regal features. Miles bowed and took his seat. Bitt was not there.

It was strange how all his plans to keep calm dissolved at the lack of her presence.

"Where's Elizabeth?" he asked in what he deemed an appropriately casual voice.

Her Grace gave him an arch look, her thin eyebrows rising as though he'd asked the most important question of the evening. He shifted uncomfortably in his seat. He downed his water. A footman instantly refilled the glass.

"My granddaughter will be down in a moment." She sipped her own drink, eyeing him above the rim. Her quizzing glass was absent, which inspired an intense relief. He'd taken a great disliking to the thing. "Did you cheer her up this afternoon?"

Throat dry, he nodded. Normally he and the duchess got on rather well, but after what felt like a reprimand earlier, he'd been second-guessing himself. How could he have forgotten the responsibilities entailed in courting a woman? All the emotions, the guesswork, needing to find out how she felt constantly and if there was anything he should do to make her feel better.

His relationship with Anastasia had been exhausting. He had hoped for something calmer with Bitt.

"Very good." The duchess straightened. "Ah, Elizabeth, come join us. We were just talking about you."

Miles stood as she came in. She sat and Miles followed suit. He tried very hard not to stare, but it was as though an invisible force had taken hold of him. Her hair had been put up in a style that framed her face. Long curls caressed her shoulders. His head told him that curls did not change anything about Elizabeth, yet somehow they made her eyes look large and luminescent. They emphasized the delicate curve of her cheekbone and the charming pink bow of her lips.

To cure his dry mouth, he took another sip of water. "Good evening, Bitt. You look lovely tonight."

The duchess released a soft sound that sounded like approval.

"Thank you, Miles." She pursed her lips, glancing at her grandmother. "I was told I must dress wisely."

"Threatened, you mean?" A faint chuckle escaped him. "I say, Bitt, I'm surprised the tactic worked."

"As am I." She scowled at her grandmother but then sent him a gentle smile that did horrible things to his pulse. "How was your afternoon?"

"Productive. We've ordered more windows and arranged the schedule to allow for more moments of fresh air."

"You are renovating the Littleshire Mill?" Lady Windermar took a serving from the plate the servant held out to her. "It has been brought to my attention that new management has improved the place. Your father would be proud." Her face took on a soft look, startling Miles.

He took his own portion, uttering a quiet thank-you to the footman who held the platter for him. He had often wondered at his father's relationship with the duchess. It had been an unlikely friendship, strange because in those days the peerage did not associate with commoners. With them both being widowed, perhaps a feeling of more than affection had sprung up between them.

The duchess was lost in thought, her lips tilting at the corners. Miles looked to Elizabeth, but she also daydreamed. She had propped her chin on her fists and stared at some point beyond him. How often he had seen her in such a pose, the crystalline quality of her eyes fringed by dark lashes and her lips slightly parted at the beauty of her daydreams.

The moment did not last long. More food was brought out and they continued eating.

"I have been researching and believe I may have information that will help you update your mills to acceptable standards," she said.

"Elizabeth, are you instructing Mr. Hawthorne on the correct way to run his cotton mill?"

Her face pinked. "Of course not, Grandmother."

"A lady's job is to—" A mild cough interrupted her words. She pressed her table napkin against her lips. "Oh, my, I do not feel well."

At once Elizabeth was out of her seat, going to her grandmother and laying a hand on her shoulder. "Are you in need of your heart medication?"

Miles stood immediately, prepared to help.

The duchess shook her head. "No, no, I shall be fine. Perhaps I shall take my meal in my room." She waved a hand, her eyes suspiciously bright. "You two continue your conversation. Elizabeth, be sure to let this whipper-snapper know exactly what you expect."

The duchess pushed back from her seat, rising firmly, and Miles bit back a smile at the tone of her voice. She did look as though she were choking a bit.

On a laugh.

She must be delighted that Elizabeth was betrothed, he realized. After all, hadn't she been the one to provide the trousseau for Elizabeth's Season? Or something to that effect? He really did not know what all went into a woman's fashions.

Once the duchess had stridden, and not hobbled, out, Elizabeth and he sat back down to their food.

"That was odd," Elizabeth remarked.

"Theatrical," he responded.

They shared a grin, and at that moment, Miles felt a release from the tension that had ridden his shoulders since this morning. Perhaps marital happiness was out of reach, but surely contentment could be attained. A companionable friendship, even. Optimistic, he told Elizabeth the rest of his plans for the factory. "And you may be interested in knowing that I saw Becky and she appeared in good spirits."

She'd actually been running up and down the hall, not working, but Elizabeth didn't need to know that particular detail.

"I am so very happy to hear that. The housekeeper's son will also rally. He strained his back and bruised his leg in a fall. I ordered him to bed and hired a man from town to temporarily overtake his duties."

Miles paused, his fork midair. "*You* hired?"

"Why, yes. I run this household, Miles. Did you not know that?"

"It seems I should have. Who will take care of your grandmother when we are married?"

Her brow crinkled. "Why, I was planning to."

"You will run two households? Three, when we are staying in London?"

Elizabeth set her fork down. "I am perfectly capable of such a feat, should the need arise, but honestly, I was under the impression that you and I were not going to share a household."

"*Share* is a strong word. We may be in a partnership, but your part of our union is as the lady of the house. You will be expected to do your part." An uncomfortable tightness invaded his chest once again. Any reprieve he'd felt fled.

Elizabeth pressed her lips together, repressing the urge to wipe the priggish look from Miles's face. "Really, Miles, there is no need to be quite so dogmatic. I am aware of your plans and how I fit into them. There will be no problems, and I shall accomplish what you have asked of me. You are worrying over nothing."

"My dear, I never worry." Struck by an impish urge, he winked at her. "But it's important to me that you abide by our agreement. When you are Mrs. Hawthorne, you will be expected to handle all the requirements of housewifery."

Bitt blinked, her fork midair. "You sound as though you are worrying. As if you do not trust my abilities."

"To be truthful, I had no idea you ran this household. Every time I have ever visited, you have been in the library or wandering the estate with a novel beneath your arm."

Elizabeth's fork clattered on the plate. "I hardly think that you have a right to criticize me when your factories are in such obvious disarray."

Too late Miles realized he was upsetting her. Taken aback, he set down his own fork. "Explain yourself, madam."

"Certainly, sir." She emphasized the *sir*, as if pointing out his lack of title. Or perhaps just his lack. Fingers clenching, he set his jaw.

"Well?"

"Your ledgers, sir, have been manipulated. By whom, I dare not say, though you are well aware of my feelings toward Mr. Grealey. Perhaps you should spend less time sporting and socializing and more time in the offices examining your books."

Shock rooted Miles to his seat. His mind spun and annoyance built, especially at the way she sat so prim and judgmental in her seat, daring him to be better, to do better. As though he wasn't enough.

At that moment, he could only remember Anastasia. Though her words had been different, the feeling behind the accusations had been the same.

You're not good enough.

It echoed through him, loud and resounding, gouging his ego and prompting a flicker of temper to race through his veins.

"You misjudge me," he said, forcing the words through gritted teeth.

"Nay, your misjudgment came first." But her eyes flickered, and uncertainty dashed across her face.

"First, if you believe I spend my time socializing and sporting, then you do not know me at all. I am surprised by you, Elizabeth. I expected better."

Her eyes flashed. He supposed it was a good thing he sat across the table from her or she might jab him with her fork. Typically, he'd find her temper amusing, but her words had hit their target and the only thing he felt was a raw wound pulsating from her dig.

"Second," he continued in a stern voice, "I examine the ledgers once a month, much like clockwork. The entries are precise, and everything is as it should be. Perhaps you should reconfigure your mathematics."

"My mathematics are error free." Her face had taken on a still look that indicated deep anger.

What right had she to be miffed? He mentally retraced his words and could find no reason for her irritation…oh, except that he'd told her he expected a wife who could handle the household. That could not be the problem. She had no reason to be angry when she was the one who had questioned his abilities. His body was rigid, anger tensing each muscle. This was exactly why he'd avoided the marital state for so many years, when most men rushed into a new marriage after being widowed.

Women! Difficult creatures and impossible to please.

"Don't look at me like that," Elizabeth snapped. "How dare you assume I spend my days in leisure, flitting about like some kind of spoiled butterfly? You have done nothing but ridicule me since we were children. I am tired of the condescension from you. Yes, I read. I adore reading. Books and imagination are far better companions than real people. Why is that so difficult for you to comprehend? But my choice of pleasure does not mean I neglect my duties nor that I am incapable of living life." She shoved to her feet, a firebrand if he ever saw one. "You can take your condescension and—"

"Perhaps you should consider your own words." Miles pushed out of his seat and strode around the table until he was face-to-face with his snarling betrothed. It wasn't fair that she looked beautiful when angry. He knew of no other who managed such a feat. Even her birthmark, the shape of a heart, he'd often thought, was beautiful because it was a part of Elizabeth. "There is no other woman I would even consider giving my name to, ruination or no. And yet you act as though I am a dumb, unworthy man."

Shock crossed her face, paling her skin, widening her eyes. "I never said such a thing."

"You implied it," he said flatly.

Her lips tightened. She threw her napkin on the table. He hadn't even seen it balled in her fist. "If I were not in such a predicament, you would be the last man I'd ever marry."

She stalked off, leaving Miles to wonder how things had turned so horribly sour so very quickly.

Chapter Eleven

Men were dastardly creatures.

Elizabeth muttered to herself as she awaited a horse to be saddled. After mailing off her article on telescopes and astronomy to the Society of Scientific Minds, she'd spent the rest of the morning writing invitations for a betrothal house party. Grandmother had kindly agreed to allow the party to be held at Windermar one month from now. Though it would be during the height of the Season, she supposed some members of the ton might enjoy a respite from London's flurry of activities.

A house party was best, she'd decided, because it gave all the guests time to know one another and relax before the main event, the ball. It also provided Elizabeth the means to work up her nerve toward such an event. Being surrounded by the same people might defuse the nerves that so often plagued her in social settings.

That was her hope, at least.

Though many of the names on the list Miles provided had been unknown to her. Business associates, perhaps? That ought to be interesting, mingling the haut ton with people who worked for a living. Perhaps her parents might refuse attendance on such a basis.

Biting back a smile, Elizabeth acknowledged to herself that if such a thing happened, she would not be disappointed.

The groom brought the horse to where she waited outside. It was a lovely day for a ride. A cool breeze gusted across the land, riding waves of sunshine and scents of summer flowers. The land sloped in emerald hills all around her and after being cooped up for so many hours in the office, she'd decided that paying a visit to the housekeeper's son would not be uncalled for.

"Thank you," she told the groom. He doffed his cap, and a twinge grabbed hold of her. She should say more. Care more. She set her shoulders back. "What is your name?"

A look of surprise crossed the young man's face. He shuffled his feet in the grass. "William, my lady."

"William," she said, tasting the name, determining to remember it. If Miles could remember names, then so could she. Thinking of him brought a gouging hurt to her chest. She mustered a smile for the young man before her. "And the horse's name?"

"Silver Lightning, my lady."

"A sweet name. Have you been with us long?"

His head tilted. "I was born here. Sally is my mother."

Sally? She had no idea who he meant. Managing a tight smile and completely convinced of her absolute lack of skills in social etiquette, she thanked him. He helped her onto Silver Lightning and then hooked the basket of goodies she'd brought onto the back of the saddle.

It was a relief to canter off toward the housekeeper's house on the estate, to feel the warm sun on her hands and the breeze playing with her riding habit. It was a new one, straight from Paris, she supposed, since her grandmother had done the ordering. All in preparation of a Season, to find a husband.

And all she'd managed to accomplish thus far was an almost ruination and the discovery that after fifteen years at Windermar, she knew no one.

What kind of person paid no attention to others? Perhaps Miles was right about her, after all?

Last night had been terrible. She'd gone to bed upset and agitated. She'd tossed and turned, the look on Miles's face at dinner plaguing her all night long. His words, oh, how they stung! And he'd had the audacity to accuse her of calling him dumb.

Just the memory brought a betraying sting to her eyelids. She blinked hard. Never mind Miles and his wretched opinions. He'd always been this way. Challenging her and making her feel as though she couldn't measure up.

She frowned. Perhaps that wasn't completely true. It was because of Miles that she'd climbed her first tree. A harrowing experience, to be sure, and it ended with him scurrying up to rescue her from a branch. But… he'd had confidence in her. He'd encouraged her to try something new.

And there was the time a village child stole her book and tossed it into a creek. She clearly remembered bawling in her grandmother's sitting room, wrapped in a warm blanket and unable to sip her hot chocolate. And then Miles pranced into the study with her book. He was sopping wet, of course, and in the beginnings of autumn it was no small feat to jump into a creek just to fetch a novel.

The memory drained her ire.

Last night must have been an anomaly in their relationship. Though it was true that they did not always see eye to eye, he was as familiar and dear to her as a beloved novel. One whose ending she could not always guess, but did that not make for the most exciting stories?

As though her thoughts summoned him, she heard a call on the horizon and looked over to see Miles riding toward her. As he neared, a hitch drew her breath short.

She had no idea what he would say. An apology lay precariously on the tip of her tongue, but every ounce of her being resisted being the first one to apologize. Pride, she knew, yet it kept her back rigid as Miles drew his horse alongside her.

A playful smile edged his well-shaped lips, and the sunlight caused his eyes to twinkle. He tipped his head toward her. "My lady, how lovely your pursed mouth appears this morn."

Miles read the annoyance on Bitt's features as easily as he read contracts.

"It takes a certain kind of man to appreciate irritation," she snipped. Facing forward, she nudged her horse to keep moving. Miles easily kept up.

"Where are you off to this morning?" he asked.

The large basket behind her suggested a picnic but he found it hard to believe she'd be eating outside. Her riding habit fit her form well. She looked every inch a duchess's granddaughter. Once again he wondered why he thought a betrothal was a good idea. Last night had proved many things. Remembering scorched his good mood.

"I'm visiting the housekeeper's son."

"Annie's son?"

She tossed him a disgruntled look, hardly discernible beneath the decorated hat she wore. And ruffles. Ruffles everywhere. "How can you see past all those trimmings?" he asked.

"How do you remember every person's name?"

"I pay attention," he said drily.

He wasn't sure how it was possible for her back to stiffen further beneath the smooth fabric of her habit, but he was certain it did. He brought his mare closer to hers.

"Really, Miles." She shot him a scowl, but he read the hesitation in her eyes.

"I'd like to join you," he said simply. "I'm not happy with how our conversation ended last night, and a ride together leaves room for more discussion."

"There is nothing to discuss. You have kindly agreed to marry me to save my family from bearing the consequences of my corrupt ways. I will do my utmost to honor your name." Her formal tone echoed the duchess, causing another unwilling smile to form.

He did not recall her being so prickly, so difficult, in years past. Last night's barbs irritated but today, riding in the spring air, the scent of leather and horse perfuming their ride, he could only think of how he enjoyed her feisty words. They added spice to a bland day.

"Thank you for pointing out any errors in the ledgers," he said. "Even though I pride myself on my mathematical skills, I have been reexamining the ledger per your advice but have yet to find your changes."

"I did not write in your book, Miles. I wrote on a separate paper. Also, it is not the addition that is erroneous. It is the prices of products. The amounts. Although there may have been one or two mathematical errors."

"I misunderstood you, then. For I thought the math was off."

"It is the prices, Miles. But perhaps I am wrong. Perhaps I was looking for deception where there is none."

"I shall look into it," he said with finality. It might require more research, but he would get to the bottom of it. Even if only to set her mind at rest. Slow clouds crept across the sky, reminding him that they'd best hurry before they were caught in a rain shower.

"It looks like rain," Elizabeth said, echoing his thoughts. She studied the sky, her profile arched upward, the line of her petite nose quite lovely. "The cottage is only a bit farther."

"Are we agreed that our squabbling should cease?" asked Miles.

"This is not squabbling. It is communication, though perhaps a tad incomplete." She pressed her heels into her mount and sprang forward.

When they arrived at the cottage, Elizabeth amazed him. In his mind, he had painted a picture of her that did not exist. With the tenants, she was gracious and courteous. Though soft-spoken and wont to say little, she listened to them, offering to help in different ways. She left a basket of goodies on their table. A surprising sense of pride undulated through him as he watched her act every inch the lady of the estate.

Who was this Elizabeth? How had he not known she existed? After promising Annie's son that she'd gather some of the other men together to patch his roof, Elizabeth said her goodbyes and followed Miles out of doors. Though the small cottage had smelled like spiced cider and yeast, the vastness of the outdoors brought relief from his aversion to closed spaces.

It was not an overly bothersome paranoia, but at times he began to feel caged and longed for a wide-open space in which to breathe.

"Are you well, Miles?" Elizabeth asked after he'd helped her mount and they began the journey home.

"I was beginning to feel the press of the walls," he admitted without thinking.

She was quiet for a moment.

The wind had picked up, carrying with it the sultry musk of impending rain. He thought of his mill workers, of the coughs that plagued those in the Littleshire factory, the fatigue. If the windows did not ease the burden, he might have to look into reconstructing the layout. Breathing in fibers every day posed a significant threat to their health.

"Is that why you avoid the library?" she asked, interrupting his thoughts.

Startled, he glanced over to find her brow quizzical and her expression compassionate. He measured the comment, searching for traces of truth. "Perhaps when I have been confined too long is when I yearn for the openness of the outdoors." He let out a short laugh as a memory surfaced. "I was locked in a trunk once, you see."

Elizabeth gasped.

"Do not alarm yourself. It was only a few minutes but it felt like eternity. Thankfully your brother found me. We'd been playing hide and seek, and I had it in my head that a trunk was the perfect place to hide."

"How terrible!"

"I remember the odor to this day. Rotting wood and mothballs." He shrugged. "Ever since, too long in a room and I get itchy."

Elizabeth shook her head. "I am certainly glad John found you, else I would have no one to argue with."

Her smile warmed him, as bright and cheerful as the day was not.

"That would be a sad loss indeed."

"I owe you an apology. Not for anything I said," she rushed on, "but for making you feel as though I think poorly of you. For making you feel as though you are deficient."

He cringed. "An apology is unnecessary. My ego is intact despite your disapproval of my ways."

"But that is just the thing, Miles…" And her lips curved in that dreamy way she had about her. "You are a lovely man, full of many fine qualities, and I shall be proud to be your wife."

Was she jesting? "Just last night you said I was the last person you'd ever choose," he pointed out carefully.

"I spoke hastily." Her head bent. "Since I am being forced to marry, you are my best choice. Despite your overbearing, superficial ways, you have a sweet disposition and truly care about me."

"Is this a compliment or an underhanded way of insulting me?" He could not even find the will to tease her. Not one person of his acquaintance had ever referred to him as overbearing. And superficial? He nudged his mare closer to her. "How is it that I'm superficial, Elizabeth Wayland?"

"It's not necessary to argue over trivial matters." She picked her head up and stared straight ahead, toward the estate, which loomed before them.

"I am merely asking you to provide evidence for your suppositions."

"And that is why you're overbearing."

Miles clenched the reins. She was maddening, simply maddening. "If we are to have any kind of comfortable marriage, perhaps we should find a way to overcome this squabbling."

She shot him a glare. "You may call this a squabble, but I feel that it is a fair indicator of our lack of compatibility in almost every way. If our marriage is to be a contractual agreement and nothing more, do you not feel that we should stop bothering with needless niceties? I have no desire to be a part of your world or to engage with you on a daily basis. The agreement is that I shall be available and able to play the part of hostess when you are in need. Other than that, I believed myself to be free to live how I want. Even if that means taking care of my grandmother. There is no reason to live with you after our marriage. I was truly shocked when you practically ordered me to do so last night."

Forceful words, and they cut him to the bone. "I see my affection for you has blinded me to the coldness in your character."

"Oh, yes, I'm well aware of how little you value my person. You are constantly reminding me of all the ways in which I am failing. Every time I see you, I must bear your unconscionable comments about my person and my hobbies."

"That is not true."

To his surprise, her chin quivered. She glanced away, drawing her reins closer as if to shield herself.

He set his jaw. "You cannot go around protecting yourself from life. You must be involved. You must reach out to others. I only say these things because of my deep affection for you. I only wish to see you happy."

"Am I not happy with my books? My life is fulfilling as it is, and it is your incessant desire to change me that wears on me."

"Change you?" Miles edged closer to her, ignoring her mare's nervous prancing. He grabbed Elizabeth's arm, gently yet firmly, forcing her to meet his gaze. "You are just right the way you are, and I regret ever making you feel as though you are not."

He hesitated, feeling the heat of Bitt's skin through her broadcloth sleeve. Her eyes were on him, wide, surprised, but she did not shrug away. And somehow their horses had stopped moving to nibble at the grass. It was the two of them on a sloping hill, sunlight and flowers their sweet companions. Beneath his sternum, his heart pulsated in quick, staccato beats.

"I know what it is to never be enough," he said quietly. The thing he most adored about Bitt was her capacity to listen. Not in a normal conversation. No, in those she flitted away like a delicate butterfly, lost in her dreams the way a monarch lost itself in a bouquet of lilacs. But when someone spoke to her of important matters, she listened with her whole self.

He saw that gift of hers now. The line of her vision did not waver from his. He found himself clutching her arm because memories spiraled through him in angry circuits, a long algorithm of mathematical codes that all ended with the same conclusion: he had never been enough.

"Miles, please tell me." Her fingers skimmed his hand, lightly, each stroke resting on his knuckles, as though comforting him.

And strangely enough, he had need of comfort, for he had never spoken of his marriage to anyone. But if Bitt was to be his wife, she should know something of what he'd gone through. He owed her that, at the very least.

"Anastasia was a great beauty," he began. Creaking words crowded his throat. Having never been spoken, perhaps they had rusted within, tarnishing him in ways he had not anticipated. "Her laugh, it was said, was reminiscent of the tinkling bells played at Hyde Park during winter months. Her eyes the sparkling blue of a clear lake, and her form comely in every way. She came from an impoverished earl's family. It was said that she had little dowry. No one in the ton cared. Perhaps you were too young to remember?"

"I was in the schoolroom still, but I heard of her. She came to a house party once, perhaps when you two were married, though you were not with her."

Miles winced. "I should have been with her more."

"Were you not working, providing for your family?"

She had been expensive, he thought, remembering the first time he'd received the bill for her clothing expenditures. But he'd believed he was making her happy.

"There is more to marriage than building a comfortable nest. Anastasia had needs I couldn't meet, and as bright as her smiles were, her frowns were far deeper and darker. I did not have the skill nor the knowledge to make her happy."

Bitt's eyes turned glossy. Her fingers crept around his until their hands were clasped. "I had no idea, and I am deeply distressed to hear you speak thus."

"I only speak so for a reason." He brought her hand to his mouth. He pressed his lips lightly against her glove, letting the touch linger. When he let her hand go, he saw that her mouth was parted. "It is never my intent to cause you harm, nor to imply that you are lacking in any way. In my eyes, you are wonderfully you."

Chapter Twelve

In my eyes, you are wonderfully you.

The words played with Elizabeth's emotions, weaving in and out of her every thought the following morn. While she ate breakfast, she thought of Miles. When she tried to read, he interrupted the story, his intense gray eyes teasing her memories. He had spoken so fiercely, as though he truly meant what he said.

She frowned at her breakfast plate. They were to leave for London in an hour, and she could not relieve herself of these intrusive, disturbing thoughts. If only she could shoo them away as easily as she swatted a fly.

Not that she swatted flies often. Why, she never even went into the barn except for making visits to the tenants or to check on their houses. She always walked to Littleshire. The barn smelled of mold, animal droppings and a broken heart.

What a fanciful notion. She wanted to swish it away, too, but it buzzed at the back of her mind, reminding her of feelings she wanted to forget, memories of unkindness better left in the darkness of a stable corner.

Groaning, she pushed her plate away and stood. Her

things should be packed by now and all that remained was to bid farewell to her grandmother.

A servant entered, head down, and set the mail plate on the table.

"Thank you." Elizabeth paused, realizing she did not know the girl's name. It really wasn't so horrible to be unfamiliar with the lesser housemaids, but seeing how Miles treated everyone as an equal stirred uncomfortable guilt. The maid turned to leave, so Elizabeth touched her shoulder. The girl's face crumpled and then quickly settled into a mask as she looked down at the floor.

Elizabeth dropped her hand to her side. It was easy to forget that this girl was raised to believe her livelihood depended on her employer's goodwill. A perfectly valid belief, for it did.

"I apologize for startling you. I simply wish...to know your name. You may look up."

"Yes, my lady." The hesitant words followed an even more reluctant action. "My name is Sara." A swift curtsy followed. Head down again.

Frustration simmered, but Elizabeth tamped it down. After all, how often had she chosen to speak to the staff? Not often at all. In fact, she only addressed Stockton, the head housemaid, White, and the most senior maid in her office twice a week. Every Monday she conferred with Cook about the menu. Except when she'd been in London. In that case, they had planned ahead.

"Sara, thank you for bringing the post."

Her eyes flew upward, dark brown orbs wide with apprehension and perhaps a touch of disgust? They flittered across Elizabeth's birthmark. She steeled herself to remain facing the young maid when all her instincts begged her to duck her face. Thankfully, Sara did not look too long upon the mark, returning her gaze to the floor instead.

"You're welcome but it is my duty, my lady," she said. "I carry the post in every morning."

Wonderful. Now she felt even more the dunce. "Well, you do a marvelous job. I shall mention so to Ms. White."

At the mention of their head housemaid's name, Sara's face colored. "Thank—thank you."

Annoyed that Sara found her so fearsome, Elizabeth waved her hand in dismissal, and the maid scurried off.

Sighing, she turned to the silver salver that Sara had forgotten on the table. How was it that she struck fear into the staff? She frowned, scooping up the multiple letters on the table to take to Grandmother. The duchess spent a goodly amount of time each day composing missives to her London friends, and perhaps friends in other places.

Elizabeth had never quite paid attention to her grandmother's communications, but now she wondered if she ought to have done so. Delved a little deeper, expressed interest. She found her Grandmother in the garden room, talking to a plant covered with fiery orange blooms.

"There, my love, you have performed marvelously. I knew that you would, of course, being an expert in all matters of horticulture. Why, dear Lindon told me to give you a bit more sunlight, just enough to warm your leaves, and he was right. The old sod." Grandmother giggled, completely unaware of Elizabeth.

She did not usually like to interrupt Grandmother, as her garden room was to her as the library was to Elizabeth, but Grandmother adored her letters. And as she planned to leave soon, now was as good a time as any to say farewell.

She set the salver on a small table near the doorway.

Grandmother turned, her outfit a frothy concoction of purple frills and pink ruffles. She looked like a pretty flower herself.

"Is that the post?" Grandmother rubbed her hands together and shuffled over. Though spry, sometimes she moved stiffly due to rheumatism in her knees. "I have been waiting for the latest on-dit regarding the princess. She is so shockingly impolite. Though I must say that Prinny deserves her crassness, after all he's put her through." Her grandmother clucked her tongue.

"I know not, only that a maid—" She caught herself. "Sara, brought the post to me."

"To you?" Grandmother's brows crinkled. "Whatever for, if the mail is mine?"

"A pertinent point," Elizabeth murmured.

"And to leave the salver with you, how perfectly uncouth and ill trained. I shall have a word with White about this Sara. It is not *your* job to deliver the post, do you understand me, Elizabeth? We pay staff to perform these duties."

Her throat closed. "Please do not say a word to White. Sara was perfectly well mannered. I took the salver of my own accord, because I wanted to see you before I leave for London."

Grandmother set down the paper she'd been holding. "Leave? Why, you only just arrived!"

"I know, but I have been planning our betrothal ball, and I am also to visit Drury Lane next week. It will be a boon for Miles and me to be seen together before the house party. The staff will need time to prepare. It is still acceptable to hold it here?" She'd spoken with Grandmother about the event yesterday, but it did not hurt to check again.

"Of course, you will have the party here. I have invited a few friends myself." Grandmother sniffed, lifting her nose. "I must say, I'm perturbed at the manner in which Mr. Hawthorne is stealing you away from me."

"You wanted me to marry," she pointed out gently, ignoring the tight ball growing in her stomach.

"I simply did not think the process through." Grandmother let out a long, shuddering sigh. "At least I shall have my flowers to keep me company. But who shall plan the menu? And direct the cleaning?"

Elizabeth stepped forward, drawing her grandmother into a hug, breathing in her familiar scent of talcum powder and lavender. "I shall help in whatever ways possible. Why, it is probable that I shall even be living here after my marriage."

Grandmother's eyebrows snapped together so fiercely that she startled Elizabeth. "Bah! I should think not. I expect grandchildren."

The knot that had been forming constricted, making her feel positively ill. "There will be no children, Grandmother. I do not dare pass on my blemish."

"My dear girl, that is hogwash of the silliest sort. There is nothing a touch of rouge or powder can't lighten. My sister had one, you know, and she was a great force in society." Grandmother lowered her voice to a conspiratorial whisper. "She turned down a prince, you see, all for the sake of true love."

True love… Elizabeth had lost her own chance for that. Regret curled through her, strong and viscous. Oh, why had she gone out to that gazebo? Why couldn't she have braved the ball instead of placing her reputation on the line? If she could only go back…but alas, the deed had been done and Lord Wrottesley had seen to it that she was compromised.

Blinking hard, she handed Grandmother the mail she still clutched, wishing desperately to be curled on her bed with a good book. Her grandmother took the stack, saying nothing though a knowing gleam lit her eyes.

"This is for you, dearie." She held out a parchment stamped with a crest Elizabeth did not recognize.

She took the missive. The paper was of fine quality, thick and stiff. Prying the letter open, she scanned the contents and then, to be sure, she read it again. Her heart crashed to her stomach, or so it felt. The strength left her legs and she moved quickly to the small couch Grandmother had set up near a potted fern. Sinking down, she closed her eyes as apprehension scuttled through her on pointed toes, piercing every nerve and bringing her breaths to quick inhalations.

"Whatever is the matter?" Grandmother glided over, concern in every syllable. "Elizabeth Wayland, you are as white as a sheet."

"I have had an invitation," she said painfully. All these years of writing articles, and now this...

"From?"

"The Society of Scientific Minds wants me to speak to them of my experiences with a telescope."

"The who?" Grandmother shook her head. "And the what? Speak English, my dear. Does this have to do with those articles you write?"

"They are merely opinion pieces, designed to explore the nature of mathematics in relation to the stars."

Grandmother waved a hand, her rings glittering in the bright light of the solarium. "So speak to them. I have never heard of anything half so dull in my life, but if it is what you wish to do, then do it well."

Elizabeth's throat felt as dry as the deserts she'd read about. "That is the very thing. I plan to decline, but in a way that will still allow me entrance to their group. They are a very closed society who study all sorts of interesting and fantastical wonders. I confess I hardly know what they are talking about at times, but to read their musings is fascinating."

"You must know enough to write what they want to read. They would not ask you to speak if it were not so."

"I am well-read, and I am the only one who has acquired a telescope. They wish to hear how the invention works."

"And this causes an attack of nerves?"

"What will I say? Their eyes will be upon me."

"You are the granddaughter of a duchess. Need I remind you how your great-grandfather was knighted for his bravery, or how I have sat at the table of kings and queens? No granddaughter of mine dare shudder at the thought of speaking to others. Chin up."

Chin up, indeed. She frowned at the paper, tucking it close. Whatever would she do?

Marriage must be the worst shackle ever created.

With a sigh of relief, Miles exited the barouche containing his friend Wiley and his wife. Their ride around Hyde Park had been horrific, thanks to his wife's constant commentary on every subject possible. Miles rubbed his forehead. He did not think he had ever met a more garrulous female.

Turning on his heel, he walked up to his townhome. Perhaps it was a good thing Bitt had turned down the invitation, after all. At first he'd been disappointed, but now he realized that if Wiley's wife drove him mad, there was no telling how his reclusive betrothed would cope.

She'd enjoy Drury Lane more. A theater was nothing if not the showcase of a story.

Their drive back to London had been mostly silent. Three days of near silence, to be exact. He did not think he had ever met a more quiet female than Bitt. She had been pensive, speaking little and even appearing to have trouble reading. He'd caught her staring out the window several times, a worried expression upon her features. When he asked her what was wrong, however, she'd shrugged him away.

Unsettled by the memory, he nodded to Powell, who opened the door and took his frock coat. While most of the London ton was still up and about, enjoying the Season, he preferred to get a good night's rest.

He was not a peer. Just a businessman who lived in modest comfort. His home, situated on a quiet street near Mayfair, offered him the best of both worlds. Access to well-made goods and crime-free living, but not so near the ton's neighborhood that their constant social visits, characterized by carriage wheels on cobblestones, broke his sleep.

And a good sleep it was.

In the morning he rose, performed his ablutions and went over various business arrangements. His report from the Littleshire factory looked promising. He had scanned the ledgers while there but found nothing out of place. Perhaps during the house party, he and Bitt could look over them together.

The thought of being in proximity to her accelerated his pulse. Perhaps he should not have kissed her hand.

The action crossed a line, taking him from old family friend to...to what? Everything within protested a romantic relationship. That had not been part of the deal.

"Sir?" Powell set a crisp invitation on the desk in front of Miles. "This just came for you."

"Thank you." He sliced the edge of the paper, unfolding it to read the message. The Society of Scientific Minds invited him to attend a special seminar to be held three days hence. Guest speaker to share experiences with telescope.

For the first time that morning, Miles smiled. The article writer known only as E.W. was to be the guest, and he would not miss his presentation for anything. The man's writings were fresh and insightful. He often shared interesting tidbits and wrote in a clear, bold voice. The society was a very secretive group, and he was fortunate indeed that they'd invited him.

"Draft a response accepting the invitation at once," he told Powell, who still lingered near the wall, awaiting direction. "Then send a post to Lady Elizabeth requesting her company on this day. Do not mention anything else."

"Very good, sir." Powell bowed and left.

Miles leaned back in his chair, the morning suddenly so much cheerier. He was not sure Elizabeth would be interested in such an event, but the idea to invite her had been spontaneous. She was inquisitive, and he thought she might like to hear about a telescope.

Perhaps it was the one thing she had not read about? Chuckling, he went back to his work.

When her refusal to go with him arrived less than an hour later, he was not so amused.

He stared at her hasty script. She wrote that she had a previous engagement. One to which he was obviously not invited. Disappointment crawled through him. He slapped the note on the desk and stood, stretching, forcing his arms upward and stomping his feet. Enough of this.

What had he expected? That she'd want to spend time with him? Just because she stared up at him with those clear blue eyes of hers? Just because she'd allowed him to kiss her hand? She had called him lovely, he recalled, right before accusing him of being overbearing.

He must stop himself from expecting more from Elizabeth. When had she ever given of herself? The unfair notion infiltrated his thoughts, dredging up memories of his marriage that he'd rather forget.

Foolishness. Was he courting Elizabeth? Falling into the habit of treating her as his betrothed in a romantic sense when the truth of the matter remained that theirs was nothing more than a contractual agreement?

Marry Elizabeth to help her keep her family's good name. That was his only reason for trapping himself. If she wanted to live with her grandmother, so be it. The dowager duchess did seem in need of looking after at times, and Elizabeth claimed to be in charge of the household.

A surprising jot of information, and entirely unexpected. It had revised his opinion of her. The household was run with efficiency.

He stalked out of the office, calling for his horse to be readied. A brisk ride along Rotten Row ought to calm his nerves and release the tension that had accumulated with her refusal to attend the event. It was only to be expected, he told himself.

Elizabeth liked reading. Not socializing nor talking. Not debating Young's theories. That particular professor spoke interestingly of natural philosophy. When he found time, Miles enjoyed attending his lectures at the Royal Institution. *Outlines of Natural Philosophy* had been a dynamic read. He supposed the ideas might be more than what Elizabeth could comprehend. She was intelligent, but he did not think she'd find that particular subject interesting.

Setting his jaw, he decided it was best she had declined his invitation. For all he knew, she had an appointment with the modiste. He could not allow himself to fall into the snare of thinking more of their relationship than he ought. He would not ask her to reschedule for him. That was beyond propriety, and then he'd certainly be the overbearing beast she liked to insinuate he was.

He would not give her the benefit of being right, and he would *not* romance her. Mind made up, he set out for a ride to clear his thoughts and forget that he'd even come close to the dastardly notion of courting Lady Elizabeth Wayland.

Chapter Thirteen

The meeting of the Society of Scientific Minds proved to be a larger event than Elizabeth expected. She hugged a corner of the salon where they met, using her favorite bonnet to shadow the part of her face that garnered attention. People milled around the room, holding small saucers of petit cakes and engaging in passionate conversation. Words filtered to her but her brain, busy with worry, could hardly understand them.

"Lady Elizabeth?" A young man with large spectacles and one protruding tooth bowed flawlessly. "We are so happy you could make our humble presentation. Have you brought the telescope?" Eagerness coated his words. He did not seem as though he even saw her birthmark. His gaze did not stray from her eyes. She liked him already.

"Are you Sir Rigby?"

"Yes. I have quite enjoyed your articles through the years, though I never guessed you to be a woman. It is a surprise."

Elizabeth stiffened, her corset cutting into her back. She had donned one for the occasion, despite her misgivings. Arching a brow, she offered him a disapproving look. "The fact that a woman wrote those articles boggles your mind? Kindly explain yourself."

"I beg pardon, my lady. I intended no offense. I simply thought you were a male author. Your thoughts are logical. Concise. When you speak of nebulae seen through your telescope, I am reminded of great astronomers such as Herschel. I assume you've read his words?"

"I am a great admirer of his sister, actually. Caroline Herschel is a noted astronomer who I had the privilege of meeting last year. She is intelligent, and I'm rather surprised you have asked me here instead of her. Unfortunately, I was unable to transport the telescope. I own an older model. It is quite large and cumbersome, but I have brought several drawings and details of my latest discoveries, including a whitish smear about the galaxy, which I believe to be a cluster of stars."

"You referred to this celestial mark in your latest article, did you not?"

Elizabeth flushed, a great beam of pleasure spreading throughout her. "Yes, that was a great discovery, though of course I did not discover the mystery myself. As you must know, that strange, milky formation has been under study for quite some time." She stopped herself from rambling, which she was wont to do when it came to subjects of great delight.

Sir Rigby's attention prompted a smile.

"I look forward to hearing more, my lady. I shall gather the company and ready them for your presentation."

A shiver borne of nerves shuddered through Elizabeth, though she believed herself to retain a measure of composure as the interesting baron left her side.

She had been determined to refuse the invitation, but

the temptation to speak about her new telescope proved irresistible. Then she had considered speaking only behind a screen. A large part of her wished to preserve her anonymity, but upon mentioning such a tactic to her grandmother, she'd been met with scorn and shock. A Wayland did not behave in such a manner, Grandmother asserted.

Elizabeth wanted to respond *this one does*, but then she recalled Miles and all of his dreadful insinuations and she longed to prove him wrong with a desperation that surprised her. It was time to be a stronger Elizabeth, worthy of her station in life.

Or so she bravely told herself.

Now that the time had come to face a large group of intellectual, scientifically minded people, the majority of them men, her courage faltered. Though it did help that Sir Rigby seemed not the least bit interested in the quality of her skin tone.

But what would she say? She patted her satchel, a leather monstrosity she carried books in when traveling. Though it did not match her dress, which Grandmother had insisted on picking out, not one person eyed her askance. In fact, not many had looked at her at all. They busied themselves debating theories and ideas.

Such an odd atmosphere, and yet she found she rather fancied the sound of conversations that did not revolve around Prinny or the state of his wife's wardrobe.

Sir Rigby appeared again, clapping his hands loudly. As if on cue, the attendees began taking seats. Once those were filled, some lounged against the wall, but all eyes were on her. Disconcerting, to be certain.

She fiddled with her satchel. Patted the sides. Assured herself that the drawings and informational pages resided within. That they had not deserted her the way her courage had.

"My fellow scientific minds, it is my pleasure to introduce to you a person of great insight and curious exploration. It has long been my belief that intelligence is not limited by gender, and today that belief is once again proved correct. Analysis has shown that the female mind is only limited by society's strictures, and even then, a woman can overcome these boundaries thrust upon her person with perseverance and intelligence." He swept her a bow, his eyes alight. Then he turned back to what seemed to her a massive crowd. Her throat closed. She dared not faint and prove to them the weakness of femininity.

She must remember Ms. Herschel and how that indomitable woman spoke and wrote without fear of remonstrance. Granted, her brother fully supported her. Elizabeth mentally shook the thought away. She had prayed before coming here tonight, and her grandmother supported her. What else had she need of?

"Today, we are joined by none other than a regular contributor to our gazette, Elizabeth Wayland."

Gasps rippled through the room. At that moment, the doors swung open, and Miles hurried in. He did not look up, so intent was he on finding a place.

Elizabeth thought then she would faint away. Surely grandmother's malady had been passed to her, for the boning in her corset felt far too tight and her breaths far too shallow.

Alas, the feeling passed just as Miles lifted his eyes. At once, she saw awareness fill him. Shock. His brows rose and though he was across the room, she felt certain his jaw tightened.

Or perhaps she imagined the reaction.

She forced her gaze to move from his to meet the stares of others in the room who looked at her expectantly. Gathering her breath, she addressed the crowded room.

As she spoke, she relaxed. It was difficult to forget that Miles watched her so intently when she passed out the drawings she'd made and shared her hypotheses on different stars, but somehow she managed to ignore his piercing attention.

Why was he here? Had he followed her? Was he angry she had refused his request for her company this evening? She could not begin to fathom the reason for his presence. His words from the other day still echoed in her mind, though... He thought her wonderful just the way she was.

A gentleman in the back of the room cleared his throat. "Miss Wayland, have you any plans to further your research in astronomy?"

She did not correct his address, as she was here not in the capacity of a lady, but as a fellow sojourner in the pursuit of knowledge. "The telescope is intriguing, to be sure, but my true love is reading. Studying the stars is a natural part of learning, of taking joy in the process of discovery. Much like a well-written novel."

A few scoffs erupted at her words, quickly tamped by manners. Feeling incredibly self-conscious, Elizabeth refused to look at Miles. He no doubt smirked, perhaps laughing at her the way several others were. Too many believed novel reading to be unscientific and unhealthy for the brain.

She squared her shoulders. Let them believe what they chose. She knew otherwise. Though everything within screamed to run away, to back out of the room and leave, she mustered strength and asked if there were any questions.

Of course, there were. People questioned her drawings, asked for examples of how the telescope worked, where best to place it, how lighting conditions affected it. The list of questions was endless.

"In less than a month, I am hosting a house party," she blurted out. Her legs shook from standing so long. Her bonnet's flowers lay heavy on her head. Wilted, she thought. This meeting was not for types such as herself.

"A house party?"

"Yes, to celebrate my betrothal. If you care to attend, leave your card with me, and I shall see you receive an invitation. It shall be ever so much easier to explain the workings of my telescope if you are able to see it in person."

Her words inspired several curious looks. She gave her grandmother's name, noting the distaste crossing several features. The fact that the party was to be held at the home of a dowager duchess would discourage many. These were not the sort to care about hobnobbing with the ton. Indeed, she had the distinct impression that her rank in the peerage discredited her in a way her gender could not.

She no longer cared.

Depleted by the energy spent speaking, she cast a desperate look to Sir Rigby, who thankfully, sweet man, rushed over and delivered a short conclusion.

Relieved to be through with the ordeal, Elizabeth sank into the nearest chair. She closed her eyes. She must leave at once. Block out the noise. Crawl into the library and soak up silence.

Perhaps speaking had not been a colossal mistake, but

it had certainly stolen the wind from her sails. She felt utterly deflated and devoid of energy. Her brain could not take another conversation.

"My lady, are you in need of a ride home?" Miles's voice intruded, as it so often did, on her silence. The gravelly quality of his tone inspired little pinpricks of awareness to rush over her in soft waves. A quite pleasant feeling, actually.

She forced her eyes open. He stood beside her, concern drawing his brows together and the usual quirk of his lips softened by worry. His hands rested in his pockets, and he looked utterly handsome and dignified.

He belonged with a beauty like Anastasia.

Pushing the unwelcome thought to the side, she stood on wobbly legs. "If you would be so kind."

The benefit of betrothal. She need not worry about anyone raising eyebrows about her riding home with Miles.

"Give me but a moment to arrange for my carriage. Did you bring a maid?"

She nodded, numbness pressing against her ears. So many people in this small room. Everything closed in on her...or perhaps it was this infernal corset. She vowed never to wear one again.

A few members walked over and spoke with her. She could scarce concentrate, but answered them as best she could. Soon Miles returned and escorted her to his carriage, a comfortably padded rig with a roof and curtains. She climbed in, quivering with the need for escape. Jenna sat on the outside, enjoying the sunshine, Elizabeth hoped. As for herself, she only wanted silence.

Her satchel rested on the seat beside her, but even the novel within could not entice her from her lethargy.

Miles settled across from her, rapped the outside and the carriage moved over the cobblestones.

A relative quiet settled in the interior, though she was too aware of his scrutiny. Through lowered lids, she studied his hands. Graceful, with long fingers, he held them clasped on his lap as though perfectly at rest.

"I am in awe of you, my lady," he said after an interminable length of time.

Curiosity stirred. Refreshed by the quiet, Elizabeth bent her head. "You flatter me, Miles. But how is it you arrived at our meeting? How did you know I would be there?"

"I could ask you the same, for you refused my invitation."

"But…" Grasping for understanding, she sat a little straighter. His invitation had been for this event? "You are a member?"

"I receive their quarterly gazette."

"So you have read my articles?"

His brow scrunched, looking ridiculously adorable. "Articles?"

For a second she was flummoxed by his surprise, and then she recalled that he had entered the room after the introduction. Oh, dear, she could have avoided this conversation altogether.

Wetting her lips, she clasped her hands and tried her best for a lofty look. "Yes, I write under the name E.W."

"You're E.W.?"

Astonishment crossed his features, and her heart sank, heavy as a novel by Milton, to the bottom of her stomach. Miles did not look happy.

Miles was not happy.

He worked like one of those mechanical automatons

he'd seen in London, signing papers, reviewing contracts and plans, but his mind could not concentrate. The date of their house party crept closer and closer like the onset of a bad megrim. When he shuffled through the papers on his desk, he found an old article by E.W.

Elizabeth Wayland.

How was it that he could be so shocked? So singularly impressed and yet completely dismayed? And then she'd invited the society members to her home... If they went, he'd be doubly surprised, though a telescope would be hard for anyone with a modicum of intelligent curiosity to resist.

He squinted at the stack in front of him. He'd managed to slog through quite a bit of work in the last few days without calling on Elizabeth. After all, there was no need for a formal courtship nor any appearance of a romance. He had decided it with finality. Their ride home from the society's meeting the other day had been quiet and without fanfare. She hardly spoke, appearing wan and drained.

Her demeanor further convinced him that their marriage must remain a rescue mission. If a few hours of social contact tired her so, she would certainly have trouble hosting events. On the upside, she would not require the social interactions in which other women of her rank indulged.

He buried his head in his hands, groaning. What had been meant to be a simple decision to keep Elizabeth from ruin had turned into a matter that twisted his gut at night and made him double guess every action.

"Mr. Hawthorne?" Powell dropped something on the desk, prompting Miles to drag his head upward. "An invitation for you, sir, and a young lady is in the hall to see you."

"A young lady?" He squinted. His head pounded.

"Your young lady, I believe." And then Powell smiled. Miles was so taken aback that his jaw dropped.

When had his valet last smiled? He could not recall. "Has she amused you in some way?"

The smile stiffened as Powell resumed his usual professional stance. "We had a conversation about Shakespeare, which I found most enlightening."

"Indeed…" Miles tapped his fingertips on his desk. "Did she say what she is here about?"

"Her arms are filled with papers, but she declined to leave them with me. She said she must see you immediately on a matter of grave importance."

Grave importance? How like her to rely on melodrama. Sighing, he stood. "Thank you, Powell. Show her to the study, and I shall be there in a minute."

When he arrived, it was to find Elizabeth draped across the sofa, a book spread before her feasting eyes. She wore a purplish dress and a bonnet with fewer frills than he'd expect from a woman of her station. Her hair was put up, but two shining curls twirled over her feminine shoulders.

His breath caught within his chest cavity, a painful pressure he could do without. She looked at home in this place, as though she belonged. An unlikely notion.

He took one more moment to study her, the girl who had blossomed into a woman when he least expected it. Her small size did nothing to detract from her womanhood. An image of her standing before the society speaking on matters he'd never expected her to even know about rushed through him. How her eyes had flashed and how her voice filled with the strength of her thoughts. There had been no self-conscious twisting of her face, no burying her gaze in the floor.

She'd met the eyes of everyone in the room while exhorting the benefits of astronomy. She had been magnificent. Uncomfortable with the direction of his thoughts, he cleared his throat.

No response.

He cleared it again, louder this time, and walked to her. She glanced up then, her eyes blinking as though wiping dreams from her mind so that she could return to the here and now. He'd seen that dreamy gaze far too often.

What must it be like to live in one's imagination? He could not fathom.

Though he'd made good headway with the pile of papers on his desk, there was still much to be done. Fingers itching, he placed his hands on his waist and gave Elizabeth a stern look. "Grave importance? Is all well with your grandmother?"

"Oh, my, why yes, she is altogether her usual self." Elizabeth pushed herself into a sitting position, closing the book and setting it to the side. "I apologize for importuning you during your workday, but I wanted to offer you important information."

His brows rose.

"Do not give me that expression, Miles Hawthorne. The past few days have been a vicious madhouse of planning and inviting and researching. All to prove to you that I will make a wife worthy of a gentleman. That your sacrifice is not in vain."

He couldn't help the smile that tickled the corners of his lips. Amused, he sat beside her on the sofa. This close he could study the pale smoothness of her complexion. Besides the mark on her face, which curiously resembled the shape of a heart, her skin held a gentle flush. Not pasty as one would expect from a young lady who cloistered herself within libraries.

Though perhaps that was an unfair assessment, as he'd seen himself that she visited the people of her grandmother's estate and often walked into the village.

"Are you laughing at me?" Eyes wide, she shifted away from him. "I don't appreciate your amusement. Are you ever serious? Oh, yes, when it comes to work you are the icon of drudgery." She sniffed, the subtle lifting of her nose an aristocratic trait he found immensely charming.

"Get to the point, Elizabeth. You are not writing a novel in my house."

Certainly it was only manners that kept her from scowling, but he couldn't resist needling her. Giving Bitt trouble had been a source of pleasure for him for as long as he could remember. A part of him wanted to go back to those days of childish freedoms, before life intruded.

University, expectations, responsibilities…

Unbidden the memory of Elizabeth crying in the stables flashed through his mind. Was that when their relationship had changed? He recalled the sound of her weeping and the accusation in her eyes as he'd tried to comfort her.

Ever since, she'd chosen to be rather prickly with him.

Even now, her nose in the air and her shoulders stiff, he noticed the distance she put between them. As though she did not want him close.

And he agreed.

Only moments ago his head had told him what was

best: a distant relationship based on nothing more than a good deed. Yet sitting next to her, the heat of her skin palpable, the sweet scent of her hair floating about his senses, made logic difficult. She fiddled with a pile of papers beside her while he ruminated. Completely oblivious to his inward struggle, he'd wager.

"Here we go." She flourished a sheet of vellum through the air and thrust it in front of his face. The words wiggled on the page without his spectacles. "Notice the part where Mr. Listley states that his factory's profits have increased. I thought that tidbit rather intriguing. He sent me much-needed information on several mills across England that have implemented these policies."

Miles stared at the paper she held. He didn't take it. "To what are you referring?"

"Why, the reforms you're making." She glanced at him then, her eyes astute and not an ounce of timidity in her manner. "The Littleshire Mill is in need of an overhaul, and I've taken the liberty of contributing a spot of research to your cause."

He didn't know why, but her words rankled. "I have another mill besides Littleshire, and I plan to follow the outline of that one."

"Ah yes, but that mill is not filled with small children." Her gaze bored into him. Accusatory.

He was becoming rather tired of these looks of hers. His eyes dropped to her lips, soft and rosy and pursed in absolute disapproval.

"The children weigh on my mind. I'm exploring options," he said stiffly, shifting his body away from hers. "Have you come here to lecture me?"

"No, not at all." She returned the vellum to the stack beside her and then heaved the entire thing up, unceremoniously dumping the pile on his lap. "Here is all the necessary information. I have included several addresses of mill owners and supervisors who have found ways to educate the children and factory workers whilst increasing production. You'll find their methods fascinating. Now, I have a modiste appointment today and must be gone. Evidently, a house party formally announcing a betrothal requires a new wardrobe."

"Is everything set for that, then?" Miles eyed the massive stack, dread sinking his gut to new lows, even as the pressure of the papers cut into his thighs.

"Invitations have been sent to a broad spectrum of persons. Despite the crossover of gentry, peers and commoners, I believe this party shall be a raging success. Grandmother will make it so."

"I'm sure she will," he muttered.

Elizabeth rose, the silk of her dress rasping against his every sense as she flounced out of the room.

Chapter Fourteen

Three weeks later, Elizabeth studied her grandmother's ballroom, admiring the sparkling chandeliers and shining fixtures. Their staff had done a magnificent job in readying the house. All of the previous days' activities had been enjoyable. Tonight was the last night of the ball, and it was moving along without a hitch.

People milled about the floor as the orchestra played a quiet Mozart piece. She spotted Lady Danvers speaking with Mrs. Johnston, wife to one of the gentleman on Miles's list.

"A varied guest list, my dear." Grandmother's perfume reached Elizabeth before the duchess herself did. "Were these…commoners…your choice or Miles's?"

"What does it matter?" Elizabeth scanned the crowd for her fiancé. They had planned to make their announcement before dinner. "This is the last night, and not a person has complained of sharing the house with those of lower stations. In fact, this party has been everything I hoped for it to be." And she prayed Miles agreed. If he ever showed up. She had much to tell him.

"Miles participated in the activities, I presume?"

"Yesterday he joined in the shooting." Not an event Elizabeth enjoyed but many of the guests found it exhilarating, and they'd brought home a few grouse for their efforts. "He's been at Littleshire much of the time." She had not liked his haggard look yesterday. Her heart squeezed painfully as she recalled the circles beneath his eyes.

Grandmother put her quizzing glass to her eye and made a tiny sound that passed for disapproval. "He should be here with you."

Elizabeth set her shoulders, prepared to defend him when she saw Lady Danvers floating their way. The elderly matron of all things respectable was a longtime friend of Grandmother's and a titled woman. By her side was Lady Kimball, a marchioness with a reputation for kindness. One of the main reasons Elizabeth had invited her.

They greeted Grandmother and then turned to Elizabeth. Lady Danvers's silvery brows rose as she inspected Elizabeth head to toe. Her gaze lingered on the birthmark, but no pity entered her expression. Then she met Elizabeth's gaze.

"Imagine my surprise when I received your invitation in the post and learned that a duke's granddaughter was to be married to a gentleman. A man with neither pedigree nor title."

"He is a respectable man of honor," Elizabeth said quickly, hardly thinking as the words poured from her mouth.

"Is that so?" A knowing look passed between Lady Danvers and Lady Kimball.

"It is." She pressed her lips firmly together, little wanting to offend these women but unwilling to allow them to disdain Miles. Certainly, she could point out his flaws to him, but she was not about to let women who did not know him one tidbit damage his reputation.

"We have heard of his charitable bent," Lady Danvers continued. "It is rumored he runs his factories with precision and fairness. His father had the reputation of being a gentleman and has obviously passed it down to his sons."

"Are you acquainted with Mr. Hawthorne's brother, then?"

"I am. He is quite the businessman. Or so I've heard. I certainly am not involved with trade, but I do take note of children and their fates. On that note, Lady Elizabeth, I have been speaking with one Sir Rigby. He is a guest of yours who is involved with a society that studies scientific developments and the impact of inventions on our world. Fascinating character. I must say that Lady Kimball and I are immensely impressed with this house party. You have created a novel mix of people." And then Lady Danvers tapped her cane against the floor, a sharp rapping that startled Elizabeth, who had begun to daydream just a smidge during the lady's monologue.

"Pay attention, Elizabeth," said Grandmother.

"We—" Lady Danvers gestured to Lady Kimball "—wanted to give you our blessing on this marriage. Mr. Hawthorne is an upstanding gentleman, and yours is clearly a love match."

Elizabeth could not stop her own brows from ratcheting upward.

"Do not look so surprised." Her smile warmed as she leaned forward, forcing Elizabeth's attention. "It was clear yesterday during our time in the salon that Mr. Hawthorne has eyes for only you. While the rest of us played with that fascinating invention called a telescope, his gaze never strayed from you."

He had played his part well, Elizabeth supposed, though that had not been part of this plan. The words *love match* had nothing to do with his agreeing to rescue her from her dire situation. She could not fathom what Lady Danvers referred to, or why Miles may have been watching her, so she nodded her head in a docile agreement.

"That is all. If you will excuse us, I see the punch has been refilled." The ladies sauntered off, leaving Elizabeth once again with her grandmother.

"I am feeling weakness in my legs," said Grandmother. The elderly lady did appear pale. Concerned, Elizabeth grasped her elbow and led her to an alcove off the ballroom, designed for fatigued dancers.

"Shall I bring you punch and perhaps one of Cook's special tarts?"

Grandmother nodded.

Feeling a nudge of apprehension over her grandmother's health, Elizabeth hurried to one of the servants stationed at the punch bowl and gave him instructions for retrieving a pastry for the duchess. Then she filled a cup and threaded her way back to Grandmother.

"Congratulations on your love match," Mrs. Shaunessy from across the way said as she passed.

And was it her imagination or did Lord Danvers wink at her?

Steadying her hand to keep the punch from spilling, she continued to the alcove where Grandmother waited. She searched for Miles, but saw him nowhere. Surely he had arrived? This had been his idea, after all. Why would he miss the party? She knew the reasons she would attempt to avoid such a crush. The loudness of conversations buzzing all around, the dance of perfumes tangling together, irritating and thick. So many people, so much talking.

She kept walking when what she longed to do was dodge to the right, through a door she knew would take her to her room. To peace and quiet.

If only Miles would get here. They could formally announce their betrothal and then she could speak with him about another idea she'd had for his Littleshire Mill. And then…plead a headache to facilitate escape.

She reached her grandmother, punch intact and emotions beginning to brim with irritation. Handing the glass to the duchess, she once again scanned the ballroom. Her parents stood cloistered with an earl and his wife. Sir Rigby held an animated conversation with Lord Danvers. Other guests swirled around the floor in cadence with music. According to Elizabeth's card, a waltz was to be played next.

The risqué dance was gaining popularity and, surprisingly, Grandmother had suggested it as part of the musical set.

She sank next to her grandmother, reaching for her gloved hand. "Are you feeling better?"

"These old legs only need a rest. I shall be fine. But where is Mr. Hawthorne? It is not like him to be so tardy." Grandmother's querulous words grated on Elizabeth's already raw nerves.

Could it be that she missed Miles? Surely not…and yet he had such a ready laugh, and his eyes crinkled at the corners in a most becoming way. He always looked at her, really looked, and listened.

As though her thoughts had spoken aloud, Miles appeared. He sauntered toward her, passing guests without removing his gaze from her own.

She felt as though she were the subject beneath a microscope. Her stomach quivered. Her fingers pressed against the wall. He wore pristine breeches and an elegantly cut waistcoat, and his cravat was neatly knotted. The look in his eyes did her in, though.

It was as though they saw only her.

Which could not be, she tried to remind herself, but her thoughts were drowned by the heady rush of feelings pulsating through her.

He came to a stop before the alcove. Looking past her, he bowed. "Your Grace," he murmured.

And then he turned to her, his eyes a tempestuous gray filled with mystery, his hand aloft. "My lady, would you join me for a waltz?"

Even as he spoke, the music swelled in the ballroom and couples crowded the floor. Heat flared through Elizabeth. Cheek to cheek, hand to hand…the dance called for a scandalous closeness, and now Miles was asking her to participate?

Ignoring his hand, which waited for hers, she glanced back at Grandmother. The duchess's lips formed a thin line but Elizabeth could not tell if she approved of waltzing with Miles or no.

Turning to him, limbs quivering, heart shaking, she placed her hand in his. He asked for a waltz, but it felt as though he asked for so much more.

And she did not know if she was capable of giving him what he deserved.

The slightness of Elizabeth's hand in Miles's stirred feelings he had longed to forget. They pinched at his chest, tightening the muscles, mingling pleasure and pain.

He drew Elizabeth onto the floor, her perfume heady,

surrounding him, reminding him of dances long past. She wore her hair in elaborate auburn curls, which cascaded around her shoulders. Her dress, an icy concoction of frills in all the right places, emphasized the beauty of her eyes and the soft tones of her skin.

Had she ever looked so beautiful? The last waltz he'd danced had been with Anastasia in France, before the dance had arrived in England. He'd been there not only for business, but to try to cheer his wife. It hadn't worked and not long after she'd… The memory clamored within, struggling for release.

But with Elizabeth in front of him, so close he only inhaled the scent of her, he could barely remember what Anastasia looked like.

The lines of her face and the color of her eyes faded from memory. Fizzled away like foam on a seashore.

He tugged Elizabeth closer. They were hand to hand, swirling around the dance floor. Music undulated within him, pulsing to the beat of their steps on the floor. She followed his lead flawlessly, every inch an earl's daughter. Her hair tickled the bottom of his chin. She smelled like roses. Reminding him of the trellis they'd stood beneath weeks ago.

Her fingers closed in his, tightening. He couldn't see her face, but he was altogether aware of the fluidity of her movements, the grace.

That terrible pinching began again, somewhere at the bottom of his sternum. An ache he struggled to ignore. Piano chords strained, the notes vaguely registering within the cloud of uncertainty that overtook him.

He'd expected marriage to be like owning factories. He would wed Bitt. Make sure she could perform the most fundamental of wifely duties. Organize their lives so that she avoided ruin, and he would never have to worry about dealing with women again. After all, marriage ensured safety from the clamoring misses looking for a man with a fortune, even though a great bulk of his wealth was tied up in his businesses.

The entire plan had seemed very clear-cut.

And it still could be, his mind insisted. Even with Bitt in his arms, warm and soft and smelling like forever, it was possible to keep their marriage strictly platonic.

Was the music still playing? Faces blurred as they danced by. Sweet notes echoed through him. Bitt's dress rustled against his legs as they twirled.

She looked up at him then, tilting her head, meeting his eyes with that dreamy directness she often employed. As though part of her existed in another realm. The look always softened him, made him want to protect her. There was a gentleness in her eyes as she smiled at him. Laughter edged the corners of her lips.

Reflexively his arms tightened around her. He was as close to her as he possibly could be and still keep propriety, but he wanted to be closer. He wanted...more.

That acknowledgment shook him as nothing else had. Deliberately he loosened his hold. Her smile faltered. They were still sweeping along the ballroom, but her body stiffened beneath his hands and her eyes clouded.

Was he doing the right thing? He had believed he was but now...he didn't know. He hated not knowing. His entire life revolved around making choices. Being in control.

But this feeling...this constriction in his throat.

He didn't like it.

Not at all.

The music ended and he found himself releasing Elizabeth quickly. She didn't seem to notice as she took his arm and rather forcefully led him to the side of the floor.

"I have been awaiting your arrival, Miles."

"There was an accident at Littleshire."

"I do hope no one was hurt."

"Thankfully not, but equipment was damaged and I had to oversee the ordering."

"Let us go outside." She cast a glance behind him. "It is too loud in here for what I've wanted to discuss with you."

Taken aback, Miles wanted to say no. Outside was private. Moonlit. Everything within resisted, but Elizabeth practically propelled him out. He allowed her to lead him onto a quiet patio that overlooked a well-manicured garden. A different one than where he'd found her last time.

Lanterns traced light along the borders of the walled patio. Elizabeth paused at its edge, her back to him as she stared out over the gardens. It was not silent out here. Faint strains from the orchestra merged with the quiet song of insects. A bright moon created deep shadows across the garden and draped Bitt in a milky glow.

Miles had never felt so uncomfortable as he did at this moment.

"You wished to speak with me?" His voice scraped the silence.

She turned slowly, her fingers tapping the rail. "I was hoping to see you earlier today. With the week's festivities, I haven't felt that we've been able to communicate and I have an idea."

He tipped his head. "For?"

"The Littleshire Mill. The children, Miles. Part of the problem is that these workers are uneducated. How can they better themselves, how can they find more stable and less dangerous occupations, if they cannot read?"

"And then who will make the cotton?"

She reared back at his words, which he supposed had sounded more cynical than intended.

He held up a hand to stop any tirade. "You are correct about education, but there will always be a need for mill labor. For able-bodied workers to perform tedious tasks. It is the way of the world, Elizabeth."

She planted her hands on her hips. "My research has shown me that mills are changing. New inventions are creating safer workplaces. Not only that, but you said able-bodied workers, and I certainly do not consider children to be *able bodied*. Do you?"

Her eyes were flashing at him, and though only inches separated them, he had the strongest inclination to reach out and haul her to himself, to kiss the indignation from her face and assure her that all would be well.

He withheld himself.

Doing such a thing would serve only to complicate an already complicated situation.

He thought of the scrawny children scampering around Littleshire. Of how often their eyes were dulled by hours of labor. "No," he said finally. "I do not consider them able bodied."

"Then we are in agreement that something must be done. It is my intention to visit at least once a week for an hour or more to teach reading and writing. I shall buy supplies. I will provide a schoolroom somewhere, even if it is out in the sunshine, though I do confess that they may find it hard to study when there is so much nature to be explored. It is doubtful they've spent their childhood as you and John did, monkeying up trees and pilfering sweets from Cook's kitchen."

Miles grimaced. "An hour a week? Who shall cover their shifts? How shall they be paid?"

"A small decline in income is a small worry when their minds shall be so enriched."

He crossed his arms. "That is no answer, my lady."

"Do you have a better one? These children are in need of nutritious food for their minds. They deserve to see that a world far greater and wider and more beautiful than theirs exists. That there is more to life than powerful, odiferous machines that never cease their infernal clanking." She wrinkled her nose as if reliving the sounds of his mills.

"Come now, Bitt. It's not so horrible as you make it out to be." Sometimes he rather found the consistent sounds comforting. "And you speak of this rich world, but reading about a place is not the same as living there."

"It is a near enough substitute. Which is why I propose to enrich their minds with great literature and grand ideas. I shall hire a tutor to help them learn sums."

"All this in an hour?"

"Cynicism solves nothing, Miles Hawthorne."

He frowned. "I am merely considering the practical aspects of your plan. Frivolous novels are not going to solve a widespread problem. These children need more than an hour of lessons, and their families will suffer from the lack of pay."

"One must start somewhere," she said coldly. "Even if it's with *frivolity*."

Sweeping her skirt up, she brushed past him, nose high, gaze averted. Telling him in no uncertain terms with her back just how much she disapproved of his response.

Not the best way to end a betrothal ball, he mused, but certainly an indicator of what marriage to Elizabeth entailed.

No matter what he'd felt while dancing with her, he must remember that a traditional marriage came with petty dramas, irritating spats and hurt feelings.

Altogether more reason to keep his distance. To reject any notions of togetherness, romance or, horror of horrors, love.

Chapter Fifteen

When would this dreadful ball end?

Elizabeth fanned herself, pressing her back against a corner and longing desperately for a story. Anything but this dream that had turned into a nightmare. Couples swished past her, lips curved and eyes alight. Much as she had done only moments ago.

Frivolous.

How dare he call her novels such a thing? She fumed in silence, tapping her toe and swishing her fan. The brush of cool air against her hot skin brought little relief because his words bounced within her mind, vexing little reminders of the kind of man she must marry. A man who did not value books. Who worked and worked and worked…

Her fingers tightened on the fan until her knuckles ached. How often she'd daydreamed of love. The kind where a man saw into a woman's heart, where he loved her for all her flaws and strengths. And what happened?

She got herself almost ruined, forcing a marriage of convenience.

Miles swirled her around the ballroom in the most

dizzying, heart-stopping fashion and she lost her senses. Her brain ceased working and suddenly she had realized that she was at great risk of feeling too much for the infernal man.

She could not, would not, allow such feelings for one who didn't enjoy novels. His imagination must be terribly stilted, she mused, scanning the ballroom for him, hating that her gaze sought him out even after he'd so cavalierly thrown her ideas into the metaphorical trash bin.

But when she spotted him near Grandmother, her pulse sped up. Pinpricks of awareness washed through her. Her stomach knotted and unknotted all as she watched him from behind the safety of her fan. The decoration served as more than just a communication or cooling device.

She spied on him, nerves thrumming. He bestowed a soft smile on her grandmother, bending near to hear her as she spoke. They engaged in conversation and he threw his head back in an open laugh. Perhaps his eyes might be a stormy gray, like a winter's eve sky. She quite enjoyed his eyes and their moody changings. He had a way of looking at her... Despite herself, she shivered.

That dance had been the most romantic moment of her life. She'd felt positive that, as he looked down at her, he must feel the same way about her as she did him.

She snapped her fan closed. And how did she feel?

Not as one should when marrying for convenience. Certainly not as one marrying to escape ruination.

She would not allow this attraction to fester into anything more than childhood affection.

He'd called her ideas for the children, her love of novels, frivolous.

Just remembering that idiocy caused her teeth to grind and her body to stiffen.

It was not reasonable to be attracted to a man who believed such foolishness. Emotions roiled, coiling within until her body strained with the effort of holding her temper back. Her neighbors from the south, a wealthy baron and his wife, stopped to greet her.

She had never met them before and for a millisecond, felt conscious of her birthmark. Did the baron's gaze stray to it? But no, both he and his wife spoke to her without allowing her disfigurement to distract them.

The realization helped her create a conversation whilst hiding all the frustration she felt toward Miles beneath a veneer of politeness.

"We have been admiring your grandmother's stable and collection of prize mares. You realize," the baroness was saying, "that my darling Edward never learned to ride until two years ago?"

"How curious," Elizabeth murmured, trying as hard as she could to rein in her riotous thoughts, to still the erratic pounding of her heart and the nervous tension that pressed upon her sternum. It was not their fault she'd realized a terrible discovery about herself. Unrequited attraction. How bothersome! She must find a way to avoid it. Miles did not fit into the box where she stored romantic daydreams.

A dark and swarthy earl was one of her favorite daydreams. She'd meet him in a library. Yes, they'd both be reading Wordsworth. Perhaps he'd recite something to her. A romantic poem filled with the sweetness of tender longings and unfulfilled dreams. His gaze would hold hers, his irises a riotous mix of mossy greens and steely grays…she straightened abruptly.

No, that had never been the color of her imaginary earl's eyes before.

"My lady?" The baroness stared at her, the question in her tone clearly stating that Elizabeth had been caught daydreaming.

She wet her lips, inclining her head to indicate attention. "I apologize. My mind snagged. You were saying?" She looked expectantly from husband to wife, hoping one of them might forgive her lapse in manners and continue talking.

The baroness graciously nodded, accepting the apology. "Only that my husband had a dreadful dislike of horses. He saw them as foul creatures and refused to enter the stables."

"Clod footed," the baron put in, giving a humorous, good-natured tug on his mustachioed mouth.

"It was only after I showed him their intelligence and gentle nature that he grew fond of them."

Elizabeth's ears perked. "And now you enjoy horses, my lord?"

"We ride every morning." The baroness patted her husband's arm, deep affection apparent in such a tiny touch. "But it took a tragedy to show him what he was missing. My favorite mare, Beauty, took sick. I'd had her since my sixteenth birthday and she had aged, of course. One morning I went into the stables and there she lay, on her side, belly heaving."

"Your stable hands did not alert you?" asked Elizabeth.

"I employ one and he stated that Beauty had been fine only moments beforehand."

Elizabeth controlled her cringe. Of course, they had only one. She was accustomed to a large staff and forgot that others required less. "Was she...did she recover?"

"No."

The baron took his wife's hand, and Elizabeth marveled at the sweetness between them. Had they been a love match then? Or had love grown over the years, fertilized by kindness and compatibility? She wanted to ask, but feared the question out of place.

Instead she murmured, "I am very sorry."

"Thank you. It was a dreadful time for me but to comfort me, Edward promised a new mare. For my sake, he overlooked his antipathy toward horseflesh, and now he is an avid rider."

"I would not use the word *avid*, my love." He chuckled.

"All due to a change in perception then?" asked Elizabeth, a strange feeling unfurling within.

"Much like your telescope," he affirmed. "Last night I saw the stars in a marvelous new way. When I shopped for a mare, I learned each one's personality. I had to see horses from a different perspective to appreciate their beauty. I do not claim to love horses as my wife does, but I respect them."

"Oh, look, there is Lady Danvers." The baroness tugged on her husband's sleeve. "Come, we must speak to her. She throws the most extravagant parties in London every year."

They offered their farewells and rushed off, leaving Elizabeth with a curiously lightened heart. Perhaps this unexpected situation with Miles was not hopeless, after all.

He only needed but to see books in a different light. If she altered his perception of them, showed him the transforming wonder of a story, then surely he would agree to her plan.

She flicked her fan open, holding it up and peering over the top. The house party had been a raging success. The ball, interesting and not altogether awkward as a part of her had feared it would be. After all, it was not every day that peerage and commoners mingled.

She searched for Miles, locating him at the other end of the room. He stood with his back to her as he spoke with Sir Rigby and a small group of men from the society.

If he shared her interest in scientific matters, surprising as it was that unbeknownst to each other, they'd read the same scientific papers, then perhaps he would not be completely closed off to the beauty of novels.

If he could but understand the potential of a story to stretch the mind, to enlighten the darkened, then he might approve her plan. For the children's sake.

Just then, he turned and his gaze immediately alighted upon her. Pinning her in place with its intensity. Had he known where she stood this entire time? Had he been watching her? Surely less than a ballroom separated them? For it seemed as though they were the only two in the room. Every part of her felt alive as she answered his look with her own. Were his eyes green right now? Gray?

Her feet itched to move forward and discover the answer. She remained in place, however, for until he changed his perception, she refused to give in to these delicious feelings melting through her, leaving her breathless.

More money owed.

Sighing, Miles signed the invoice to install windows in the Littleshire Mill. He had spent two days at his brother's mills, touring the grounds and sharing information. They both wished to carry on their father's tradition of being fair employers. No mill worker would become affluent, but Miles hoped that what he paid was enough for his workers to put food on the table and to clothe their children.

The Littleshire Mill was the only factory in the Hawthorne family to employ children under the age of twelve. Miles had gone to his brother for advice. He brought the information Bitt gave him, which proved immensely helpful.

The honorable course involved taking her for a ride, offering his gratitude for her research, but after that night at the ball…a curious tug in the vicinity of his heart brought a frown to his face. He finished signing the invoice and set it in the stack for Powell to put in the post for Mr. Shapely.

He did not dare remember the feel of Elizabeth in his arms as they waltzed, nor the scent of her hair, nor the lustrous shimmer of her eyes.

There had been that second when their eyes met across the ballroom. When the temptation to cross the room and kiss her silly accosted him.

Thankfully, he had not, for if she'd been on the brink of ruination before, a public kiss certainly would have pushed her reputation beyond repair.

She had broken their visual connection. Had pivoted, severing the invisible thread that inevitably drew him to her. Shortly after the formal announcement of their betrothal, she left the ballroom, exiting the room with the grace of royalty.

And he'd known that to follow her would be a mistake.

The next day consisted of farewells, packing. He'd made his excuses early and left to visit his brother, Bitt's papers safely stowed within his trunks.

"My Lord?" Powell stood at the door. "Lady Elizabeth has arrived."

Of course. No request for an audience. She showed up uninvited. He nodded to his valet. "Show her in."

"There is no need." Bitt appeared behind Powell, a mere slip of a woman with a giant-sized expression of stubbornness. "If you will just—" She nudged his valet, actually nudged him, and managed to slide into the room.

Miles glowered at her, any vestige of good mood abandoning him. Powell, traitor, still stood in the doorway, his face a blank mask and his shoulders shaking with mirth. Miles flicked his hand and the servant disappeared. Ostensibly to procure a refreshment and show Bitt's lady's maid to the servant's quarters.

Elizabeth sailed across his office and paused at the family portrait hanging on the far wall. She held a massive book in her hands. Just looking at it made him feel queasy.

All those words… He pressed his thumbs against his temples to ease the sudden ache.

"You're in an energetic state," he remarked for lack of a better thing to say.

She didn't respond, only peered up at the painting. "Your brother is so much older than you."

He joined her, careful to maintain enough distance that he would not be forced to inhale any remnants of her perfume. The painting showcased his father, his brother and himself.

"I did not know Peter well," she continued. "Though I recall your father being a great laughing beast of a man."

Miles couldn't help the tug that pinched the corner of his lips. "A beast, you say."

"Well, yes, he was so very large and hairy. He always brought me a sweet." She said the last words in a wistful tone, as though she missed him.

Swallowing the lump that had grown in his throat, Miles studied the painting. "I suppose he had a tender side. By the time I came along, he was already teaching Peter the run of the factories. With my mother lost in childbirth, he had to grow up quickly. I only knew my father as a businessman. A good and honorable man, but life for him was all business."

"Oh, Miles." She turned and placed her hand on his arm. Warmth seeped through his sleeve. "You must never turn into your father."

He stepped away from her. His gut twisted at her words. "Why are you here, Elizabeth?"

As though realizing her faux pas, she dropped her hand to the book she still pressed against one side. "I came to show you something."

He gestured to his desk, piled with papers. "I spend my days working. In the future, please send a note requesting my company so that I can adequately plan ahead."

Elizabeth flinched. Her eyes flickered up, then lowered in a subservient manner. One that he'd always tried to tease her out of. She held her head to the side, the cheek with the birthmark lowered so as to be hidden.

Even to his own ears, his words sounded unkind. An urge to apologize trampled through him. He could not bring himself to do so, though. Better to set boundaries now. He waited for her to speak.

"I shall remember that in the future," she said quietly. Her hands twisted the novel. "I was hoping I might take a bit of your time to proposition you about something."

"The last time you came here with a proposition, I ended up betrothed," he said drily.

"No one forced you to offer in the first place." A hint of steel entered her voice.

"True." He cleared his throat. How he wished the scent of her perfume would not fill his office. "I do have much to accomplish. My father was a great businessman. He earned the title of gentleman, which he passed on to Peter and me. If that means I must work as hard as he did, or harder still, then I shall."

Finally she lifted her gaze to his. Concern shadowed her irises. "It worried me to see you so tired at the house party. Grandmother missed you, as well."

His jaw tightened. "You are not to worry for me. What is it you wish to speak to me about?"

She held out the book. A navy blue monstrosity of a novel. "This. It is the collected plays of William Shakespeare. Not the tragedies, mind you, but the comedies, the romances. I wish to read it to you."

Because she was holding out the book as though she wanted him to take it, he did. The weight of it sank his heart to the floor. "I have no time, Elizabeth, for such a venture. And are not plays meant to be watched?"

Her brows furrowed and her eyes clouded. "I considered the difficulty in that, yes, but it is my deepest desire to show you how much a story can mean. How beautiful and lovely a tale can be. I want you to understand why I love reading. If we are to be married—"

"We will be married, and not long from now." He handed the book back to her. "There is no need for me to understand why you love reading. I accept you as you are, but you must do the same for me."

"Sharing what I love with you in order to expose you to a new perspective does not mean I don't accept you, Miles. I simply want you to understand the beautifully great scope of stories. Their extraordinary ability to draw out the imagination, to teach life lessons and to inspire one to greater heights of creativity." She moved past him and set the book on his overcrowded desk. "Won't you consider allowing me to read to you? Perhaps only a few minutes per day? I would greatly enjoy it."

Her eyes, so innocent and bright, fastened on him, pleading. He groaned. "Wrottesley will pay for this."

"Is that a yes?" Her rosy lips curved becomingly. "You shall not regret it."

"I already do." He pulled out his pocket watch and tapped it sternly. "Thirty minutes a day, at the most. I haven't time for more than that."

"You will see that reading is not frivolous. I can assure you that reading is like peering at the world through a telescope."

Paperwork awaited. He glanced at the mounds, then back to Elizabeth, who glowed as if she'd accomplished some miraculous feat. "Is that all?"

She moved a bit closer to him. "I wonder how I could have known you for so long and yet never realized what a serious man you are. So serious. Working all the time. What do you do for fun, Miles?" A teasing lilt flavored her words.

"Poking fun at me? For shame, Bitt."

"It's not as though you don't deserve it." She turned and began touring his study. Touching the various objects he'd placed around the room. "After all those years you teased me."

Miles rapped his fingers against his thighs. "Are we finished here?"

She cast him a disgruntled look. "Really, Mr. Hawthorne. That is not the way to speak to an old family friend. Shouldn't we get to know each other more?"

"No."

She pursed her lips. "I disagree. A marriage must needs some measure of knowing, don't you think?"

"What I think has no bearing, but since you showed up unannounced and you're draining the time I have to work, let me remind you that the last time I saw you, you were miffed with me. There was no talk of getting to know each other nor special reading times." As he spoke, his frustration mounted. He shoved one hand through his hair. Words pounded through him. "Our marriage is for convenience's sake. Nothing else."

She stopped walking the room to face him, chin lifted. "You need not constantly remind me of your honorable choice. If I had known it would be such a heavy burden, I would have married Wrottesley instead."

"Don't be ridiculous," he growled.

"I could say the same for you." She glared at him. "I am trying to make the best of a situation I would not wish on my mortal enemy. I have ideas and thoughts. Perhaps I prefer solitude and books to people and talking, but that does not mean I am without a brain. Is it so terrible to consider my opinions? They have merit." She walked closer to him, invading his space, pressing the boundaries of propriety. "This delicate situation requires a bit of finesse and a changing of plans. Perhaps you should bear in mind the ways I have grown in order to meet your standards. And expectations." She waved her free hand through the air. "Your horrific expectations. What have I asked of you? Nothing. Absolutely nothing."

"Beyond marriage?"

"Only because the alternative was…" She expelled the last words on a soft breath, as though her speech had exhausted her.

"Unacceptable." Miles touched her shoulders. Her head jerked up, her eyes lifting to his, and he knew he would do almost anything to make her happy.

Stunned at the realization, he released her and stepped back. Took an extra inch as a precaution. "Nevertheless, our marriage remains a business arrangement. There is no need to know each other beyond what is necessary." He gave her a soft look, quelling the urge to reach for her. "Thank you for the information about the mills. I spoke with my brother and together we devised a plan for creating a more healthy work environment. I have decided that your ideas for the children are beneficial."

"Thank you." Elizabeth clasped her hands in delight.

"Now, if you don't mind, I have work to do." He looked past her to the door. "Remember that two nights hence is the theater with Langford and his wife."

She blinked, her features tightening. "I do not know them."

"He is a business associate. As my future wife, you will often meet people you do not know," he said sternly.

Blanching, she became completely and utterly still. Giving him a slow, appraising look, she nodded once, curtsied and left.

Groaning, he returned to his desk. This hasty betrothal was doomed to failure, and it was all his fault.

Chapter Sixteen

The Littleshire Mill sounded just as dreadful as Elizabeth remembered. Clutching her books to her bosom, she marched up the front steps to the entrance. Behind her, Miss Townsley struggled to keep up. The young governess had answered Elizabeth's ad for employment. Her serious air convinced Elizabeth that she was the best candidate for the job.

She wet her lips and waited for Jenna to open the door for them. The mill manager met them, a supercilious expression upon his weaselly features. How she'd hoped he'd be dismissed. Sucking back her disappointment, she squared her shoulders.

"Good day," Elizabeth said in her most brisk tone. "We've come to teach the children."

He made a little bow, probably to hide his displeasure. "I've assembled them in the lunch room."

They followed him to the room. Children crowded within, standing against the walls, the tallest in the back and the smallest up front. Becky wiggled, her cleft lip hardly noticeable she was so covered in grime. Beside her, Katie giggled.

Elizabeth looked for Louise but did not see her. "Miss Townsley, please stay in here with the boys. Jenna, will you take the girls outside for fresh air and sunshine? Mr. Grealey, a word if you will."

Without waiting for his answer, she pivoted and went into the hall. She walked toward the doors that led to the other rooms and then stopped to wait. Jenna led the girls outside. The sounds of snickers and shoes scraping the floor echoed in the long hall, though somewhat muted by the other sounds of the mill.

Little boy laughs filtered out, as well. Elizabeth was not concerned. Miss Townsley came with the highest references and much teaching experience. No doubt she would soon have those boys in hand.

Mr. Grealey came skulking out of the room. Unfortunately, he stood a head taller than her. She would prefer to loom over him but the Lord had made her Lilliputian.

That would be a most excellent novel to read to Miles. What man would not enjoy *Gulliver's Travels*?

Thinking about reading softened her ire as Mr. Grealey neared.

"My lady," he said, the sound of his voice causing her teeth to grate.

"Children are missing. Bring them up, please." She used her most haughty tone.

Grealey squinted at her, and inevitably, his attention moved to her cheek. Something near to a smirk twisted his lips. "I've brought all under the age of twelve."

"But the ones who need to learn the most are the older children."

"You are welcome to read my letter from Mr. Hawthorne, in which he instructed those beneath the age of twelve to be given precisely an hour of study."

How utterly frustrating! She peered closely at him, but his eyes did not so much as flicker from her birthmark. In the past, she might have dropped her gaze and hidden from him. Perhaps scuttled off as some demeaned victim.

But the remembrance of Miles and his words regarding Becky filled her with strength. God made all things beautiful. Besides, Grealey's vile nature did not deserve one second of her thoughts. She ducked down, moving so that his gaze must meet her eyes.

"I realize that my birthmark is distracting, but do try to look me in the eyes when I speak to you. I shall contact Mr. Hawthorne as I'm sure his stipulation of age is a mere oversight. Be prepared in the coming weeks to have all the children assembled to learn."

Mr. Grealey's mouth dropped open, rather like a stunned toad. Or what she imagined one might look like. Slimy man. Barely repressing a shudder, she brushed past him.

Within the room, Miss Townsley had captivated the children. They each bent over a slate as she instructed them in a quietly modulated voice on how to form the letter *A*. Flashing her a gratified smile, Elizabeth went outside in search of the girls.

She found them on a sunny square of grass, picking flowers. The mill sounded more soothing out here, the water wheel constantly gushing as it powered the machines within. Hundreds of yards away, the River Irwell glistened. There were places where the smell of pollution overwhelmed the senses, she'd been told, but her lady's maid had chosen to take the girls to a high part of the land, away from the stifling odor of the river.

"Ladies, I have a story for you." Beckoning the girls, she settled down onto the grass. They followed her example. Jenna sat and two little ones climbed onto her lap. "After I read to you, I shall take you back to the room so that you may learn your letters. Listen closely."

"I want to play," piped up Becky.

"As you shall, when it is time. But every week or so I shall be visiting and we will read this magnificent adventure so that all of you may understand that life is not merely about the job you go to, but about the life you live."

"Stories are boring."

"You may go in and work if you do not wish to listen." Elizabeth gave Becky what she hoped was a scolding look, though her heart pinched at the thought of the little girl leaving them to go into that odiferous factory.

Scrunching her face, Becky shook her head and settled onto the grass.

What transpired in that hour was more than Elizabeth could have ever hoped for. Halfway through the time, the girls and boys switched so that the boys could have a turn listening to a story. First they ran circles in the grass, somersaulting and whooping. Bittersweet, as they all knew the joy would be short-lived.

Still, a great feeling of accomplishment swelled through her as she read the book to them. The bright sun warmed her fingers and nary a sound from the boys could be heard as they listened to the story.

Why had she waited so long to help others? Though it was true the children did sometimes stare at her birthmark, overall, being out of the house and doing a useful good deed already felt as though it enriched her life. Miles had been right to prod her, she mused.

If being his wife opened the doors to helping others, then she had made the right decision. Whether he agreed or not. She thought of his coldness the last time they'd met, his distance when they'd gone to the theater with his friends.

He was the Miles she'd always known. From childhood he had been a brooding sort. Something bothered him, and now that she'd successfully implemented her idea, she would corner him and get to the bottom of his rottenness.

When Miles arrived at the Littlshire Mill, the first carriage he noticed bore the Windermar crest. So Bitt had come, after all.

Pensive, he strode to the factory and let himself in. Usually the faint clamor of machines and the water rush of the mill greeted him, but today another sound filtered into the entranceway. Hushed giggles and a soft, feminine voice.

Interest piqued, he inched toward the room where his employees normally ate and peeked in. His betrothed sat in a puddle of skirt, surrounded by children. They all giggled at something she said. He peered closer.

A huge book nestled in her lap. He supposed she didn't own a small novel.

He must have made a noise, for she looked up, beaming him a smile that indicated nothing of the way she'd left his study only days ago. At the theater she'd been quiet and only spoke when spoken to. When Langford mentioned her shyness, Miles simply nodded.

He did not know how much of her timidity was due to shyness and how much to self-consciousness, but looking at her now, she appeared to be neither.

Her eyes sparkled at him. She closed the book and addressed the children. "I have already used more time than allotted by reading to you beyond our outdoor lessons. You must work now, but I shall return."

"Tomorrow, tomorrow," lisped Becky.

Bitt flashed him a helpless look and then shrugged. "I will try, but I cannot promise anything. Only you all must do your very best to read everything that comes into sight, and if you find a book, hold on to it, stow it safely, for it is your entry into another world."

She rose to her feet, and everyone followed her lead. Rustles and thuds resulted as children knocked into each other. Two women, one of whom Miles recognized as Elizabeth's lady's maid, waded into the crush of children and began ushering them out the door.

They waved to him as they stumbled by. He watched their exit and frowned. It did seem a shame to see them heading toward the main part of the mill rather than outside to play.

"I have to thank you, Miles. The children enjoyed their lesson immensely, and I feel it will not be long until each and every one is fully literate."

Elizabeth moved past him, beckoning to the women. "You two may wait in the carriage while I speak with Mr. Hawthorne."

Curtsying, the women left.

That left Miles and Elizabeth. He cleared his throat, feeling a strange itch at the back of it. "I'm happy the class proved productive."

"Oh, it was. I confess to being…" She paused, looking furtively past him. Voice lowered, she continued, "Gravely disappointed that you still keep Mr. Grealey on hand. He is altogether unsettling, Miles. I do not care for him at all."

"You must forgive his crass words. The man is doing his job."

"This has nothing to do with forgiveness." She hiked up her chin.

"I believe it does, but that is between you and God."

"How very condescending." She glared at him. Fortunately, he was well used to these looks of hers.

Winking at her, he gestured for her to follow him as he started down the narrow hall. "Come with me. I wish for you to look at my ledger again."

She let loose a puffy exhale, most likely to express her displeasure with him, but the sound of her dainty steps echoed behind him. Once in the office, he went straight to the cabinet where Mr. Shapely kept the ledger. Behind him, Elizabeth plopped her book on his desk. Or so he assumed, based on the smacking sound the leather binding made against the wooden surface.

"Do you plan to always be peevish with me, Bitt?" he asked mildly as he drew out the book.

"Forever" came the snappish answer.

He turned. She lounged against his desk, a disgruntled slant to her lips. On her, it was adorable. But would she be like Anastasia? He wondered how often she cried, for his first wife had wept at the drop of a hat pin. She'd been very tenderhearted, and it had been the ruin of her.

Besides that time in the stables, a memory that never failed to twist his gut, he could not recall Elizabeth actually weeping. He studied her now, bringing the ledger to the desk and setting it beside her.

"Since I am incapable of making you happy, please take a look at this and show me the errors, for I have not found a one." Obviously, he was incapable of pleasing women. The knowledge vexed him in unexpected ways.

Elizabeth had been trying so hard to prove her mettle, but he feared in the end, *he'd* be the disappointment, not her.

The unpleasant conclusion tried his patience even more.

She flipped open the ledger but her eyes were on him. "Did you have a difficult day?"

"No harder than any other."

"Come now, it is easy to see that you're worn and irritable. Perhaps we should stop by Grandmother's. I'm sure Cook has a tasty dish at the ready."

"Eating solves nothing."

"That is not what Grandmother says."

"Must you always argue?" Miles threaded his fingers through his hair. "In truth, it has been a harder day than most. There was another machinery malfunction at my other mill and the costs are hefty."

"Another one?" Elizabeth frowned, her empathetic tone making his arms ache to hold her.

A perfectly natural response, he assured himself. It was normal to seek comfort when agitated.

"Yes," he said shortly. "I have a suspicion that someone is out to sabotage me, but I'm not sure who or why."

"That is a strange thought, but it is true that all of these sudden problems are rather suspicious." She paused, her finger to her chin. "Grandmother says that food comforts the soul and prayer comforts the spirit. Perhaps you ought to pray?"

He let out a short laugh. "I pray every day." His relationship with the Lord was the only thing that kept him sane after Anastasia died.

"Well, that is very good of you. I did not use to, but when that dreadful Wrottesley accosted me in the gardens, I prayed hard indeed and God sent you. I was amazed by how quickly He responded. Perhaps if you pray now, He shall send you a quick answer."

"He is not a math problem. Praying isn't an equation to solve to get what you want."

"Don't be cross with me, Miles Hawthorne. I know that God is not my personal wishing well. I simply was surprised. I had expected a more distant being." She propped her chin on her fist, her eyes taking on that faraway look. "I had almost hoped to get a glimpse of heaven through my telescope."

Miles squinted at her, his chest constricting. Thinking about Wrottesley increased his pique exponentially, but Bitt was already dreaming of something else. She really had no idea, or refused to think about, the ramifications of what could have happened. But perhaps this was better.

She believed God to have rescued her, and as far as he remembered, Elizabeth had never spoken of God. He did not think she even attended any chapels, unless for a special occasion. With all her book learning, had she ever read the Bible?

He moved to the desk and propped himself on the corner. "My father believed deeply in God. He brought us up to have faith in the darkest of circumstances. Perhaps that is why he and your grandmother were great friends?"

"I'd like to believe they were secretly in love. Rather like Romeo and Juliet, but without the tragedy. Grandmother only speaks of him fondly. If she felt more for him than friendship, she does not let on. You know they were the same age. She simply had my mother before your father was even married. Perhaps they shared a similar faith."

"What do you think of religion?" He studied her carefully, noting the thoughtful expression that crept into her eyes and the relaxed posture of her shoulders. What a fascinating woman Elizabeth had turned out to be.

"I have no use for religion," she said. "But faith, on the other hand, seems to have served Grandmother well. Except when it comes to her moments of shock. I confess I find her fainting spells puzzling. And utterly convenient. I should rather like to learn how to faint, for I believe it might stand me in good stead during moments of abject boredom." She slanted him a crooked smile, which he thought surprisingly irresistible.

"I attend a quaint little chapel on the outskirts of London," he found himself saying. "Perhaps this Sunday you'd like to attend with me?"

"Why, of course…" Her face fell. "I don't know. New places are…uncomfortable. You are used to this—" her hand fluttered toward her birthmark "—but it is alarming to some. I do not care to be stared at nor to embarrass you."

Miles started, surprise shooting through him with all the force of a steam engine. "Whatever are you talking about? You could never embarrass me."

"I assure you that I could."

"What I am saying is that you are beautiful and graceful. You will be my wife," he said in a stern voice. "I will never be ashamed to have you by my side."

She blinked, looking down at the ledger. "Those are strong words."

"I mean every one of them. As I told you, God has designed you just as you are. I shall be proud to have you on my arm."

She made the slightest of sounds that might have been a sniffle. He frowned. Had he made her cry? Now his gut really knotted. He stood, unable to sit any longer.

"Check the ledger, please," he said gruffly. "I wish to know exactly where you spotted the errors."

Her head bent, the dark strands shining in the room's candlelight. In the silence, he became aware of the faint sounds of the mill that so often comforted, reminding him of long nights spent at his father's knee while some issue was attended to.

She shook her head. "This isn't right."

He came over, bending to see closer. He should have brought his spectacles. The numbers blurred. He bent closer, searching where her finger pointed. "What is the problem?"

"These aren't the same values."

He straightened. "What do you mean?"

She looked up, her expression confused. "I mean, this is not the same ledger I read before."

Chapter Seventeen

Someone had traded the ledgers.

Elizabeth could hardly believe it, but the evidence glared at her from Miles's desktop. His face scrunched while he bent to look at the book. She caught a faint whiff of soap and woodsy cologne. She allowed herself an appreciative sniff.

"How can you tell?" he asked.

She pointed to the numbers. "What I thought odd was the cost of your new carding machines. I had read an article several months ago promoting the use of them, and I remember the price being far cheaper. There were also more entries in the other book for miscellaneous items."

"I shall ring Grealey. Perhaps Mr. Shapely keeps two and has not updated this one."

A terrible suspicion was taking root in Elizabeth's stomach. What if Grealey were up to no good? What if he were stealing from Miles? As she pushed back from the desk and stood, she wondered how feasible it would be to share the thought with Miles.

His agitated stance, the tension radiating from him as

he strode to the door, decided for her. She needn't add to his worries. A good wife soothed her husband.

A hot burn scalded her cheeks. She wasn't his wife yet, but the prospect seemed less and less horrendous. She studied him carefully, recalling the gangly youth of childhood now fleshed into a mature man. So much more serious than she'd ever anticipated.

He had been right, she mused, while they waited for Grealey. Locking herself up at Windermar, shutting herself off from the world, had taken much more from her than experience. His hair, mussed from nervous fingers, stuck up in different directions.

What would he do if she walked over and casually straightened his unruly locks? Or if she leaned up and kissed his freshly shaven cheek?

His gaze met hers then, and every part of her trembled at the look he gave her. Did he know her thoughts? Though he stood at the door and she at the desk, the distance between them shrank beneath the power of their shared glance.

To know someone since childhood, to see him young and then grown, and yet…she felt as though she hardly knew him at all. His marriage to Anastasia had truly hurt him in ways she could not fathom.

"Grealey shall arrive in a moment," he said, his voice a rumble that soothed her senses.

What was wrong with her? Just because he called her beautiful did not mean she should overthink his feelings toward her. And yet her heart would not stop its confounded pitter-pattering.

Elizabeth moved toward Miles. "Though I should like to stay and confront that odious man, Miss Townsley and Jenna await. I am so happy I was able to see you today.

I should like to attend your chapel and perhaps then you may share with me Mr. Shapely's response."

"I will send a post to your London address with the name and location of the church." He stepped to the side, allowing her to exit.

She was altogether too aware of the breadth of his shoulders and scent of his skin. She swept by, head up, when what she wanted the most was to hold him close and assure him that she would never hurt him as Anastasia had.

The ladies waited for her outside. During their two day journey, they chatted about what had been successful in their approach with the children and what needed more work. Miss Townsley was full of practical ideas, but Elizabeth scrambled to pay attention. Her mind kept wandering, skipping all over the place.

From Miles and his impassioned words about her beauty to the strangeness of the accounts. Something was dreadfully wrong, but what?

If only she could stay and help him, but duties called. She struggled to put an ear to the conversation. They spoke of obtaining better writing utensils, more books. Of engaging the Littleshire community in helping the children.

All grand plans.

She gazed out the window at the passing trees, the verdant grasses and the air that grew fresher the farther they traveled from Littleshire. Soon she'd be married, but only as a countermeasure. Though it had seemed the right choice at the time, now she wondered if it might be even more lonely to be a wife without love than a ruined woman.

It was all so very confusing. At times Miles eyed her

with a strange intensity, but then he returned to his laughing self. And he'd invited her to church.

Church, of all places.

Her faith had wilted long ago, bent beneath the harsh blows of reality, but lately a change had been taking place within. A softening, and as she watched the land pass, covered in cloud-shaped shadows, the newly blooming flowers ripening the air, she couldn't help but feel that this Sunday might be an exciting moment for her. As if flowers bloomed within her.

How would Shakespeare write this feeling? More adeptly than she, certainly.

Attending chapel was another scary step into a world unaccustomed to her looks. The very thought quivered her spine and brought up the urge to bury herself so deeply in a library that she need never claw her way out.

Her thoughts traveled to the young stable hand so long ago. *Luke.* Just a boy, really, but his incredulity that she had thought he found her pretty still stung.

He had been so kind to her, which was what had confused her. Made her think he found her attractive, but in the end, he had only been trying to do his job well.

Which brought her thoughts circling back to today, to the oddness of agreeing to be seen publicly. But wasn't that what being betrothed meant? What else would be required when she married? Certainly she'd attend church with him once in a while.

Going to church with Miles… She sighed. They would sit together in the pew, she supposed. Only a month before she had not seen a future beyond living with Grandmother and finding new novels to read and writing articles about fascinating advances in technology.

"Heavy thoughts, my lady?" Miss Townsley asked.

Her inquisitive brown eyes gave the impression of seeing too much.

Elizabeth forced a smile. "Always heavy, as worries tend to be."

Miss Townsley laughed. "That is positively true. Which is why for the longest time I tried very hard to never think at all."

Despite herself, curiosity rose. "And then something happened?"

Miss Townsley cocked her head, expression sobering. "Life, my lady. Life forced my hand."

"As it does to us all," murmured Elizabeth.

And she wondered what Sunday would bring.

Sunday brought Miles a measure of anxiety in heaping doses. He readied for church, hands unsteady and mood sour. Elizabeth might not show up. That would be for the best. Or so he told himself as he climbed into the rig. Powell joined him, and so did the upper housemaids.

The misty morning threatened rain, but it was too late to change vehicles. His mood dampened even more.

"Are you all right, sir?" Powell slid him a questioning look, his used Bible slipping precariously across his lap as they rounded a corner toward the south London area. He stopped it with the flat of his palm.

Miles hesitated. Powell had been with him since he turned eighteen. The man was not much older than he, though he behaved like an old man sometimes. Confiding in a servant was not the wisest choice, but then again, they knew all the goings-on anyway.

"What do you think of my betrothal to Lady Elizabeth?" he asked carefully.

"Very sudden, sir, and unlike you."

Miles nodded, gratified by the honest words. "She is not Anastasia."

"Not in any way, sir." The words, spoken with vehemence, rippled through Miles.

"You think not?"

"Absolutely not."

Somewhat comforted, though he knew not why, Miles nodded his thanks. "She may be at chapel this morning," he finally said. His voice sounded rough in the early morning.

"That is good news. The lady does not strike me as the type who cares for the pomp and circumstance of a London church."

"That is true. I believe she prefers a smaller, more quiet church experience."

"This may be out of place, but what weighs on your mind, Mr. Hawthorne?"

Miles sighed. He slid a glance to Powell. Faithful valet for so long. "Your discretion has always been greatly appreciated. I value your service. Forgive me for waiting until now to ask this of you, but I believe I may need to make some serious inquiries. Perhaps even engage the services of a runner."

"Bow Street?"

"Possibly. There have been odd incidents at the factories. Mysterious equipment failures and a discrepancy in the books. Do you know how to go about engaging a detective?" His specialty lay in business, not law. And all of his instincts were screaming that something was amiss.

"I believe I can find out, sir."

"Excellent." They were nearing the chapel. Traveling through a pretty little part of London filled with small homes and clean streets. The smell of the Thames was not so strong here and the chapel's tall structure could be seen from the street.

"Only pray I do not make a muck out of this situation."

"Sir, if I may." Powell placed his hand on Miles's shoulders, a gesture completely out of the ordinary for his usually staid valet. "I shall be praying for you daily, but do not forget that Lady Elizabeth is unusual, different than others of the ton."

"Thank you, Powell." Miles exited the rig and together they walked up the stone pathway to the chapel, which sat on a little hill above the homes. The mist gathered about the steeple, a protective shroud of silver droplets. At the door, two figures huddled, one small of stature with hair the color of an aged rose.

Elizabeth.

His pulse quickened despite every instinct to tamp it down. As they neared, he heard Powell draw in a deep breath. Distracted, his gaze shifted to the woman next to Elizabeth. She looked familiar. Her lady's maid, a pretty woman with a great poof of blond hair twisted into a chignon.

He glanced at Powell. His butler wore a rapt expression. The bell tolled, chiming through the air in sweet, melodic notes.

"At last." Elizabeth rushed forward. "I believe we may be late, but I did not want to go in without you. I thought it best for Powell to escort Jenna to the servant's gallery."

Powell and he exchanged a glance.

"My dear, this is a small chapel. There is no servant's gallery, for inside those walls, all are equal."

Elizabeth's brows rose. "I have never heard of such a thing."

Miles grinned. "Not once, my lady? Surely a woman

of your book learning has read of places in which social standing is irrelevant."

"Only in *Utopia*, sir." But she answered his grin with a shy smile of her own, and in that very second, all felt right with his world. They entered the chapel together, and though the service had started, some turned to wave. A few curious glances flickered toward them, but they quietly found seats in the very back without causing any great disturbance.

The pastor's voice, flavored with a thick Scottish accent, spoke of worries and casting them all on the Lord. It was a good service, and at the end, his shoulders felt lighter.

As their group left the church, his friend Langford approached them. His wife followed behind. "Miles, are we still on for next week at Vauxhall Gardens?"

"We are. You remember Lady Elizabeth, my betrothed?" He watched her closely.

Her face flushed but she kept her gaze steady as she murmured a greeting.

"My darling Sarah will be going, as well. How many in our party, Miles?"

As they talked, they meandered to where the curricles were parked. Like Miles, Langford lived in London. He worked in investments.

They exchanged pleasantries and Miles was proud to see Bitt hold her own in the conversation, even finding a shared enthusiasm with Langford's wife about some lady writer he had never heard of.

After they had left, he faced Elizabeth. "Vauxhall Gardens next week."

"I shall look forward to it. Did you hear anything about the ledgers?"

"Looking into it." Miles grimaced. "I confess to finding the entire matter surprising. It's odd. You would think Shapely would have told me if he carries more than one ledger."

"It's a possibility I hadn't considered."

"But why all of the accidents?" He shook his head, surprised that he felt the liberty to tell her these things. "Something doesn't add up."

She gave him a winsome smile. "I have every confidence that you shall resolve the matter."

Her faith in him was rewarding. Would he live up to her expectations?

Chapter Eighteen

Miles paced the entrance to Vauxhall. He was early, he knew, but he'd wanted to make sure to be there when Elizabeth arrived. It was her final bow to his whims. She'd visited his factories and planned their betrothal ball flawlessly. He felt certain that tonight was to be a success, as well. She had seemed more comfortable with Langford's wife at church. Perhaps because they had already met at Drury Lane. Althought tonight, there were others in the group with whom she might feel uncomfortable. Lord and Lady Maxwell often intimidated people, but Lord Maxwell was one of his closest friends.

He scanned the crowded entrance and then pulled out his pocket watch. Almost eight o'clock. They should be arriving at any time. His overcoat warmed him. Perhaps it had been a bad choice.

He dropped the watch back into the pocket of his buckskins and flexed his fingers.

"Miles, old chap." Lord Maxwell appeared out of a group of the fashionably dressed peerage. His wife, a raven-haired beauty who'd had her come out when Anastasia did, was at his side. She gave him a cool nod.

"Jonathon, glad you made it. Langford is on his way."

"Are the Curleys joining us, as well?"

Miles glanced at Lady Maxwell, knowing that Mrs. Curley was a particular friend of hers. "Yes, I made sure to invite them."

He exchanged a knowing look with Jonathon. His friend's marriage had not been a love match and often the two were in discord. Thankfully, Mrs. Curley's presence might soften the tension and distract Lady Maxwell, leaving the rest of them to enjoy the entertainment Vauxhall Gardens offered.

The subject of their conversation arrived just then. Miles shook Jacob Curley's hand. His wife immediately joined Lady Maxwell, moving off to the side to engage in gossipy whispers. Langford and his wife came on the heels of the Curleys.

"Have you seen Lady Elizabeth?"

"You did not pick her up?" Lady Maxwell's voice held a touch of scorn that set his teeth on edge. "I suppose you were busy working."

"Ignore her." Lord Maxwell took Miles's arm and steered him to the right. "I believe I saw your lady hovering near the pavement. Perhaps you should fetch her? We will wait here for you."

Miles nodded, setting off to where carriages dropped their passengers. In the midst of all the finery, the top hats and skirts, he thought she'd be hard to find but, no, he spotted her almost immediately.

Her dark red hair stood out, two curls trailing down her shoulders, standing out against a wispy dress that gave her an ethereal glow. When she saw him, her eyes widened and she rushed forward.

"I am so happy to see you." Her usual reserve faded beneath the panic he saw in her eyes.

"Why didn't you let me escort you?" He took her arm, tucking it under his as he led her toward their party.

"Mother insisted I meet her charity group."

A chuckle escaped, rumbling through him. He could only imagine her discomfort. "You should have mentioned prior plans."

"They were last-minute." Her voice took on a thoughtful tone. "Mother wanted me there. I didn't know how long the entanglement might last... It is so very lovely here. Have you been before?"

The darkening evening cast muted light upon her features, capturing the piquant turn of her nose and deep guilelessness of her eyes.

"Many times." He gestured to where their group awaited. "I take it you have not."

"I always considered Vauxhall Gardens a shallow entertainment. I believed I could read of it and experience what I needed, but perhaps I was wrong. Just look how beautiful they have decorated everything."

Indeed, Vauxhall Gardens, a prominent London venue, offered paying guests great value in amusement. Fireworks, a light supper, desserts, gardens, the pleasures knew no bounds. Great lanterns of light decorated the various pathways. Miles knew from past experience that the food was overpriced but nothing could compare to the shows inside.

"I want to thank you, Elizabeth." He paused in walking.

"Whatever for?"

"For performing admirably the silly favors I asked of

you. I see now the fear behind my requests, but you have rarely chided me over it."

"You are the one who has rearranged your life for my sake. There are no thanks needed."

Their eyes met. A mutual recognition passed between them before they continued walking.

When they reached his friends, he introduced Bitt. Her manners were impeccable, though he sensed tension in her words. She seemed unusually stiff. He only hoped the darkness of night might relax her. If she was worried about her birthmark, it was not so noticeable in this lighting.

They entered the gardens and his schedule went according to plan. They ate thinly sliced meats and delicious tarts. When they watched the fireworks, he could not help but notice Bitt's rapt expression. She clutched her hands to herself, eyes wide and unblinking as colors exploded against the inky sky.

Anastasia had been bored, he recalled, just as Lady Maxwell looked. She'd made a few snide references to his marriage to her friend during the evening, but thankfully Bitt had been involved in conversation with Langford's wife about Shakespeare and which works were his greatest. He was not surprised that Elizabeth preferred the ones that weren't named after characters. Apparently most of the named plays were tragedies.

His Elizabeth longed for hope and happy endings. He was sorry that she had lost her chance at love, thanks to Wrottesley. And thanks to him, for he knew he was incapable of being the kind of husband she deserved.

After the fireworks, their group walked to where boats waited to ferry visitors across the Thames to see the gardens.

"Did you walk Westminster bridge when you arrived?" asked Lord Maxwell of Miles.

"The bridge was our best opportunity to be seen," put in his wife.

Artifice was quite unbecoming. "I did not." Changing the subject, he said, "A boat ride is ideal on this starry night." They filed into the boats and Miles searched for Bitt. Despite the glow of lanterns and stars, she was nowhere to be seen.

"Where is Lady Elizabeth?" Langford's wife stared up at him from where she sat in the boat. Miles glanced down the shoreline, but did not see his betrothed. He looked in the other direction, the muscles at the back of his neck straining. A tic picked at the corner of his eyelid.

"The last I saw her, she looked like a marred little bird staring off into space," Lady Maxwell drawled. She tittered and Curley's wife joined in, though quietly.

A giant swell of anger bowled through Miles, locking his jaw so tight he could barely speak. "And that was?"

"Near the palace," she supplied, her eyes unreadable in the black night.

"You all go on without me," he said tightly.

"Shall we wait for you anywhere?" At least Langford's wife showed some kind of concern. The other two talked amongst themselves. The men waited for his answer.

He clasped the back of his neck. In a place as crowded as Vauxhall, it could be hours until he found her. If he found her at all.

How had things turned so sour so suddenly?

"Go on ahead," he said at last. "The night is nearly over for me. I shall find her and then leave for home. I've a busy schedule tomorrow."

He bid his friends farewell and then turned back to the

paths that led to the palace structure. Nothing showed him just how much a failure he was as this night had.

His wife had died from a broken spirit. He had not been able to save her.

Elizabeth was alone in this place, possibly scared out of her wits, and he had been the one who was supposed to protect her.

The third test for his betrothed, but he realized that it had also tested him.

And he'd been found wanting.

He had to find Elizabeth, he realized. Heart pounding, he strode forward. Determination roared through him, strengthening his legs, fisting his hands. He would find her and keep her safe.

He could not fail this time.

She was too important.

Flowers everywhere. They hung in the trees, floating clouds of suspended fragrance. Elizabeth inhaled deeply, pausing at the juncture of a path to appreciate their beauty. The group meandered ahead. She would catch up. She wanted this moment to just breathe in the exotic chaos of this place.

The Grand Walk had been interesting. She'd seen the more fashionable members of the ton promenading in their fine silks and furs, showcasing the most recent styles from Paris. Their supper box had been surprisingly comfortable. The food had not been as tasty as she expected. The meat had been thinly sliced, but the dessert had been delicious and there had been quite a variety of puddings served.

She moved closer to the path, which veered to the right. Its serene, gently lit serpentine curve beckoned her. How oft she had read of Vauxhall in the paper. No amount of words could describe the experience, though. Her senses had been regaled with the smell of fireworks, the booming explosion of light behind her eyelids and the entrancing shower of colors raining down to earth. The echo still filled her mind.

And the music. Oh, the music here had been worth every shilling spent. Miles had paid for the outing, and she must be sure to thank him.

She blinked and looked down the path. Her party was nowhere in sight. She set a brisk pace, passing another pavilion swirling with colorful arrays of costumed entertainers. Panic edged her throat, suturing her windpipe closed. The walkway seemed unbearably crowded, each person not the one she sought.

If she didn't find Miles, should she go home?

Yes, her brain insisted. Go home. Do not allow nerves to win. Clutching her dress, she passed a large tower surrounded by a thick mix of people. She skirted around them. Surely she must reach Miles soon.

Perhaps it would be better to wait to the side. If he came looking for her, she would not want them to pass each other by. That idea relieved her panic. She walked to the side, standing near a rainbow triad of lamps. Though she hated being in the light, where everyone might stare, the position provided the best opportunity for Miles to see her should he walk past.

And so she waited, her thoughts circling in lunatic patterns, her heartbeat tripled by nerves. Her knuckles ached from squeezing her purse, but she could not seem to relax.

Moments passed, in which she ruminated on the night. The pleasures and gallantries, the underlying tension she believed to be caused by Lady Maxwell and Mrs. Curley.

Those two had not fit with the rest of them. Mrs. Langford presented an amiable and intelligent nature. The men held interesting conversations about the state of politics, France and the Prince Regent. Mr. Curley, in particular, had been quite knowledgeable about the myriad of original paintings in Vauxhall.

But the two women…their snickers and sidelong glances dampened the mood at times. Elizabeth could not help but feel that Lady Maxwell's words carried an underlying scorn when she spoke to Miles. She'd even commented about Anastasia in Elizabeth's hearing…a tiny comment about beauty being wasted, but she wasn't sure what the lady had meant. Only that she seemed to blame Miles for Anastasia's great sadness.

Elizabeth had discreetly looked into Miles's first marriage and discovered that Anastasia had been deeply unhappy. But surely he was not to blame? From all accounts, he had loved her dearly.

Elizabeth shifted, her feet aching and the cool breeze from the nearby Thames coaxing goose bumps to her skin. The sounds that had been so exciting now clawed at her serenity, grating on her nerves. She searched the crowd for Miles, for his broad-shouldered physique and perfect top hat.

He had looked so dapper when she arrived. So very much the gentleman. One might never guess that his father had been raised in squalor and worked himself into the realms of wealth and high society.

Sometimes she could hardly believe that they were to be wed. Married, in actuality. Yes, it was for convenience, but she would not deny the part of her that longed for caring, that thought perhaps, within a few years, he might feel something toward her beyond friendship.

She touched her birthmark, feeling the uneven ridges even through her kid gloves. Could she risk passing this on to a child, though? She dropped her hand and stared unseeingly at the lamps.

It would be most selfish of her.

"Elizabeth, I am so relieved I've found you." Miles appeared out of the mill of people, his long legs eating up the ground between them.

A violent rush of gratitude pulsed through her. She could not stop the exhalation of breath nor the way her shoulders dropped as all of the anxiety she'd been carrying faded.

"Come," he said, taking her arm and drawing her onto a pathway behind her. "Let us speak where we might hear each other."

She followed wordlessly, the heavy weight of his clutch on her arm welcome and reassuring. They walked down the path, which curved before them in colorful shadows from the lamps.

Perhaps it had been specifically designed for privacy. She felt certain she'd read something to that effect, that the quiet little paths were perfect for a rendezvous. Their footsteps scuffed, whispery as they left the revelry behind. Muted darkness closed around them, a soft blanket of silence that shrouded her uneven breaths.

Miles did not look at her, but she felt the tightness of his grip and the deliberateness to his steps that had not been there before. They rounded a bend, coming upon a tiny bench hidden in an alcove to the right.

If anyone caught them out here… Elizabeth shoved the thought away. Miles had found her. He'd left their group to look for her.

Milky shadows, moonlight hued, draped the bench.

Miles stopped at it, turning to face her with an expression of intensity she'd never seen.

Not even when he'd found her in the stable years ago. She well recalled his anger then. His tightly controlled emotions.

He reminded her of that young man now. Her breath fluttered in her throat, a trapped butterfly struggling for release, but she couldn't exhale. His fingers found hers. They interlocked, joining in a silent dance. His eyes were so very dark, hidden by the shadows. His jaw a marble sculpture, clenched in sharp relief.

She wanted to speak, to say something, but her heart thudded desperately against her rib cage. Her knees shook. Who was this Miles? A dangerous antagonist come alive from a novel, or a moody hero intent on saving the damsel?

"I was worried." His voice cut through her thoughts, low and rough.

Her gaze flew up to his. The way his eyes bored into her… She shivered.

"Are you cold?" Immediately he moved closer, his arm sliding around her in a welcome, warm embrace.

"I am fine, Miles." She shivered again, relief rippling through her. "I am so glad you found me."

"And if I hadn't?"

The measured words, careful and slow, drained her last ounce of willpower.

"You would, because when you want something, you do it," she said quietly. Why resist what was so very obvious? She was marrying this man. Could it be so bad to be attracted to him?

"Not always, Bitt," he rasped. Leaning forward, his breath a kiss in the air between them, he rested his forehead against hers. It was an utterly foreign sensation to feel his skin against hers, and yet natural. "Sometimes I don't get what I want."

Strains of piano undulated in quiet waves, wrapping around them. Without questioning herself, Elizabeth brought her arms up to circle Miles's neck. Their faces shifted, his cheek pressing against hers, his lips searching until she offered her own.

How very often she had read of stolen kisses. Of rendezvous and secret loves. But no amount of reading had prepared her for the shock of Miles's lips upon her own. The way his mouth pressed against hers, warm and inviting, crisped with the taste of strawberry from their dessert. His arms possessed her. Capturing her against himself.

Every sense heightened, discovering the scrape of his chin against hers, the pressure of his palms on her back, the emotions streaming through her in unrelenting currents.

And then he drew back, taking his lips from hers. Removing his hands. Leaving her alone and breathless and shivering.

She dared not speak. Was not sure she could, for every part of her thrummed. And her heart hurt. Oh, it hurt. Every beat seemed too loud and she wondered if Miles could hear the tortured cadence. But no, he appeared in his own agony, his cheekbones cut into harsh angles and planes, his eyes buried beneath the veil of shadows.

For the moment, their heaving chests and whispery exhales mingled with the night's noises. Footsteps sounded upon the walk. Quickly, Miles drew her to him, pivoting so that they were shadowed upon the lane. The party passed by, a group of laughing men and women so intent on their own fun that they did not notice two souls beside a bench.

After the path had cleared, Miles released her. She felt more steady now, though there was the shock of his kiss still echoing on her lips, in her heart.

"I am very happy you're well and unharmed," he said at last. "We should return to the Grand Path. The others went across the Thames to see the gardens."

"I should have liked to do that. I was distracted," she admitted. Knowing whatever they'd just shared had been shattered by reality, she walked away from the benches. Miles moved beside her, his steps mirroring hers. After that kiss, could she really enjoy the night? She wanted to go home, to bury herself in her bed and relive every special moment.

She glanced at her companion, annoyance surging when she realized how unaffected he looked. He winked at her.

Infernal man.

But she couldn't quite dredge up irritation, for her lips still ached from the press of his kiss, and it was as though the warm imprint of his hand still lingered on her back. How would she ever look at him the same?

"I will escort you home," he said finally.

"Jenna awaits me. There is no need for your presence." She did not think she could sit in a carriage with him. Not with how she felt, as though her entire being adored him. Her fingers longed to stroke his cheek, to tell him she would be the best wife he could have ever asked for. But he looked distant, even walking a smidge farther ahead, as though trying to escape.

Perhaps the kiss *had* affected him, after all. Hope enflamed. Putting aside the concern of future children bearing her marred skin, the dream of being loved bloomed within. A fragile dream but it unfurled nonetheless.

As they neared the entrance, passing throngs of revelers and pavilions of entertainment and songs, she reached for his arm. His muscles jumped at her touch but she did not remove her hand.

"I have fulfilled all three of your requests," she said inanely, a part of her desperately grasping at a semblance of normality. "Is there anything else you want from me?"

"No." Miles faced her, and gone were the crinkles at his eyes, replaced by a sober look that chilled Elizabeth and chased every warm feeling from her soul. "Nothing at all."

Chapter Nineteen

When Elizabeth awoke, it was to Jenna's quiet hum as she prepared for the morning. Elizabeth squinted out from beneath the covers, which gathered in a warm nest about her head.

"Is it time to awake?"

"Lady Danvers wishes to call in two hours. I am laying out your clothes." Jenna came over, eyes worried. "I'm sorry for waking you, my lady. Shall I bring you something?"

Elizabeth groaned, her eyes gritty, her imagination still teeming with dreams, all revolving around Miles. "No, that is not necessary." She rolled onto her back and stared up at the ceiling. "Have you ever been in love, Jenna?"

Her maid rustled the coverlets, smoothing them. "Twice, my lady. The first time when I was a young woman."

Unbidden, Elizabeth felt stirrings of curiosity. Jenna had been with her since she was thirteen, and this was the first she'd heard of a romance. "How did I not know of this young man?"

Jenna flushed. "It did not interfere with my duties, I promise you that."

Dumbfounded, Elizabeth could only stare at her maid, who looked truly frightened. Did she think Elizabeth a monster? Unfeeling? Shaken, she sat up, letting the covers fall to her waist.

"Of course, it did not. You are a quality lady's maid, Jenna, and I do apologize if I've never told you so."

She dipped her head. "Thank you, my lady. I suppose I did not think you interested in my life."

Elizabeth grimaced. "What happened to him?"

"He was sent to France during the war. He didn't return." Jenna gazed down at her hands.

Pain lanced Elizabeth's chest. While she had been reading and dreaming her way through life, Jenna had quietly suffered a broken heart. "I am so very sorry."

"There is no need to apologize. It was a long time ago and we were very young." Jenna curled her fingers around her skirt. "Perhaps my heart has healed, for…" She hesitated, as though questioning the prudence of sharing secrets with her mistress.

"For?" Elizabeth prompted.

"I have met someone. He is so very handsome and composed. An older man with a gentle smile and kind eyes."

"Those are fine attributes, indeed." Why did falling in love bring Jenna so much happiness when all Elizabeth felt was pain? Chest tight, she wet her lips. "Do I know him?"

Her lady's maid nodded, but her eyes filled with what looked like worry. "When you marry, my lady, and perhaps this is out of place, but I feel that I must plan for my future…"

"I shall be taking you with me," Elizabeth said quickly. "That is, if you wish to stay on."

Jenna's face cracked into a wide smile. "Nicholas is his name. You know him as Powell. He is surely the most wonderful man I've ever met."

"But when did you meet him?" She picked at the coverlet as she awaited the maid's reply.

"Several months ago." Jenna sighed heartily. "He is Mr. Hawthorne's valet."

"Oh, my. Powell. Yes, he is quite a good choice." An image of the man flashed through her mind. He had been easy to talk to, a creative thinker with a thoughtful smile. "You seem…confident that your situation will end on a positive note."

"One must always be optimistic with love. You can never give up nor lose hope." Jenna patted Elizabeth on the knee. "Come now, my lady. We shall ready you for the day. There are several callers to be seen and then a small get-together at Lady Charleston's this evening. Do you wish to wear your teal or your champagne day dress?"

As Jenna riffled through Elizabeth's clothing, Elizabeth hauled herself out of the bed. She dearly wanted to gush about her first kiss, but unlike Jenna, she had no way of knowing if Miles reciprocated her feelings.

She supposed she could ask.

Yes, that seemed the obvious solution.

Beating around the proverbial bush never suited her. Reading and quiet nights at home, yes. Avoiding difficult conversations with her betrothed, never. In fact, Miles was probably the only person she had ever felt comfortable losing her temper with.

Perhaps he was as on edge as she. There was only one way to find out.

"Jenna—" Elizabeth walked to her desk and plucked the quill from its container "—could you see that a note is delivered to Mr. Hawthorne today? I would like for you to personally give it to him. Tell him I do not need a response, but to simply expect me at four."

"Lady Ewell is arriving, my lady, at that time."

"Fiddle-faddle," she muttered. She'd forgotten today was the day reserved for callers. Scrawling a quick message to Miles, she handed the parchment to her maid. "Very well, wait for his answer. If I must arrive sooner, I shall. Could you arrange this for me?"

"Yes, my lady."

"Oh, and do tell Powell I say hello."

Jenna's face turned pastel pink and Elizabeth could not help but smile. Life tossed unexpected twists. At least they made some people happy.

The afternoon passed uneventfully. When Lady Danvers called, she regaled Elizabeth with the latest on-dits, including the still-circulating tales of Lady Elizabeth and Mr. Hawthorne's love match. Elizabeth had neither the heart nor the inclination to explain the real situation, and a sigh of relief passed her lips as soon as the matriarch left.

She called for Jenna and learned that Miles could receive her at five thirty. Nervousness plagued her all day, for she longed to see him but could not help but remember his coldness when they parted. Surely today he might be in a better mood. She needed to see what he thought about their kiss. If perhaps he might kiss her again.

Last night she should have asked, but her emotions had been roiling like unruly waves. She had hardly been able to think clearly. Even now, as she readied to leave, as she pulled on a shawl and arranged her bonnet, she remembered the tenderness of his embrace.

The ride to his house was torturous. She clutched her reticule and a copy of *Gulliver's Travels*. She found herself praying to God that all would go well. Not sure of the specific details she should ask for, she simply prayed for wisdom.

The prayer comforted.

When she arrived, Powell showed her into Miles's study. She offered him a conspiratorial smile, to which his normally staid expression broke into a beaming grin. They said nothing, but she could not help but feel a kinship with the man. He had, after all, been charmed by Jenna.

As she settled into one of Miles's great wingback chairs, she mused on how lonely Powell must have felt all these years. And then he met Jenna and fell in love. Uttering a heartfelt sigh, she hugged her reticule.

True love.

A gift that always seemed outside her grasp. A sound at the doorway caught her unawares. She looked up. Miles strode into the room, his hair unkempt, his eyes a mottled green.

And every ounce of her melted.

Was this how Hermia had felt for Lysander? Such a riveting love that she risked death to be with him?

"Miles," she breathed, her heartbeat a sonata as she remembered the feel of his arms about her waist when they waltzed.

"Elizabeth." His gaze flickered.

The sonata came to an unromantic halt. Flustered by his unemotional greeting, she hugged the book tighter. It was her excuse for the visit, a way to lead up to what had happened the previous evening. "I have brought a different story to read you. Something other than Shakespeare. Just a chapter. Please."

He laughed. A dry, hollow sound. Frowning, she slapped the book on her lap and glared at him.

"Have I said something to amuse you?"

"Your request to see me is merely to read me a *book*?" His last word held so much surprise that Elizabeth flinched.

"There is more to the request than that." She paused. "I wished to speak to you of several things. First, Miss Townsley and I plan to visit Littleshire this week and stay for a few days. This is the novel I am reading the children."

"You think me so ignorant you would read me a children's book?"

Elizabeth tightened her grip on the novel. He was positively in a wicked mood. Why did he sound so very defensive? "This is fine literature, I assure you. There is no age constraint on imagination. I completed three requests for you, and all quite successfully, I'd say. Now I simply ask for a few moments of your day. Surely you can spare that, to humor me."

In the past, when she used this tone, he flashed her a mischievous smile. He teased. Today he gave her a long, measured look. Taking the seat beside her, he released a pained sigh.

"I am marrying you for convenience's sake, Elizabeth. Those requests were to prove that you could rise to the occasion of being my wife. A task that might be unwieldy for one used to being cosseted and waited upon her entire life." He steepled his fingers, his eyes guarded. "You performed magnificently. You will be an excellent wife, and we will get along just fine as long as you understand one thing. I owe you nothing."

Elizabeth felt as though she'd been slapped. His tone burned, twisting her heart and scouring away any hope she might've felt for their union. "There are so many offensive words you just uttered, that I know not where to begin in refutation."

He shrugged. "There is nothing to refute. Simply understand that I shall care for you and protect you, but do not think that I will humor you. You forget that I have been married once before, and I well know the machinations of a wife."

Machinations? Elizabeth was sure her tongue had stopped working, right along with her heart. Her throat constricted and telltale prickles crept along her eyelids. She would *not* cry in front of Miles. She would not give him the satisfaction of knowing how deeply his words stung.

Though looking at him now, at the proud jut of his jaw and the stiff posture, hinted that everything he said came from a wounded place she knew little about. And she had trod upon the wound somehow, with such force that he had turned into this heartless cad of a man.

Asking him about their kiss no longer concerned her. She did not want to hear what he might say because it surely would heap more hurtful words upon the pile he'd just created. She wet her lips.

"Very well, Miles, you owe me nothing. I thank you for agreeing to marry me on such short notice."

His expression further darkened into a brooding mask.

"I take it that I may continue my lessons with the children in Littleshire, or is that beyond the scope of what is expected of me?"

"Lessons are fine." He was looking at her warily, awaiting a verbal tirade, she supposed.

She stood. The desire for anything from this man had fled. How utterly silly she had been to think a kiss meant more to him than it did. Even though the deepest parts of her protested that it must have meant *something*, she did not have the nerve to ask. Not with him in this mood.

"I will confess to being entirely surprised when you came to offer marriage. Indeed, you were so opposed to the institution that I could not believe you would do such a thing simply to keep me from ruin." She clutched her reticule so tightly her knuckles ached. "You said my parents did not put you up to it. You said John was worried. Did he pressure you to marry me? Tell me the truth. You do owe me something, Miles, and it is honesty. I shall always expect such from you."

He dipped his head in concession. "Try not to lose your temper, Bitt, for what I have to say shall surely irritate you." He paused, and it seemed as though her breaths paused with him. "Your brother did indeed request that I marry you."

"I knew it." She reeled beneath tremors of anger. "John was behind your proposal."

Miles uncurled from the chair, rising in a beautifully lazy elegance that almost distracted Elizabeth from her rapidly rising pique.

She shook her head, mind racing. "Why would he ask you to do such a thing? I hardly ever speak to him. I cannot believe he told you to marry me. Is he that concerned with his reputation?"

"Dearest, you must understand. He wanted to save you the distress of scandal, and since the article implied my involvement, he held me responsible for your plight. I didn't tell him about Wrottesley because I could not allow your betrothal to such a man, and I knew John would demand that he do you right by marriage. You must know, I owe your brother a great deal for his help in a past situation." He shoved his fingers through his hair, thoroughly mussing the blond strands. "There is nothing to worry about nor to be upset over. John wanted you safe and happy. Asking for your hand was simply an obligation I felt duty bound to fulfill."

Elizabeth clutched her reticule, every response locked tight beneath the pressure of her diaphragm. Surely she had misheard. She replayed his words in her mind.

His cold, emotionless words.

An *obligation*.

Drawing herself as tall as possible, she skewered him with a glare. "One does not simply go around kissing obligations."

Her words brought a rouge flush to his cheeks.

He moved forward, grasping her by the shoulders, his irises a swirling mass of greens and grays, his fingers digging into her flesh. "I was worried about you. It was a mistake."

Her heart swelled, battling between so many feelings. He had worried about her. It almost took the sting from their argument. Oh, how tempting to stay, to lift her face and place a kiss upon his lips. To show him how she cared for him.

But he had called their kiss a mistake. Her an obligation. That is all, he had said. Simply an obligation.

Heart twisting in tight, painful spasms, she jerked from his grip. The reticule swung from the force of her movement, knocking against her knees in an angry protest.

"I am a grown woman," she said stiffly. "No one has

asked you to worry over me. My parents can pressure me to marry, but certainly no one can be forced into marriage. If I choose to live in quietude with Grandmother, it is not because I am helpless or in need of rescuing. I could have found another suitor, especially with the pounds attached to my name."

Miles nodded, mouth grim. His hands dropped to his sides. "I am fully in awe of you, Elizabeth. My proposal had more to do with what I owe John than any concern on my part for your ability to handle your situation."

Every fiber of her being urged her to call off her betrothal to this antagonizing man. That would be an unwise reaction, though. She had wanted to quell the ton's gossip, but instead they now chattered about her "love match." To call off the marriage would only set tongues wagging more.

She was well and truly stuck with him.

"Believe me, your meaning is taken," she said in a cold voice. "I do not wish to bother you any longer with duty. Please, return to the work that you never cease doing, and I shall retire to my home to be cosseted whilst I read a dreadful, horribly meaningless piece of literature, the likes of which is too immature for your well-seasoned ears."

"Bitt." The low timbre of his voice scraped her emotions further. He sounded disapproving. "You are overreacting."

"Nonsense. I knew from the beginning that you were making a sacrifice to marry me. What I did not fully realize was that you felt an obligation to my brother to do so. To say that I am a duty you must fulfill… If not for Wrottesley and his obnoxious nature, I wouldn't be in this quandary of marrying a man who finds me a mere item on his list of accomplishments. Well, never fear, Miles. I shall not disturb you anymore. You may have your mundane, unimaginative life in which you prance around scoffing at other people's dreams—" At that her voice caught. Horrified, she stopped ranting because she had a betraying stinging in her eyes and her throat had stopped producing sounds. "It is altogether insulting," she choked out.

She spun around, intending to flee, but Powell appeared in the doorway, unwittingly blocking her exit. His eyes flickered to her then landed on Miles.

"Sir, I would not interrupt but there has been an emergency." He held out a paper. Miles snatched it.

Donning a pair of spectacles, he unfolded the paper. Beneath the tan of his skin, he paled. Without a word, he gave it back to Powell and turned to Elizabeth.

The pained expression on his face drained the anger from her. She reached out, clasped his hands. "What is it? Your brother?"

"Littleshire Mill." His fingers spasmed over hers. "Burned down last night. Everything is destroyed."

Chapter Twenty

Miles found he could not release Bitt's hand.

He'd been working so hard and now…gone. Everything gone. No one had been hurt, though, and for that he thanked God. His people were the most important part of his factories.

A haze settled over his mind. He had put a large chunk of his cash toward that mill.

"What will happen to the families?" Her whisper filtered through his consciousness.

"I must see my solicitor at once. I'll visit the bank in the morning. Powell," he barked. His valet stepped forward. "Get word to Mr. Shapely that I will arrive in three days. I'll need both books available. Instruct him to contact all the employees… I shall write instructions."

"Both books?" Bitt looked up at him, her eyes wide. She still held his hand tightly within hers. He found the strength of her clasp warm, comforting.

"I verified that he keeps one with him and sporadically updates the one you saw. Which explains why we saw differing amounts."

"Have you compared them?"

The question spiked the pounding pressure in his head. With his other hand, he massaged his temples. "Not yet, but I will. Once we see him, we will get everything in order. In the meantime, I must tender instructions to our employees regarding wages."

Miles spent the next hour arranging for instructions to be sent to both Mr. Shapely and Grealey. During the entire process, Elizabeth sat in his study, calm and reassuring, offering a quiet solace that he found immensely relieving. He did not have the inclination to order her home nor the time to apologize for hurting her feelings earlier.

He would make his insensitivity up to her. Once this situation was resolved. Somehow he would show her that even though he could never be the husband she wanted, he would care for her as best as he was able. He would explain what he owed John. She deserved to know, though the idea of confessing his failings to Anastasia stoked a panic he found hard to ignore.

But Elizabeth could be trusted. She was, after all, an old childhood friend. Forgetting that fact in the wake of kissing her had been a mistake. He blocked from his mind the memory of last night. What good could it do to remember the sweetness of her embrace?

He shoved papers to the side of his desk until he found what he was looking for. "In the morning, I must go to the bank. I will need an idea of what is available to rebuild the mill."

"You're going to keep the factory still?"

"Of course." He paused in his rummaging. "Did you expect otherwise?"

"I am merely surprised. The other mill produces income, does it not?"

"It does, but I have several investments that have tied up my funds as well as a bulk of monies put into the Littleshire Mill. The income from my other factory is not enough. The people of Littleshire are going to be desperate for work. This is a tragedy, Elizabeth." He pressed his palms flat against the desk. "I shall contact the insurance company to begin the work of restoring the mill."

Her pretty lips relaxed. "I understand. What can I do?"

"There is nothing at this point."

"I shall go with you to the bank."

He told her no, but the next morning found her waiting on his doorstep. Her appearance was a welcome surprise. He'd spent the night sleepless. Worried.

They decided she would wait in the carriage while he completed his business. Her proximity reminded him again of the responsibilities of having a wife. She was inserting herself into his life, and it felt too comforting. What happened when she tired of him? When he proved himself unworthy just as he had with Anastasia?

He shut out the thoughts. She was *not* Anastasia, and this circumstance was not a repeat of his former marriage. Anastasia had been prone to fits of great sadness. He had tried so very hard to please her… Grimacing, he helped Elizabeth into his carriage.

He must trust God. At this juncture, it was his only peaceful option.

During the ride to the bank, the scent of her perfume filled the carriage. The rustle of her dress accompanied the nervous silence. He could not bring himself to speak, and she did not do so either, but he felt her voice within his heart.

Before he went into the bank, as the carriage jostled

to the curb and stopped, he held out his hand. "Will you pray with me?"

Her brows arched up, but she nodded and placed her small hand within his.

"Lord, I ask for your bountiful mercy today. Your blessing and your wisdom. I am in need of the peace only you can give. Amen."

"Amen," she said softly. "Should I send a message to have a bag packed for our travel to Littleshire?"

"There is no need for you to go," he said. "Your presence is appreciated, but there is nothing you can do there."

"Nonsense. Grandmother will be happy to see me. Not only that, I can organize the women and children into groups. They shall help clean up the debris and scrub any machines that are still usable. Did the fire spread to the town?"

"No, the note said it remained contained and burned itself out." Miles frowned. "A very odd thing in and of itself."

"How do you suppose it started?"

"We shall conjecture later." He gave her a farewell wave and exited the carriage. The door let in a fair amount of light, revealing the tight anxiety on Bitt's face. "Try not to worry, dear. I shall have this taken care of, and all will be well."

He gave instructions for his driver to wait and then turned to face his bank. Drummond's rose above him in solid splendor, as if reassuring him that despite the loss of his mill, his money still remained safe. He strode into the large entry, where an intricate clock ticked away the time and quills greeted guests.

"Mr. Hawthorne, what brings you in today?"

Miles addressed the clerk, told him what he wanted and within a matter of minutes, his world crashed into pieces around him.

In a daze, his pockets empty, he walked to the carriage. He told the coachman to take them to the shipyard. He barely registered climbing into the carriage.

"Where are we going?" Elizabeth's voice pierced the fog coating his mind. "Whatever is wrong?"

"Gone," he said hoarsely, his future suddenly empty of everything he'd worked so hard for. "Everything is gone."

"Gone?" Elizabeth repeated.

"Yes. Stolen. Every last pound." Miles sat still as a rock in his seat. The carriage jostled through the streets while Elizabeth tried to absorb his words.

"But how? Who?" she finally asked.

He shook his head, his eyes eerily blank. "William Shapely, my steward. He came in yesterday morning with a supposed letter from me to withdraw funds."

"But why would they not verify with you? Surely he does not have the authority to access your money?"

"He's my steward. He has more authority than you realize. He can't access my personal funds, but everything for the business…he had a letter signed by Grealey and me regarding the fire and the need for all available funds."

A terrible dread settled over them as they clattered through the London streets. The stench of the Thames grew, salted with the odor of manure-lined streets and rotten fish. Indignation swelled within Elizabeth as they drew closer to the shipyard.

"Why would he do such a thing? He has not put you in the poorhouse, has he?"

"I have my property and personal funds, but the monies in those accounts…they comprised the bulk of my liquidity." Miles buried his head in his hands, alarming Elizabeth so deeply that she reached out to touch his hair. The strands felt smooth and foreign to her fingers, on which she'd neglected to wear gloves. After all, she had not anticipated the turn of this afternoon nor that she might need them for an outing.

"All shall be well," she said firmly. "We will retrieve your stolen funds."

"Only if we can catch his ship. I believe he may have already sailed" came the muffled answer.

Aghast, Elizabeth could find no words of comfort. "Grealey must have known something was amiss. Turncoat. Traitor. Maleficent being."

Miles clasped her wrists with long fingers. "While you are busy calling names, could you kindly release my hair?"

"Oh, dear." She immediately let go of the strands, which she'd been fisting in her irritation. "I do apologize, but he has me so upset. How could he do this to you? After all the wonderful kindnesses you show your employees? And who is this Shapely fellow? I shall make sure he is caught and that justice is brought to bear upon his deceitful head. Why, this is simply villainous. An act worthy of any Shakespearean antagonist."

Indeed, a fiery heat of anger trailed through her body.

Miles turned his grip so that he held her hand within his. His head lifted and a trace of a smile tipped his lips. "Such vilification from my sweet Bitt."

His words swirled the heat within to something different, something infinitely more dangerous.

She withdrew her hand. "You are a close family friend

and my betrothed. Of course, I am positively horrified for your sake. This shall be rectified. Grandmother has contacts in high places. Her duchess friends, you know. They shall help."

Miles sighed. "I'll fix this myself, Elizabeth."

"There is no need to be prideful. If you can marry me to help my unfortunate situation, by all means, allow me to return the kindness. My family is more than capable of coming to your aid."

"Why don't we just pray? I think for now that is the best we can do." Taking her hand without waiting for a response, he bowed his head. "Heavenly Father, we thank You for Your goodness and ask for wisdom in this situation. Please help us deal with the matter in a way honoring You…"

He continued the prayer as she held his hand tightly. When he ended, she said amen and their eyes met. Dearest Miles, who must be so worried right now, yet he put his trust in God.

Swallowing tightly, she released his hand as the carriage shuddered to a stop.

Miles jumped out of the carriage.

"I am coming," she said.

"This is no place for a lady." He looked up at her from a street caked with dirt and worse unmentionables.

"My place is beside you." She held out her hand. "Help me out or I shall jump and undoubtedly twist my ankle."

A torn expression twisted his features, and she felt the slightest ping of guilt for forcing his hand. But she did not relent nor give in to the feeling. Sighing, he took her fingers and helped her from the carriage. She withdrew a linen from her pocket and held it to her nose.

"Where are we going?" She pressed the cloth more closely to her face.

"To find out if he has booked passage on any of these vessels."

"And if he used a different name?"

Miles's face shuttered. "Then the lives of my employees will be radically changed, for I cannot afford to pay them for long when there are no funds."

Elizabeth followed him, her eyes and nose stinging from the stench. The shipyard teemed with movement, curses and belligerent, unkempt men who said nothing of her birthmark nor even looked at her. They went about their business, and she could scarcely tell what that business was for their erratic movements.

It was all she could do to keep up with Miles, who set a brisk pace. He stopped when he found a man dressed in colorful regalia. A captain, perhaps?

"Aye, I know of who you speak." The man's attention wandered to Elizabeth. He perused her thoroughly. Rude creature. "The man left yesterday on a ship bound for the Americas. The *Lady of the Seas*, I believe. Is he a wanted man?"

"In a manner of speaking." Miles massaged the back of his neck. "Do you have any other ships leaving for the Americas?"

"Not until next week." A shout pulled the man's attention and he dismissed himself, swaggering off.

"Next week?" Elizabeth frowned in dismay. "How are you going to retrieve your money?"

"I can solve nothing here. We will go to Littleshire." A deep thread of tension lined Miles's voice. He surged ahead, forcing Elizabeth to extend her legs in a more determined stride.

She wanted to ask more questions, but now was obviously not the time. Poor Miles. All of the anger she had felt earlier toward him temporarily melted beneath sympathy for his plight. Whatever would he do? Surely he had funds elsewhere, but for the ones slated for his factories to be stolen…right beneath his nose. He would need to go down to Bow Street, she imagined, and file paperwork regarding the thief.

"Are you going to hire an investigator?" she asked.

"Yes, there is much to be done."

The withdrawn quality of his voice drew her thoughts back to their argument last night. How distant he had shown himself. His scorn for her desire to read to him. And to ask her for her hand merely because John demanded it…the thought shook her to the very core.

She could not allow herself to forget that while she was discovering feelings for Miles that were far from convenient, he only saw her as an old family friend. He felt nothing more and had made it quite clear that her only relationship to him could be one of convenience. A joining to benefit them both.

As they rode in the carriage, as he conducted his business and she returned home to instruct Jenna to pack her bags, she kept the knowledge uppermost in her mind that no matter what she felt for Miles, he would never feel the same.

Yesterday evening had proved him to be what she'd always thought him: a businessman who dismissed the softer feelings with a casual wave of his oh-so-elegant hand.

What a pickle she'd gotten herself into.

Explaining to her parents why she was leaving for Windermar proved a dreadful experience. Once again, her mother subjected her to disapproving frowns while her father stood silently in their ornate, overdressed sitting room. They had not been happy with her marrying Miles in the first place.

They were even less happy that she planned to help him reorganize his mill.

"It is the Season, darling," her mother said. "Certainly he does not expect the help of a lady in such mundane matters. There are operas to be seen, balls to be danced and you have already accepted invitations."

"Write them my sincerest apologies," Elizabeth responded. She had not personally accepted any invitations. Her mother had responded on her behalf. "And send this to John if you would." She handed them the letter she had quickly composed. She and John had been close once, and she appreciated his concern, but his meddling in her affairs was unacceptable.

Her parents had no choice but to accept that she was leaving. Miles was her betrothed, after all. Whether or not it was a love match had no bearing on the fact that she planned to be involved with the factory children.

How he had changed her with his challenges, with his derision of her reclusiveness. How very right he had been to show her that life involved so much more than dreaming. Living demanded action. To be in relationship with others. To see people as more than characters prancing across the pages of her world.

Perhaps she had been wrong to avoid truly living in order to spare her heart. That was a coward's way, and she had discovered that she no longer wished to be a shadow in her own life. She no longer liked playing the narrator, the one in the wings observing but not participating.

She thought of how much she enjoyed reading to the

children. How beautiful the light in their eyes when they mastered a new letter. There was so much potential for greatness, for something more than laboring twelve hours a day in a factory, producing meaningless work. There would always be a need for clothing, but how much better for these children to at least have the resources to choose a different way. To see an opportunity and take it rather than being trapped by an ignorance foisted upon them by their superiors.

Yesterday she had written to Parliament, beseeching them to look into reforms for child labor. She referenced Samuel Greg of Quarry Bank Mill, whom, she had discovered during the course of her research, ran a family-friendly mill and practiced kindness and fairness toward his workers. The man even went so far as to build nice cottages for the workers he imported from other cities. As she had suspected, his mill was doing very well. If he could make a success out of his factory and yet treat his employees in a fair way, then anyone could do so.

Yes, she was going to change her life, and it was all because of Miles. And yet, as she and Jenna departed for Littleshire in her parents' carriage, she could not help but think of Miles and how she had hoped for more from their marriage, despite the circumstances.

Their kiss…it had shown her that her emotions for him were far from the ordinary. Perhaps she could make him fall in love with her? If she was going to change, then perhaps it was best to start with how she approached her relationships. Miles knew her as an old friend. But maybe if he saw her as a woman…then he might change his mind. True love could be hers, after all, and what was more romantic than a marriage of convenience turned into a love match?

Chapter Twenty-One

Miles could not marry Elizabeth now. No daughter of an earl should marry a man who had just lost half his livelihood. He would still be able to meet the terms of the settlement he'd discussed with her father, but there was more at stake than contractual considerations.

As he had expected, insurance covered the cost of rebuilding the mill, but the scandal of his steward running off with his funds... Would word spread in London? And how would such a story affect Bitt?

Not only was there the possibility of scandal, but he still needed to find a way to take care of his employees. They might move on, leaving him fewer workers, if he didn't. A few of his employees lived in cottages near the mill, cottages he'd been in the process of renovating as they'd fallen into disrepair beneath the previous owner's administration. Those employees had been imported from other cities.

If they left...

He brooded all the way to Littleshire, refusing to stop at Windermar even though he knew Elizabeth must already be there. It had taken him a day after she left to get his affairs in order. He'd contacted his older brother for advice on how to best proceed but he didn't wish to take money from him.

A gentleman was not only known for being honorable and owning property, but also for having money. His other factory provided an income, but he had sunk so much of his monies into this one... How had this happened? Why had he not paid closer attention when Elizabeth told him his books were off?

He could not expect her to marry him now. Not with this situation brewing. There was no telling who knew of Shapely's perfidy. No one would look down on her for begging off the marriage once the ton got wind of things. Certainly he could track Shapely and recover the funds, but how long would that take? A year at best, and he'd have to find a trustworthy person to chase the man down.

Best to take the insurance money, rebuild within six to eight weeks and move on. He might have to let a few servants go, though he'd keep Powell.

When he reached Littleshire three days later, the full implication of everything he'd lost thundered down on him. The silence of the mill struck him. The heavy skies drew the silhouette of his burnt-to-a-crisp factory in sharp lines and blackened angles. Behind the hollowed-out factory flowed the river. A bitter smell tinged every breath he took. Employees huddled nearby. Their children asked questions, but he had no answers.

He would meet with them all tomorrow, he told them.

Tomorrow...and still no word from Grealey. Where was the man?

If Elizabeth still wanted to marry him, her massive inheritance could set things to rights. But he could not ask that of her. He had not proposed marriage for her money.

This problem that had set him back considerably could possibly be the best solution for her dilemma. While crying off the marriage might cause her a smidge of social distress, considering his circumstances, no one in the snobbish beau monde would blame her for backing out. He doubted any harm would come to her family's reputation.

In fact, she could retire to the countryside without a whisper of ruination to her name.

He didn't feel cheered, but he supposed it was the dreadfulness of everything weighing him down. His earlier prayers seemed inconsequential. It was as though God had not heard him at all.

He returned to the small inn. He had decided to stay there rather than at Windermar or his other estate, both for convenience's sake and because he had an irrational urge to avoid Elizabeth at all costs.

He asked to speak to the owner, a wizened man of questionable age.

"Have you seen Mr. Grealey?" He dove right into it. No sense in beating around the bush.

"Grealey?" The inn owner squinted up at him. "That old curmudgeon left a few nights ago. Took one of the best horses from the livery, too."

"Stole it?"

"That's what I mean."

"Thank you." The situation only grew more dark and twisted. Miles spun on his heel, retiring to his room. Did this mean both ledgers were gone? He had assumed one burned in the fire but now he could only conclude that Grealey had been fixing the books with the help of Shapely. And now there was nothing to examine. Had they been intending thievery all along? Perhaps they had set the fire to distract from their getaway. Or when the fire occurred, they took it as an opportunity to make good their escape with his money.

Groaning, he pressed his forehead into his hands.

A knock sounded on his door. A letter slid beneath the rough-hewn wood. After fetching his spectacles, he read the contents with trepidation.

The Dowager Duchess of Windermar requested that he dine with them tonight and stay as her guest. Miles let out a short laugh. He wanted to decline, but the wording suggested that the invitation was more in line with a command.

Considering Elizabeth's grandmother's place in the world, he could ill afford to offend her. She was also a kind lady whose feelings he would not hurt for the world. He remembered her from childhood, faint wisps of memories here and there, a haughty presence who always snuck him and John candy. He seemed to recall her laughing with his grandfather, as well. They had been good friends, despite the great divide in their social status.

Elizabeth's grandmother had married a duke, after all.

How did the dowager duchess feel about their betrothal? She had encouraged him the last time he'd stayed to forge a bond with Elizabeth, to go out and speak with her. Look at how that had finally turned out. With him almost kissing her and compromising the peace he'd worked so hard for since Anastasia died.

Sighing, he called for his carriage. The sooner he allowed Bitt to break things off with him, the sooner he could return to the comfortable life he'd been enjoying before Wrottesley's bad behavior and John's insistence that he fix the situation. Well, he had done so. His debt had been fulfilled.

The ride to Windermar chilled him. A dank wind had picked up and the sky had darkened, turning the evening ride into an uncomfortable portent of the night to come. His carriage ambled up the long, curving drive to where Windermar sat, shrouded by heavy clouds. The sloping lawn boasted thick oaks barely visible in the mist.

He felt a strange foreboding, as though tonight the path of his life would be oddly altered. It was an altogether too serious feeling, quite unlike his usual self. With this heaviness weighing on him, he could not even imagine striding into Cook's kitchen to snag a tart. He had lost all hunger, he realized, and found the discovery most depressing.

Had he been looking forward to companionship? To having a wife once again? Surely not… But the disappointment spiraling through him at even the tiniest thought of saying goodbye to Bitt told him otherwise.

When the carriage pulled up to the grand entrance, worthy of any duke's widow, he alighted. The butler had the door open before he could even knock. After refreshing himself in the room a housemaid led him to, he followed the girl down to the dining room.

Only Her Grace awaited him. The Duchess eyed him through her quizzing glass when he entered the room, and did he detect disapproval? He met her look with an inclined head as salutation.

"Your Grace," he said, bowing. "Thank you for the invitation, though it was quite unnecessary."

"Nonsense," she responded in the crisp tone he knew too well. "You are Elizabeth's betrothed. Of course you shall stay here."

He took the seat next to her, where a plate had been set out for him, he presumed. Though a grown man, when she gave him that look, he felt once more like the boy she'd reprimanded for climbing her cherry trees. "It is very kind of you."

"Have you resolved matters, young man?"

"Not to my satisfaction, but I shall, as time passes."

"Harrumph." The disapproving noise followed the lowering of her quizzing glass. He wondered if she truly needed the eyepiece or merely used it as a means of intimidation.

Not that she intimidated him. He eyed the empty space across from him. "Is Elizabeth indisposed?"

The duchess waved a ring-laden hand, which caught the candlelight and flashed colors across the white linen cloth. "Late again, no doubt finishing a novel. She shall be down shortly, I'm sure. But let us discuss this unfortunate fire. However shall you recoup? My granddaughter does not deserve to be saddled with a man riddled in debt."

He gave her a cool look. "Insurance shall cover the costs of rebuilding, and there is no reason any debt shall be incurred." Obviously Elizabeth had not told her grandmother about the thievery. If she had, Her Grace would be much more stern toward him. He was certain of that.

"That is good to know." The duchess shifted her gaze behind him. "Ah, Elizabeth, so happy you decided to join us."

Miles rose, and as he took in Elizabeth's state, the strangest panic knotted his gut and traveled through his legs until every muscle in his body seemed bunched and tight. She wore her hair loose. The shining auburn strands spilled over her shoulders, which were covered by a silky, iridescent green dress that flowed over her figure in graceful waves. She offered him a shy smile, her eyes wide and fathomless. Her lips were rosebud pink, and she held a dainty fan with slender fingers.

She glided into the room, finding her seat. An uncomfortable lump stuck in his throat. He had seen Elizabeth look lovely before, but tonight there was something different about her. An unnamed sparkle or look…he could not pinpoint the difference but nonetheless, one existed.

He sat after she sank into her seat, wanting his gaze to leave hers, but lacking the willpower to pull it away. Whatever she had changed on herself tonight, it was extremely distracting.

The servants brought in the courses, and the duchess kept up a steady discourse on the quality of elderberries and tarts in general. Miles barely heard. This might be the last time he set eyes on Elizabeth. Breaking a betrothal was serious, indeed. Though circumstances might soften the blow, there would be a small reaction from the ton.

Then again, with it being the height of the Season and engagement announcements popping up every day and scandals constantly whispered about in over-filled drawing rooms, their separation may not even be noted. But at least she'd be free, and for a smaller price than if Wrottesley had been allowed to ruin her.

The man had moved on to another heiress, he'd heard. Poor gel.

His eyes met Elizabeth's. Her lips tipped at the corners, her head tilted ever so slightly… Was she flirting with him? Elizabeth and coquetry? Doubtful.

And yet, throughout the meal, she sent him sidelong glances. When he caught them, she blushed. During the course of the conversation, she insisted on giggling and pulling his name into the conversation. She boasted on his accomplishments at the factory, the quality of his work, how quickly he had arranged to rebuild.

The duchess, in turn, shared more stories of his father.

Not the most comfortable dinner conversation, Miles thought, but he wisely said nothing. At the least, it was somewhat entertaining. Elizabeth rested her chin on her knuckles as Lady Windermar recounted his father's numerous faux pas when entering society.

"He knew nothing, absolutely nothing, of how a gentleman should speak and act. I took him under my wing, so to speak," she said. A reminiscent glint glittered in her eyes. "I turned him into a good deed and no one gave the barest hint of disapproval. He had saved my life, you see."

"He saved your life? How very romantic." Elizabeth bestowed one of her odd smiles on Miles before returning her attention to her grandmother. "You have never shared this story. I thought he was simply a neighbor."

"Well, he was, once upon a time." The dowager took on a faraway look. "Once when I was a child, I wandered off our property. Too far. I could not find my way home. He found me and brought me back. A hoity-toity little girl dressed in silks and ribbons, crying my eyes out. Nanny, bless her soul, had fallen asleep, and when she awoke, I was nowhere to be found. My parents released her, of course. I went through several nannies, you see, for I had a spark of mischievousness that has not been passed down to my daughter. Perhaps my grandchild, though…" She gave Elizabeth a deliberate look, as though daring her to break the mold she'd caged herself within.

Miles hid his smile behind a linen.

"It is there, though. Mark my words." The duchess waggled her finger precariously close to Elizabeth's face.

"What is?" The rapture on her face had turned to something akin to being hunted.

"The backbone, my girl, that pushes a person into the world to do great things. The spark that prompts a quiet woman to take risks with a—" at that, she sniffed "—debatable gentleman." She pushed her plate to the side. "I'm tired and feeling the beginnings of a megrim. Go take a walk in the garden. I wish a vase of roses on my nightstand, and Jane never picks them the way I'd like."

They all stood as the duchess took her leave.

A stroll in the garden... He had hoped to speak to Elizabeth in the study, to ascertain her willingness to break their betrothal before formally retracting the contract.

But the garden would be dark. She would not see the unexpected regret roiling through him. He did not want her pity. He merely wanted to release her from their contract and continue the life he was living before Wrottesley attacked her, before any of this insanity ensued.

As they took their leave, as she told him with a shining smile that she'd meet him at the trellis in fifteen minutes, he was certain that he'd be happier anywhere else but here.

Whoever loved that loved not at first sight?
Shakespeare had certainly said it right.

Elizabeth touched a gently furled rose, marveling at its deep color and velvet petal, while waiting for Miles. She had put her plan to make him fall in love with her into motion tonight, and already she felt an utter failure. He had hardly seemed to notice her, though she'd giggled and smiled and enacted every flirtatious movement she'd seen other women employ.

All for nothing, even though Grandmother had finagled for them to be together out here. The wherefore was beyond Elizabeth. To prove something? To give her mettle? A backbone? She dropped her hand and turned to stare at the house. One only needed a strong will for a pleasurable evening of novel reading.

For that is all she wanted to do tonight. Curl up in a chair and find another world in which the heroine won the hero, in which he felt for her as she did for him. A world in which the story ended as it should, with the villain destroyed and the hero triumphant.

Ironically. Miles had become her hero when Luke the stable hand had fallen off his proverbial charger. She still remembered his laughter when she confessed her love to him. A dreamy-eyed fifteen year old girl who had been too naive to realize that he was simply being kind to her because she was his employer's granddaughter.

How very relieved she'd been to find out he'd been dismissed.

Until she'd discovered that Miles was behind Luke's dismissal. It had been humiliating to discover that Miles knew what had happened. When he'd seen her weeping in the stables, she refused to explain and infernal man that he was, he had gone snooping.

The worst was that a mere servant had been punished for her unexpected affection.

It had not been Luke's fault that she fancied herself in love with him. Perhaps he could have been kinder, yes, but in the end, it had all been an extremely painful misunderstanding.

That was the year she'd lost all patience with Miles. He became an irritant she vowed to avoid. Yet his defense of her had also inspired a confusing devotion.

She felt no pain now over the situation, only an understanding that Luke had been toying with the emotions of a naive young girl for his own reasons, reasons she would never understand.

She shook out the folds of her dress, patted her hair to make sure all was straight. The cool evening left the faintest touch of chill on her arms. Perhaps she should remark upon the cold so that Miles would offer his jacket.

If she put him in the role of protector again, maybe he would fall in love with her...

An irritated breath escaped her pursed lips. It would not be true love, though. She was silly to think otherwise. All of her attempts at dinner to attract him had been complete failures.

She had debated using her fan... Her fingers found the thing of their own accord. She snapped it up, admiring the delicate colors and lace. She waved it one way, and then the other. Supposedly a secret code existed for the use of fans, though she'd never studied such foolishness as she had no need to use the information.

"Are you planning to slap someone with that?"

Startled, she dropped the fan to the cobblestone path. Miles stood in front of her, his casual smile coaxing good-natured creases to the corners of his eyes. They sparkled at her.

"Only those who so rudely sneak up on a woman," she retorted, fluster tarting her words.

"Perhaps the woman should stop daydreaming all the time." He bent and picked up the fan. "This is yours, my lady. Pray do not swat me with it."

"Do not earn a swat, and you shall be safe."

"I brought a basket for the roses, and shears." He held out the shears and she took them, letting her fingers graze his.

Perhaps she wasn't quite done with flirting, even if he

had snuck up on her in a most annoying fashion. "Thank you, Miles, and will you be a dear and hold the basket for me? It shall make the process ever so much easier."

His forehead crinkled, and she hid her wince. That had been a laying it on a bit thick, she supposed, but he truly was ever so handsome and soon to be her husband.

A husband in name only, she reminded herself firmly. They walked in silence for several moments, pausing when she found suitable roses to snip. Grandmother liked the deep red ones best.

"You are quite adept at this, my lady."

"I took the job over when I was eleven. Grandmother feels I have an eye for artistic arrangements."

"When we are finished here, perhaps I can speak to you about a serious matter."

She stopped, the cutters hovering near the stem of a particularly long rose. Its aromatic bouquet curled around her senses. "You may always speak to me of serious matters, Miles. I am a dreary daydreamer, remember?"

With great concentration, she snipped the rose. As it fell into her other hand, a thorn scratched her palm. Biting back a whimper, she carefully placed it into the basket Miles held out.

"Your hand." He shifted the basket and took her hand within his. A dreadful buzzing spread through her mind and her heart flittered as he studied her palm with concern.

"It is only a tiny prick. I shall be fine." But she did not remove her hand from his. After all, flirtation required a certain degree of physicality. Or so she'd read. A rather lovely warmth seeped into her skin.

Surely he must feel more for her than mere friendship and duty. Surely...

"Elizabeth," he said, his voice sounding hoarse to her ears, "considering my recent circumstances, I wish to release you from your contract of marrying me."

Chapter Twenty-Two

It was as though her heartbeats slowly came to a painful stop, each thump a terrible death knell to what she'd been hoping.

"Release me?" she repeated. A stray drop of rain plopped against her nose.

Miles took her by the arm and led her up the path. "We have enough roses. Yes, release you. There might be a slight stir amongst the ton but most likely no one shall bat an eye. My reduced circumstances allow you the freedom to break our contract with very little repercussion to your family. It is true that you might need to sit out in the country for a while, but that is your goal at any rate, is it not?"

"I…" She could hardly speak. She pulled her arm free. This was the last topic she had expected to encounter. "In truth, I have not given the situation much thought. I suppose, were it to be bandied about that you could not meet the settlement you had promised in our betrothal agreement, that we could most assuredly dissolve the contract. But Miles, that would not bode well for your status."

Another raindrop rolled down her nose. She brushed

it away, hurrying after Miles, whose broad back looked oddly stiff. He had not even turned to respond to her comment. She followed him into the house, growing more irritated by the moment. She instructed a maid to put the roses in a vase until she could get to them. They shed their coats, leaving them with another servant, and then walked to the library.

Or rather, he walked.

She marched behind him, her lack of stature keeping her a stride's length behind him despite her attempts to keep up. Thoughts rattled around her head and a steady dose of temper thrummed through her. But she kept her silence until they entered the library.

She wanted to give him a good tongue-lashing, though she did not know which subject she should start with.

His ridiculous offer to end their betrothal or the way he'd manhandled her in the rain. For all he knew, she liked standing in a spring rain shower.

A shiver trembled through her and belatedly she realized how wet her skirts were.

"You should change," Miles said in a very dark way. Indeed, he almost looked to be glowering at her. As though his pronouncement were her fault.

Oh, stuff and nonsense. Who knew why he was really upset? She could not even begin to fathom.

She shook her skirts, watching as droplets splattered against Grandmother's rug. The shelves of books remained safely out of reach. She sniffed appreciatively. No matter what else happened, the library always remained the same. The smell of leather-bound books intoxicated far more than some stuffy ball or soiree.

Perhaps Miles had things correct. Perhaps she should retire to the country permanently.

"I suppose that heavy brow of yours means you will not be refreshing yourself before our conversation?" Miles leaned against the desk, crossing one boot-clad foot over another. He looked rather dashing despite the long face.

"I declare, Miles Hawthorne, if you ever refer to my brow as heavy again, I shall throw a book at you."

Surprise flitted across his features, followed by what looked to be an unwilling upward tilt to the lips. "My lady, I should never want to cause you to harm your precious books."

"Good." She walked toward him, feeling a steel in her spine that could only be inherited from the duchess herself. "I have given the hasty words you uttered in the garden deep thought."

"Surely not that deep, as it has only been ten minutes at the most since I uttered them."

"I assure you that my thoughts are always deep and please do not impose a time limit on them. Now then…" She stopped in front of him, a minx-like urge pushing her to run a forefinger down his right arm. Yes, there was a sleeve between them, but the action seemed appropriately flirtatious. She smiled sweetly up at him. "I refuse your offer. You shall marry me and stand by your word."

"And if I can't meet the settlement?"

"Of course you can. Such nonsense from a gentleman."

A fine blush started up his cheeks, which caused her a moment's pause. Was her flirtation working? It must be, for his throat moved up and down in a convulsive way, as though he could not quite swallow, and his gaze pinned hers so that, for a moment, she thought perhaps she would not be able to swallow either.

"You are consigning yourself to a marriage of lesser

means," he said roughly. The green in his eyes appeared deeper, meaning his emotions had been stirred.

She shrugged. "As long as you can afford to buy me books, I shall be quite happy."

"I believe you mean that."

"Miles…" She placed her hand on his arm again, her previous touch not enough, for now that she had tasted boldness, she realized how very sweet it was. And affection should be shown. She understood that now, as she never had before. "You are a very old and dear friend. I was wrong to have been so resistant to your offer when you first asked, for you have proven yourself to be a Godly man, given to kindness and generosity. I am honored to be your wife, and I will not accept your breach of our contract. End of story."

"End of story?" But a smile tipped his lips. His hands cupped her face and he gazed deeply into her eyes. "Are you sure? For I cannot promise—"

"I know," she breathed, hardly able to think for the feel of his palms against her skin. He could not promise love. So how was it that she felt loved?

And she loved him indeed.

Every ounce of her being fairly burst with the feeling. "All shall be well. I am an heiress, remember, and our hasty betrothal shall in no way endanger our marriage. We have known each other since childhood, and now we shall know each other into old age."

"I cannot imagine your lovely skin lined with wrinkles, but I assure you that when they appear, you will be even more lovely to me." The words, delivered on a husky note, tore any breath she had left from her body.

Would he kiss her now? Their faces were so close, his

pupils enlarged within irises of stormy green. Her fingers tightened on his sleeve.

A sharp rapping interrupted. He ripped his gaze away, dropping his hands quickly. She spun around. Grandmother stood in the doorway, a cane poised in her hands against the door frame where she'd evidently felt the need to announce her presence.

"Mr. Hawthorne, I presume you will be obtaining a special license promptly?"

A special license, indeed.

The procurement of such took several days, actually, which Elizabeth's mother and grandmother used to plan the wedding. It would be a small affair consisting only of her parents, Grandmother, John and Miles's brother. Her cousin Jane, with whom she exchanged letters regarding novels they were reading, had wanted to attend but weak lungs kept her abed. No matter. Elizabeth planned to write every detail down to share with her cousin later.

Married.

She could not believe it. Sooner than expected due to circumstances. The more quickly she received her inheritance, the sooner it could be used.

Though she did not expect true love from Miles, what she had felt from him several times caused her mind to race and her breath to constrict. She simply could not have imagined his response to her. Deep within, she felt certain that he must love her, too.

And so she met with the cook and the maids and allowed her mother to decorate how she wished. Her wedding dress was to be a light green silk with cascading rose-colored ribbons and French lace at the hems.

"London is abuzz, my lady," Jenna told her while dressing her hair.

"About?"

"Why, what they believe to be your love match." She pulled at Elizabeth's hair, gently tilting her head.

Elizabeth winced. "I don't need a fancy hairstyle, Jenna. Just something simple. What do you mean by 'what they believe'?"

"It's been bandied about how you and Mr. Hawthorne fell madly in love, and that is why you are marrying so very quickly."

"Has anyone said a word about his factory burning down?"

"There is talk, but as you were betrothed beforehand, I don't believe anyone thinks it pertinent."

At least there was that, she thought ruefully. "How is Powell? Has there been any talk of a more permanent relationship between the two of you?"

Jenna's fingers stilled in her hands. "Well… I meant to speak with you about it. As we will be living in the same house after you are married, Nic— Powell, that is, and I, well…we…also want to marry."

Elizabeth smiled broadly but made sure she did not move her head. "You should marry, Jenna, just as soon as you can. It is ever so lovely to be in love, is it not?"

"Yes, my lady, it is." And they both sighed.

The afternoon of the wedding arrived. Elizabeth had not seen Miles since that day in the library, but she hoped she would get a kiss from him like he had given her in Vauxhall. That daydream uppermost, she scarcely paid attention, but floated through whatever her mother instructed her to do.

The ceremony was brief. Her mother had chosen

the front lawn of Windermar in which to hold the tiny service. The weather cooperated. A sunny sky greeted them all, and a lone violinist welcomed Elizabeth as she stepped from the house. Sunlight bloomed against her skin, and she squinted.

There was Miles, standing several feet away, dressed in a dapper suit that included coattails. It suddenly struck Elizabeth that she should have insisted on an evening wedding. Her skin stung from the strong light pouring against it, and suddenly she was aware of how noticeable her birthmark must be.

She had lightly powdered her face, but oftentimes the powder settled into the creases and only made the deficiency more glaring. By the time she'd reached Miles, her nerves jangled. She positioned herself so that her unblemished cheek was to him.

He had never seemed bothered by the mark before, she reminded herself. She tapped a foot against the grass, willing the service to move faster. Not only did the bright sunlight cause her eyes to water, but every moment she grew more and more nervous.

She was marrying Miles.

Miles Hawthorne.

Childhood nemesis grown into a man who secreted kisses at night and teased her about books. Every reason she shouldn't marry him crowded her mind. He didn't read. Worse, he scoffed at her books. He worked too much. He teased often and avoided serious matters frequently.

Her fingers twisted in her skirts. She looked at him from beneath lowered lids. His jaw was firm. His eyes facing forward. Was he having second thoughts?

He said the vows. She repeated them, though she stumbled through the words. Did she imagine Miles staring at her birthmark? She resisted the urge to touch it, to see if it was still there or if somehow she might have willed it away.

Why did she want him to kiss her? She could never pass this detriment on to their children. But then she thought of little Becky at the mill and how lovely she was. No outward difference should have the ability to define the worth of a person. If she had children and they all inherited the mark, they would be just as beautiful to her.

And then the reverend was telling Miles to kiss her, that it was time. All of her thoughts halted. She slowly turned, heartbeat a roaring rush in her ears, her palms clammy and every sense attuned to Miles. His eyes searched hers, slow, lingering, heavy lidded.

She wet her lips. Would this be the moment he said he loved her? She looked up at him, waiting. He leaned down. His lids flickered.

She felt his breath, so very close, so very near, and her heart longed to reach out and touch his. Her eyes fluttered shut, she lifted her face and then…she felt his lips upon her cheek.

The cheek without the birthmark.

Her eyes flew open. He was staring at her and the expression on his face…had she ever seen such a look?

He straightened, turning away from her.

She discovered something in that second of his turning away, in that half moment in which she'd seen fear and disgust upon his face. As she forced her lips to remain still and unquivering, as she blinked away excess moisture from her eyes that, if asked about, she would blame on the sun, she filed the discovery away.

People could not hear a heart shatter.

Chapter Twenty-Three

One must never underestimate a mother's penchant for meddling.

Elizabeth barely suppressed her sigh as she reached for the next book in the pile she'd created in Grandmother's library. The dowager duchess would not be pleased with the mess, but Elizabeth could not summon the energy to care.

She had just shelved a tome about India when Grandmother sailed into the room.

"There you are." There was no mistaking the miff in Grandmother's voice. She pressed her quizzing glass against her eyes and scowled. "Hiding in the library. I should have known. And with this riffraff." She gave the books a disapproving grimace as she waved her quizzing glass toward Elizabeth. "How long do you plan to mope about the estate? Don't think I haven't seen you avoiding me. It's been five weeks since you married, and you're still here organizing. You are dillydallying with these novels as though your entire future did not depend upon your ability to produce an heir. I utterly despair of you."

That last sentence was Grandmother's equivalent of a dagger aimed at Elizabeth's conscience. Meant to intimidate more than wound, perhaps, but there was still no sense in paying Grandmother any heed when the letter she'd received this morning begged her attention. Her mother was on her way to Windermar.

She barely suppressed a shudder. She'd much prefer the wilds of India to having a conversation with her mother. India was a steaming continent, certainly. Unknown and wild. Filled with dark-eyed men and women, turbans and cobras. Elizabeth searched her memory for any books she'd stumbled across regarding that mysterious country. Foreign scents, scandalous clothing and wide varieties of colors...

"...mind wandering, as usual." Grandmother's querulous tones interrupted her daydream.

Sighing, she set the book to the side, scooped up her mother's letter and opened it. She scanned the contents, but they had not changed. She was worried. She wanted Elizabeth to come to London with her for the rest of the Season.

Elizabeth could think of nothing more terrible than to run into her husband there.

"Elizabeth, do pay attention."

"I'm sorry, Grandmother, I truly am, but my mind is occupied."

"Fiddle-faddle, I'll not have it." Grandmother plied the letter from Elizabeth's fingers, forcing her to the present.

She focused on her grandmother, a petite woman who resembled a fearsome dragon. It was Grandmother's personality, Elizabeth feared, that had forever ruined her grandmother's ability to be content.

Elizabeth took a deep breath. "Please, give me that."

"This piece of paper takes precedence over my opinion?" Grandmother's jowls, well-powdered and soft, shook with emotion. "I hosted your betrothal ball, allowed your wedding to take place here and now you've decided to live here without your husband? I won't have it, Elizabeth. Look how I am repaid? A disastrous library. A timid bookworm of a granddaughter and no elderberries for tarts. Bah!" She shoved the letter toward Elizabeth, who took it quickly.

Clutching it to her bodice, she frowned. "But I clearly wrote *elderberries* on my list before I went into town."

"And yet they are nowhere to be found." Grandmother's quizzing glass swept the room.

"Do sit down, Grandmother. I shall remedy this at once."

The elderly lady sank into the plush couch reserved for afternoon reading and put a hand on her forehead. The quizzing glass lay forgotten against her voluminous skirts. "My constitution cannot take this upset. A dowager duchess has ever so many responsibilities, and I merely wanted a respite from them all. A spot of sugar to calm my nerves."

"Do not fret." Skirting the mess on the floor, Elizabeth headed toward the door.

"Stop." Sternness punctuated the duchess's tone and brooked no argument.

Drawing a deep breath, Elizabeth prepared herself for a dressing down. The look on Grandmother's face was not unkind, however. Her keen eyes studied Elizabeth.

"You deserve a proper marriage. You should be with your husband."

"Miles does not want me." Elizabeth controlled her flinch, the knowledge penetrating the defenses she'd so carefully erected. "It was a marriage in name only. I do not care to ever see him again."

"Because you love him."

She kept her voice steady. "How I feel for him has no bearing on anything."

"Nonsense. It changes everything." Grandmother sighed long and loud.

Elizabeth shifted in the doorway, waiting for permission to leave. She'd instruct a servant to find the tarts and she would retire to her room. It had been such a long five weeks. The mill was almost up and running. She'd visited frequently in the past weeks, reading to the children in the sun. Once she resumed their regular teaching, she'd feel better.

She simply must.

"You are frowning, my dear."

"Fatigue." Watching Miles ride away the morning after their wedding had felt like a dagger slicing her heart wide open. Even though she'd said her grandmother needed her, she'd hoped he would refuse to leave without her. But no, he had looked relieved. He had left speedily.

After that day, she spent hours in her bedroom here at Windermar, wanting to cry yet unable to produce a single relieving tear. Sleep eluded her.

"Fatigue? Is that the most you have to say for yourself?" Grandmother straightened into a sitting position, eyes narrowed. "I never would have thought you one to succumb to such a thing. Bah." She sniffed in disdain. "That young man of yours deserves a strong woman, a lady in the truest sense, not a ninny hiding in a library."

Elizabeth's jaw dropped. "Grandmother!"

"Do not *Grandmother* me," she said crossly. "We are made of sterner stuff, young lady. Do you want Miles? Do you love him? Are you willing to fight for your love?

Surely the story of your life is infinitely more important than these dusty pieces of leather and paper."

The story of her life?

And it was as though light sprang forth in her mind, clearing her thoughts, bringing clarity. She was no heroine.

Secluding herself away, licking her wounds, so to speak.

Wilting, she sank into a large chair positioned to the side of the doorway. "You're right. I am not who I want to be."

Grandmother harrumphed. "I do not wish to tittle-tattle, but you should know something of your new husband." And then she told Elizabeth about Anastasia, a diamond of the first water who practically disappeared from society the last year of her life.

Elizabeth learned that Miles had exhausted himself trying to make his wife better. He had hired endless rounds of physicians, traveled to Bath to breathe in the fresh air and bathe in the healing waters. In the end, Anastasia was said to have died from a weakness of the lungs, but some whispered that she'd ended her own life.

"Oh, Miles," Elizabeth breathed. The story of his first wife's plight brought about an empathy for her childhood friend. Perhaps Miles felt the pressure of being his wife was too great for her? After all, why else would he have insisted on those "tasks" she had performed?

His reticence to marry made more sense. How his heart must have broken. Though her chest ached knowing he was disgusted at having to kiss her, she ignored the feeling.

She must persevere and live her life. Not continue hiding. Which meant being his wife and making a home. Regardless of whether they ever kissed again. He might not love her in the same way that she loved him, but that did not matter. All that mattered is that she lived. Well and truly lived. And she would show him that his heart would be safe with her.

She pushed up from the chair, the movement making her head light. Or perhaps it was the sudden optimism filling her soul. "Will you give Mother my regrets that I missed her?"

Grandmother eyed her. "And where are you going?"

Elizabeth could not keep the grin from her face. "To London, for my story has just begun."

"The files you requested, sir." Powell placed a stack of papers on the desk.

"Thank you," Miles murmured. He studied the contract at hand, a request for funds to order new machines. After four weeks of continuous construction, the factory was almost finished. He needed only to stock the thing and then processing could resume. Finally.

Powell did not leave.

Miles looked up. "Is there something else?"

His valet shifted on his feet, wearing the annoying smile he'd worn ever since he'd begun courting Elizabeth's lady's maid. "Sir, might I ask a personal question?"

Miles bristled. "If this is about Mrs. Hawthorne, then no." As Powell blanched, Miles gave him a hard look. "You may go."

Not everyone could be as happy as Powell and Jenna. Though they'd been apart for a lengthy amount of time, no thanks to their employers, Miles had not missed the flurry of letters coming and going between Windermar and London.

He slammed his quill down too hard and broke the tip.

Ink leaked out in a messy puddle. Clenching his jaw, he dropped the thing and yelled for Powell to return.

Mrs. Hawthorne.

Suppressing a growl, Miles paced the room, barely registering when Powell came in or who cleaned up the mess. Where was Elizabeth? At her grandmother's, he supposed.

Their wedding day had been a disaster. He'd seen the whiteness of her face after he didn't kiss her. He'd known she wanted more from him. But he couldn't give more. It wasn't in him.

He'd saved her from ruination and, in turn, she'd kept him a wealthy gentleman. That fair trade should have sufficed.

Instead the remainder of the wedding day she hardly spoke to him. Because of the situation with the factory, it had been agreed they'd postpone the honeymoon. A marriage of convenience did not need such a thing, after all. In a few weeks, no one would even remember that they had not taken one. It would be presumed that they were happily married.

The next morning when it was time to return to London, reality set in. Elizabeth refused to leave her grandmother's house. She said the dowager duchess needed her, and Miles promptly agreed. He hadn't spoken to her since.

If that was her idea of housewifery, and perhaps it was what she'd planned all along, then good riddance to her. He had poured himself into work, procuring a new steward and righting the books.

A bleakness followed him about. Emptiness. He prayed and read his Bible, which helped, but something still wasn't right. He had altered things, he supposed, by not kissing Bitt.

For the best, he told himself, going back to his desk. The room was his alone again. He scratched out numbers, signatures, losing himself in his work. Until somewhere in the house, a door shut. And then voices echoed in the hall.

He looked up.

Bitt entered his office with a flourish, tossing a huge satchel to the floor. It made a thud like thunder. Or perhaps it was only his heart, stuttering to a halt at her presence.

She wore her anger well. Two spots of pink rouged her cheeks and her eyes flashed at him as she came nearer. Or should he say strode, for she practically flew to his desk. No small feat for a woman of her stature.

She slapped her palms upon the myriad of papers. "What do you have to say for yourself, Mr. Hawthorne?"

Glints of reddish gold highlighted her hair, which she had put up in a messy bun atop her head. Her bonnet hung from her arm. Had she been in the sun? His eyes narrowed.

"Regarding?" he asked.

"Oh, are you to be that way with me, then?" She straightened, folding her arms across her bosom and fixing him with a glare she'd certainly learned from her grandmother.

"I'm working, Elizabeth. If there is something you wish to speak to me of, then say so." Though he delivered the words in a calm manner, his palms had suddenly turned to sweat and his throat tightened. With a start, he understood that he had missed her.

The realization stiffened his shoulders.

"I hired Grandmother a companion who excels in conversation and who is a poor relation to Prinny. She shall be taken care of and quite entertained. I am here for the rest of the Season. I shall accompany you when you visit Littleshire. In the meantime, I wish for you to show me our home."

Miles did not know if he had been struck mute or if his tongue simply stopped working. His Bitt, library mouse, had just barged into his home as if she owned it.

"In the meantime," she continued in a tone a little too priggish for his liking, "I've seen that you are putting my fortune to good use. I have been out to the mill and noticed that you repaired the cottages, as well."

"You've been busy," he finally managed. That explained the highlights in her hair. Which, he conceded, were rather attractive. Like burnt gold.

"Did you expect me to wither away in the country simply because you could not bring yourself to kiss me? I'm made of sterner stuff, Miles, though perhaps I just realized so."

Miles frowned. He wasn't sure he liked this Bitt. Aggressive and demanding and yet…she was not withering away, as she pointed out. The fire in her words warmed his temper.

"What has crawled up your corset, my dear?"

Her brows rose. "Wouldn't you like to know? But you shan't, for it is obvious that you are far too busy signing papers to be bothered with the likes of a wife. I shall leave you alone while I explore the household. Alone. If you have need of me, simply send word. Oh, and be ready to leave at eight o'clock this evening. I've accepted a dinner invitation."

"Now, that's nonsense." Miles stood quickly. "I am too busy for social niceties."

She waved a hand. "Don't wrinkle the starch out of your spine, husband. It is an event we shall both enjoy. A soiree at Lady Compton's. She is a great student of astronomy, if you remember. I am here to do my duties as your wife, Miles. We shall retire to the country soon enough, I suppose." She bent over and hefted up that ridiculous bag she'd dropped on the floor earlier. "In the meantime, do not think to evade our societal duties."

"Wait just a second." He rounded the desk, irritation and confusion rushing through him. And another emotion, one he couldn't quite put his finger on, but it felt unaccountably close to relief. "What is your purpose in coming here? To order me about and tell me to go places? I won't have it, Bitt."

Her chin lifted and her slender fingers pulled the reticule up like armor. "I am simply letting you know that I'm home. That I'm not going to spend the rest of my life hiding in a library." On the last words, he thought he heard a tremble, which had the effect of dampening all of his irritation.

"I'm happy to hear that," he said quietly. How was it that after days of travel, she still smelled like roses? Before he realized what he was going to do or say, he brushed a strand of hair from her face. "I did entertain an irrational thought that perhaps you might choose to sequester yourself away from life forever."

"Like Anastasia?"

He jerked, his hand falling to his side.

"Miles…" Her smile drooped. Her eyes were great orbs, shining with what looked like compassion. "I know about Anastasia's battles with melancholia. It must have been very difficult for you."

"But how?" He felt as though she'd slammed that satchel, which was no doubt filled with books, across his head.

She winced, looking a tad guilty. "Grandmother took me to task and told me more of your marriage. That I had better prove to have more mettle than…" Her voice trailed off.

"Anastasia was a bright light," he said hoarsely. "She burned so hotly with all that she felt that she could not keep the emotions from consuming her. She had a great many fine qualities, including a deep compassion for others."

Elizabeth nodded slowly, her face pale. "You loved her dearly. I understand that. I never expect you to love me the same way, but I ask that you pay me a kindness. Do not compare me to your first wife. If, as I suspect, you worked as hard at being a good husband as you do at being an employer, than I have no doubt that there was nothing you could have done to save your wife."

Miles crossed his arms. Inside his chest, there was only the icy awareness that Elizabeth *knew*. She knew and she had married him anyway. "I hired doctors." He had spent thousands of pounds trying to woo Anastasia back to laughter. To rekindle the light in her eyes. But in the end, to no avail.

"Simply understand that I am not her," Bitt was saying, gently. "Ours is a different relationship and a different marriage. I shall never take her place in your heart nor would I ever try. Now, if you will excuse me, I am in need of refreshment."

Before he could stop her, she was leaving him, his mouth dry, his feet rooted to the floor.

Bitt didn't blame him for what happened. She *knew*. And she had chosen to come to London anyway, to give him another chance to prove himself worthy. Had God forgiven him, then? For it was true, he had loved Anastasia deeply and her death had carved a wound he thought might never heal.

He had never meant to make Elizabeth feel as though she were being compared to his first wife, but now he understood that he had done exactly that. He had pushed away his feelings for Bitt because he did not want to fail her.

Or rather, he did not want her to fail him. To hurt him even more.

He remembered the look on her face on their wedding day. The shock, the disillusionment. Had she fancied herself in love with him? Quiet, reserved Bitt? Not so reserved when he thought of it, though. For she had smacked him with a reticule, yelled at him and returned his kiss with an intensity that had shaken him to his very core.

And now she was his bride. Married to him.

Squaring his jaw, he followed her. He had been given another chance to love, and he would not waste it.

How very exhausting to be the heroine in one's own story.

Elizabeth found the library behind the next door over and took refuge there. It had been rather tiring, stomping into Miles's office that way. He had looked up, all surprised maleness, his hair a wild riot on his head from where his fingers had been digging through it as he worked. So handsome that it had taken her several seconds to gather her faculties. How very shocked he'd looked to see her.

The memory brought a smile to her lips. She did so enjoy shocking him. He deserved it, too, after all his years of teasing her.

"Ah, a smile upon lips the color of a rose."

She gasped, as Miles strode into the library, a crooked smile lighting up his face. This was the Miles she remembered, crinkles and sparkles and a laissez-faire attitude.

He dwarfed the small room, shrinking the space further as he advanced. She waited, her heart fluttering like a tiny butterfly dancing upon a flower petal. Why did he look at her so?

Without meaning to, she touched her birthmark, covering it with her palm.

"Nay, Bitt." He took her hand and removed it from her cheek. "You are lovely in every way. Do not cover yourself."

"But," she stammered, deeply conscious of how neatly her hand fit within his. "Our wedding day. You couldn't kiss me…" Ashamed, hot flushes of self-consciousness washing through her, she averted her eyes.

"Bitt—" His voice broke. He tipped her chin with his forefinger, bringing her gaze back to his. A green intensity worked in his irises. "I have been wandering this house, doing infernal paperwork for over a month, feeling miserable. Trying to ignore how much I want you as my wife in every way."

"You were afraid."

"Yes, to fail another woman. To not be the husband you need."

"About Anastasia," she blurted out. "I'm so very sorry,

Miles, but you must understand." She curled her fingers more tightly around his, willing him to see the earnestness in her eyes, the utter conviction. "It wasn't your fault."

His throat worked. "Perhaps not, but I will always feel that I could have done more." He drew closer. "And that is why, when you burst into my office, reality knocked me on the head. I refuse to live my life afraid that I shall make the same mistakes, nor can I live expecting the same behavior from a different person."

"I am me, Miles."

"Yes." His lips curved upward. "You are beautifully you, and I adore every facet, from your dreamy escapes to your haughty disdain."

"I am far from haughty."

"Not that far, sweetums." His grin widened. "It has taken your courage to make me realize what I should have known long ago. You're intelligent and compassionate, and this entire time it's been right beneath my nose. How did I not see it?"

"You hadn't your spectacles handy," she said lightly, but her knees were quivering and her pulse rioting because Miles looked at her so deeply, as he had at Vauxhall. He looked as though he would kiss her again, just as she so desperately wanted him to.

He traced the ragged edges of her birthmark. And then he leaned forward, cupping her cheeks. Her eyes fluttered closed as she felt the warmth of his breath upon her cheek, his lips settling upon the awful blemish that for so long had marred her confidence.

"Have you ever noticed," he whispered, his voice a husky caress, "how the shape of your birthmark looks like a heart? Indeed, when I look at you, I am reminded of that tender organ, of how it pumps within you, sweet and caring. When I look at you, Elizabeth, I see love."

She had not opened her eyes. She was afraid. Her heart drummed within, uneven, cacophonous, drowning out her thoughts. Making her forget the reality in which she loved him and he did not love her.

"Open your eyes, Bitt."

Reluctantly, she did so.

"Do you understand what I am telling you?" His closeness rattled her senses.

She shook her head, unable to will her vocal cords into movement.

He chuckled then, a throaty sound that chimed through her in silvery, happy notes. "I thought not. What I am telling you, Elizabeth Hawthorne, is that I love you deeply and dearly, as a man who cannot imagine his world without you in it. Always, I have wanted to see you. Always, I have looked forward to finding you in the library so that I might tease you and make you laugh. Or even irritate you, for you are quite beautiful when you frown at me."

Elizabeth blinked, but her eyes did not cooperate, choosing instead to sting and to burn and to be traitorous in every way.

"You have always been beautiful to me, and I have been a fool. A scared fool, but no longer." He grasped her hands, his thumbs moving in long strokes across the skin. "Will you marry me for more than convenience's sake? Will you join your heart to mine?"

"I love you, Miles." The admission was a welcome relief.

"And I love you, my sweet bibliophile. I have loved

you in many ways, and now I shall love you as a husband loves his dearest wife."

He leaned forward, captured her mouth with his own and, in that moment, Elizabeth's story truly began.

* * * * *

If you enjoyed A HASTY BETROTHAL,
look for THE MATCHMAKER'S MATCH
by Jessica Nelson from Love Inspired Historical.

Dear Reader,

Little did I know when I started *A Hasty Betrothal* how tragedy would affect my family.

Lady Elizabeth came to me fully formed, a flawed heroine in need of a new perspective. I empathized with her self-consciousness because of my own personal struggles with skin issues. I could only imagine how she felt in the Regency upper class, where vanity and superficiality were rampant.

But then her childhood nemesis, Mr. Miles Hawthorne, appeared in my imagination, and I liked him immediately. Strong and confident, with a touch of charm, I knew he was the perfect man to woo her from her self-induced isolation.

I didn't know much about him, only that he had a great trauma in his past that had forever poisoned him against marriage. His first wife was a shadowy, selfish figure to me. But then, halfway through the book, a tragic loss occurred in my family's life. Suddenly Miles's hurt and that of his first wife's were magnified. I had not fully comprehended the pain *both* of them had felt until suffering through it myself.

I didn't anticipate that what I alluded to in fiction would become a reality in my own life. But it happened, and now my world, my perspective, is different.

If you know someone struggling with depression, take note! There are many places to find help. I am learning that it is better to be uncomfortable with interfering than to be grief stricken that I didn't.

I pray peace and blessings for you. Thank you for

reading this story! I love to hear from readers, so feel free to contact me via Facebook, Twitter or email, jessica_nelson7590@yahoo.com.

Sincerely,
Jessica Nelson